DISAPPEARANCE

DISAPPEARANCE

A novel by

MICHAEL JOYCE

Preface by STUART MOULTHROP

Paperback edition:
ISBN-10: 0983632642
ISBN-13: 978-0-9836326-4-1

Kindle edition:
ISBN-10: 0983632650
ISBN-13: 978-0-9836326-5-8

Cover design by Ariel Braverman

~ STEERAGE PRESS ~
steeragepress.com
Boulder, Colorado and Normal, Illinois

This book is Jeremiah's,
stern quizmaster of the multileveled gameworlds
that he drew on huge sketchbook pages as a child,
who showed me the hidden stairs to heaven in SuperMario

Hacer esta ficcion para darlo a entender

Set off in this story so as to come to know the truth

• Teresa of Ávila, *El Camino de Perfección*

In Flucht geschlagen,
wähnt er zu jagen;
hört nicht sein eigen Schmerzgekreisch,
wenn er sich wühlt ins eig'ne Fleisch,
wähnt Lust sich zu erzeigen!

In the midst of his flight,
he thinks himself hunting;
not recognizing his own cries,
when he tears at himself,
he mistakes what he feels for desire!

• Richard Wagner, *Die Meistersinger*

CONTENTS

Acknowledgments

Writers talk about trying to understand something in what they do, but few are as clueless as I was in setting out to try to understand gameworlds and what they mean to people I know and love and who play and study games. To do so, of course, involved a journey into my own unknowingness, one that risks seeming foolish, lost, and even more clueless.

The journey was a good one for me but I emerged dazed and uncertain and reached out to a group of what might be thought of as spirit guides whom I knew would honestly tell me whether where I had gone were places they recognized and whether what I thought I had come to understand was "real." Thus the people whose words appear in the preface and on the cover as blurbs are something more than the usual collection of names one seeks in hopes of promoting a book (although they are extraordinary figures and truly what one means by "names" in the marketing sense). I've learned from each of them over the years—most of all, of course, from Stuart Moulthrop, with whom the journey has extended twenty-five years and whom I've watched from a distance as he explored play both as an artist—in works from *Victory Garden* to *Hegirascope*, *Reagan Library* and *Deep Surface*—and as a theorist and guru for a generation of game scholars, in essays and talks from "'This is Not a Game' and Other Foolish Statements" (where I was the one who made the foolish statement) to "Games and the New Literacy," to "After the Last Generation: Rethinking Theory, Writing, and Scholarship in the Days of Serious Play," to "Playing with Worlds: Narrative, Fiction, and the Cultural Reception of Videogames" (all available at http://iat.ubalt.edu/moulthrop/talks/). To say the least, I feared his judgment, and so you can imagine my joy as I explored it in what appears here as preface.

Jenny Sundén, whom I met in my earliest trip to Sweden when she was still a graduate student, has not only become a close friend and dinner companion at the best Stockholm restos, but also a major international theorist in feminist accounts of gender and sexuality in games, and in performance, performativity, positionality, and embodiment. She read the novel as I was completing revisions during a Fulbright term in Uppsala in 2010 and, as with Stuart, I awaited her judgment with trepidation and benefitted extraordinarily from her support, comments and suggestions as well as her friendship.

I met Robert Nashak through another great friend, the visual artist, Alexandra Grant, my longtime collaborator, who was herself a generous and scrupulous reader and editor of earlier drafts of this novel. Early on Alexandra asked whether she could share it with her dear friend, Robert, who like Stuart, wears two hats, as a theorist at USC and a VP and producer at BBC worldwide interactive entertainment. Robert's enthusiasm for the novel—and, more importantly, his confidence that it would find publication—got me through some tough times as the novel bounced from place to place.

For giving me not just that place to publish, but whose multiple forms suit both our age and the novel's modalities, I have Kass Fleisher and Joe Amato, both gifted and courageous writers themselves, to thank for their long friendship and efforts here. I am honored to be among the first authors of Steerage, their important venture into a sea of stories.

I should also thank my students in Vassar's media studies program over the years, who, moving easily from so-called high literature, to manga, comix, games, and so on, led me to understand how little I know about culture and media and how lucky I am to have had their challenges and guidance. Among them, one especially, Ariel Braverman, who designed the cover for this book, deserves special thanks.

My two sons, Eamon and Jeremiah—the latter known as "electronic boy" during his boyhood, and to whom this book is dedicated—both taught me about the deeper matters of mortality which this novel, like many games and digital works, explores. I have loved them from the moment of their births and think of them each as counselors and senseis.

And then, always already, first and ever, there is Caro, life force, my dearest love and deepest companion in this journey.

About the Cover

Ariel Braverman's cover design, "Rose," proceeds from her current work making labor-intensive screen prints, reducing a digital image of a flower into its essential pixels, and printing them by hand, one square at a time. This print required 13 individual screens and films, and 19 hours to execute.

Ariel sees her work as exploring "the relationship between femininity and technology, a sense of the pixel as the essential unit of the self (replacing the cell or the atom) and above all, a loss of fidelity to the sensory natural world." The cover design built upon her perception of "the abundance of flower imagery, allusions and symbolism in *Disappearance*, from the women's names to references to specific flowers," and "especially the image of everything coming together described as petals of a tightly bundled rose." These images for her recall "layered selves and dissolving memory—bits and pieces of identities reforming and rearranging and showing up at unexpected times," a notion that for her "resonated with this idea of the game as a digital world in which events occur and agents take action on bodies without discrete physicality (which isn't to say they don't have physical form, but rather that those forms blend into one another)."

Lastly, she intends the design to reference classic gaming aesthetics, noting that "the feedback I hear most often about my flower prints is that they look like 8-bit video game errors."

Preface

Another World Everywhere

Greetings are always more than personal, as Michael Joyce well knows. Our opening words convey not only particular but also cultural identity; they are not just speech in the moment but *Sprache*, expressing our bespoken-ness. So the Celestial Kingdom wants to know if you have eaten rice today, while the more calculating or paranoid West asks about health or status, or how your business goes. In this book, people repeatedly start an encounter with the words, "your story." I do not know in what part of the nominally real world strangers hail each other with this expression. Maybe nowhere. The chronotope of this novel seems near-futuristic and vaguely Middle European, not far perhaps from Truffaut's setting for his *Fahrenheit 451*, and similarly non-specific. Perhaps we are simply in noplace, a police state where smiling, punctilious agents can take over your body at will, a dystopia in latex velvet gloves. It may be nowhere we know, just yet.

"Your story" may indeed signify nothing but the practice of fiction. Desultory (if not due) diligence yields only an unprovable negative. Queried with *your story greeting*, Google returns endless come-ons from greeting card companies, but no anthropological leads. Not for the first time, I cannot say where my little learning ends and Joyce's vast imagination begins—possibly somewhere beyond the fifteenth or fiftieth results page, or wherever I stopped looking.

Yet whether *your story* counts as erudition or plain invention, the phrase seems deeply suggestive. I imagine the words were once a genuine question, worn down in time to phatic reflex. In the beginning, perhaps people said something like, "Hello, stranger; how do you happen to be here? What's your story?" Over time out of mind, the phrase has blurred to simple acknowledgement, losing its question mark. You have your story; I have mine; we accept our ignorance, our known unknowns, and work from there.

Or, shrugging into ignorance like an inevitable jacket, consider another conjecture. Perhaps the phrase was never a question, but instead a performative conjunction: "Your story now includes me"; or "I join your story"; or even, "This is your story now." In these cases the context lost to time would be not query but ontology, the unvoiced assumption of a world constituted as a bubbling froth of linked, interpenetrating narratives.

Done there, been that; and yet, aren't we still (always) in story space?

However one reads *your story*, the phrase carries obligation. The hearer is meant to hand the token back:

> "Your story," I offered in return.
>
> It was the old greeting and marked us as being from another world where the thing of most value was something kept within you and not to be sought at the bottom of these wells of bright light before which her customers sat mesmerized.
>
> "What will it be?" she asked, moving behind the counter. "Another run at dreams? An investigation?"

By now we never-so-modern readers may be accustomed both to dream-runs and investigations, or rather, the intersection of those sets, where we find stories that change each time we play them. Storyspace™ indeed. Likewise, some of us may bring to this book another pan-Joycean convention: the end-and-beginningless tale of Here Comes Everybody, whether in its original commodious vicus, or the post-hypertextual dance-around-the-planet that is Michael Joyce's *Was*. Both pretexts imply the now familiar décor of writerly reading, puzzle palaces of incommensurability that map the world onto a series of incomplete, peculiarized figures—the fiction of ontology in both senses of the *of*.

Yet what we find in this book is not just the postmodern idyll of cross-configuration, or as the poet says, complicated shadows. Or rather, the old play on worlds is certainly on offer here, but under a certain onus or anxiety, the looming presence of another order of signs, something that lurks inside those drowning wells of light, as well as other places:

> There used to be a game when I was very young, one not played on a screen but rather on an actual table, a game not unlike the logic dreams that sometimes assailed my sleep, where you shook a canister of brightly colored sticks and spilled them on the green felt of the table and then tried to extract as many of them as you could before the resulting pile collapsed and you had to begin again. It was like that for me during those days.

Whatever else it may be, this is a novel about certain conditions under which story is haunted by game. Many games thread through the piece, offering themselves (as games will do) as possible signatures or metaphors for the larger enterprise: Pick-Up-Sticks; Chutes and Ladders; chess; as well as games of more modern vintage, and one so advanced that it counts as vaporware. This is a fantasy game (in every sense) called Ynys Gutrin or Isle of Glass, of which one character reports:

> "I mean I spent all of the last three days or so trying to find some game called Ynys Gutrin, goin' in and out more stores and bazaars and market stalls, searching more network game boutiques and online stores than you can imagine, only to find what you want is something they ain't even released yet, in fact just started developing! Damn thing won't be available for years and the folks who told me what they knew said it was top secret."

Secrets drive narrative (as much as they do games), through their gravitational loading of peripety or unwinding. Secrets also imply anxiety or vexation in their kinetic potential for full disclosure, as witness the tremor in any hand about to turn over the card of What Will Be. Yet perhaps we should be a little worried about this anxiety. For good reasons, it has become unfashionable to speak of antipathy between games and stories, after some defining schoolyard moments in which early ludologists faced down their literary harassers, winning a grudgingly respectful truce. Yet there remains a necessary and inevitable tension between these sharply different forms of fiction.

As is the case with most deep conflicts, the root of the problem is not difference at all, but at the limits of difference, in equivalency or conversion. If a game of glass or mirrors comprises the ultimate open secret of this novel, then it might follow, as in a "logic dream," that story and game converge—that, in other words, the game of worlds in this ontoludic fiction might be a game in the strict sense, answering all relevant specifications. If this novel is informed or patterned by a game, then we may assume it has discoverable rules, principles of transformation or transition, discrete states, and some economy of reward in which acts of play (that is, interpretation) have definable consequences. If this book embodies a game, we ought to be able not merely to lose our way in it, but ultimately to win.

What would that mean? What could we win? Could *Disappearance* be parsed, successfully traversed or walked-through? Could the book be well and truly spoiled by some brilliantly attentive reader, like Jane Y. Douglas, N. Katherine Hayles, Marie-Laure Ryan, or Alice Bell? No doubt someone could spend great effort sorting out the various layers and correspondences of what may be an entirely logical dream, explaining what its various detectives seek to discover, the conundrum of the dream-murder that may have been an actual death, the contours and limits of its episodes and fugue states. We could take a stab at rationalizing the shifting dis/appearances of characters like Mr. Dee, Beckmesser, Franky, Candido, Rosaria, and all the rest, who sometimes bear a Kansas-farmhand resemblance to people we have seen before. We could hunt for themes, parallelisms, echoes and aporias. We could, in other words, choose "an investigation" over "another run at dreams," and perhaps produce some plausibly final report.

And yet, perhaps such success would never be the end this text desires.

Speaking of games, *Disappearance* has something interesting to say about what happens when a game (at least a certain game) is won. In the world-bubble where Ynys Gutrin exists as more than rumor, we learn more of its particulars:

> "It's not a sex game," Candido said.
>
> "Nor did anyone say it was." Irina gestured for him to stay silent. "If you win, there is an interlude like a dream, where you are in the arms of the queen and she tells you stories from your past, weaving in what details they can glean from the bioscan. It's very sweet. Like opium. If you like, the stories can continue, you only have to pay. That's where it is important to wager well."
>
> "And win," Candido said. Irina did not object.

To the extent that it fictively exists, Ynys Gutrin appears to be a consensually hallucinatory quest fantasy, set in some misty, monomythic Avalon, presumably a massively-multiplayer online role-play augmented by "bioscans" and other brain-machine tricks. According to Irina, there is also an element of the casino, since the game seems to involve a wager on its outcome, pay-in as well as pay-out. Indeed, it is the end or payoff that seems most remarkable. Ynys Gutrin is not a sex game, Irina assures us; yet if it lacks a money shot, there is the promise of a post-action cuddle, involving a blissed-out return to the mother, an extended sleep in the arms of the queen. Along with a certain swipe at gamer culture, this scenario evokes the dream machine from Wim Wenders' *Until the End of the World*, a device that records images produced by the brain in sleep: the ultimate gadget-love toy, or Narcissus narcosis.

The fantastic Easter Egg at the end of Ynys Gutrin may have particular resonance for those who know the game business. Its dreamy reward suggests the great desideratum of commercial game design: a quest which on fulfillment unfolds into infinite, opioid story space—a game which, once traversed, becomes endless or evergreen, replayable many times over in a no-space of un-time, the dream of a game that turns into an endless spring of stories, and an endless flow of cash. As they say each year in San Jose and Vegas, *the stories will continue, you only have to pay*.

What do we pay for a story, or a game? What does it cost to abstract a dream of a world from the world outside our dreams? With these questions, the anxious relation of story and game can no longer be assuaged, denied, or otherwise held in check. If like most people these days, you occupy the failed hallucinations of neo-liberalism, then your daily story will be about reckoning, if not paying: counting up the costs of political and corporate insanity, trying with perhaps increasing desperation to convince heirs and assigns that our culture still has vital meaning—that *your story* is not a horribly empty phrase, but a genuine extension of interest in history and posterity.

Much indeed has disappeared since expectations of cyberspace burned out so brightly at the end of the old century, as the batteries failed on our dream machines and the virtual faded all around us to an ever more starkly real. We may find ourselves like Wenders' Claire Tourneur, sobbing over a dead appliance, begging someone to make it work again. Reckonings are hard to face.

Indeed, endwardness is a common problem for both games and stories, but perhaps all the more keenly for games. A logic dream (which is, after all, another name for game) converges on a final if not singular state or solution. Performance is evaluated, then delivered up in terms of victory or defeat, agonized win or epic fail. Play always implies pay.

Stories—at least the sort of multiply-cosmologic dream-narratives we have here—may be much less susceptible to these economies of delimited value—they may indeed be more aligned with economies of the general type, emanating from a *part maudite* of surplus world production, also known as imagination. Stories are not games. We are not obligated to solve them out or reckon them up. A reader's experience need not be the same thing as a walk-through or universal solution. Dee may be Beckmesser, or not Beckmesser, but his nemesis or ghost. He may be an Alzheimer's patient, an experimental subject, a fugitive from the cops, or someone otherwise unstuck in time. He may be all those things and nothing more. Stories can handle such ontologic play better than games, at least games of the type currently in fashion.

Had *Disappearance* appeared ten years ago, or fifteen, there might have been more compelling interest in its inventions of a ludic or cyberspatial world—more game to the way it is haunted by games. Today, for this reader at least, the book seems more valuable for its evasions of logical solution, for the chance it affords to share the awareness of its main narrator, the mysteriously rootless philosoph known to the police as Mr. Dee. There is something satisfying, especially in these deepening seasons of discontent, about his Chaplinesque scufflings, his persistence in conditions where power and reason operate at dim removes, and both property and memory seem identical with theft. There is pathetic and sympathetic value in his stumblings-along, his picaresque attempts to negotiate a world where everyone seems to know more about his life than he; where he must live with the "parity" of memory and invention; where, as he puts it, "my dreams go forward and my life goes back."

Ultimately, though, there is a rare wisdom in this character and his struggles—a quality that may be reducible in the end to simple inertia, an unwillingness or incapacity to settle. This vagrant sensibility offers a certain contrast to the dire rationality of the casino or arcade.

"Play," his young companion invites him at one point, the first of many seductions. "There is another world there," the young man hints.

To which Dee responds with one of the more memorable lines in this unforgettable text:

> "You can bloody well say that again," I said. "There's another world everywhere."

Stuart Moulthrop
Milwaukee, 2012

DISAPPEARANCE

1

And so the wheel spun round again, past the double zeros, and left me here where I began, or rather where some form of who I am began to veer away from all I knew and led me toward the end where I lost you, my love. But first, well before I lost you, and indeed how I found you, I lost the boy, or he left me, I still do not know which.

I'll try to explain more slowly.

I told the boy to wait outside but when I came out he was not there. I knew no one in this city and could not go to the authorities, although of course I did not know yet that he had been accused of murder.

The few children on the street were more or less his age, but they had seen nothing.

"You," I said to the one who sat guiding a sprite around a tiny screen with his thumbs while the others looked on, "what can you discover on that screen of yours?"

He ignored me.

I might have asked what he knew of the roulette wheel and how it slows time and then speeds it up again, but I suspect that none of them had ever seen one, or if they did, only on a video screen, in some ancient spy film which they would have screened to laugh at the ancient gadgets. Although perhaps a wheel might have appeared as décor among the furnishings in a game world, I suppose.

"What do you mean?" one of them finally asked. He was a sniffly creature with the round black eyes of sentimental paintings.

Still they were boys after all, as curious as they were sullen.

"Could you find a character named Franky Ali in a gameworld?"

The whole group sniggered, including the boy thumbing the screen.

"You mean the matador?" he asked. "The killer?"

The boys all laughed. They sat along the curb in a half-circle squinting toward the screen propped against the sun on the knees of this fellow in the middle.

"Why don't you call him?" he said.

So they had seen him.

There was never a question of calling him because he changed SIMs almost daily and gave his numbers to no one. His phone was from a market stall, much better than mine, its face a dark screen, deep as a pool, where he played his game.

"If you are a cop, you are a terrible version of one," this fellow said, still thumbing away at his game. "I suppose they told you at your headquarters that this wayfarer costume was all the rage, but you look like a bargain basement avatar someone's bought second hand for game credits on the network."

"You should try a chrome theme next," the sniffly fellow laughed. "They say us boys go for chrome."

Again the others laughed.

"Which way did he go?"

None of the boys paid any mind. It was like speaking to carp at the bottom of a pond.

I cuffed the sniffly boy on the back of the head in parting, his scruffy skull dull as a coconut. I did not look back at them and heard no footsteps behind me.

"You better watch out, grandpa!" one of them shouted after. "Once a matador gets used to killing old bulls like you, it's hard for him to stop."

Franky had just showed up out of nowhere, but when exactly I could not recall. My sense was that we had been together for a long time, long enough that we had traveled through several cities and the spaces between them; long enough also that the annoyance of his constant presence had lapsed into an unlikely habit, if not what someone could call affection. Still it seemed as if something was missing without him now. He could show up once again, I knew, and so was not as much worried as unsettled, especially given what these boys had said about him, although no one could be sure how much of what they said was real and how much occurred within their many screens.

I was tired of looking for him. There was a long afternoon ahead and the sun beat down and there was little shade in this city except in the small public square we had already once been rousted from that morning.

Had he been on the run already then? Or was this accusation, his matador status, something that had happened in just half a day?

Really what did it matter? If he did not return, it would be no different than before he had appeared.

"Hey mister, you want to buy a rubber?" he had said then.

The condom in his grubby palm looked like a packaged candy, the brand name "Lucky Boy" below a smiling anime face.

"What the fuck would I do with that?"

"You very funny, boss, what the fuck exactly."

And that was that. We were walking together, that day and the next, until today.

At first I tried to drive him away, but then, when flailing at him a few times and connecting more than once did not dissuade him from following behind me, I ignored him as best I could. Midway that first day I stopped by a bridge and bought a shawarma from a Korean lady who sold them from a little shack along the river. He sat on the cindery path beyond the bench watching me while I watched the barges and chewed at the sandwich. I offered him nothing, nor did he ask. A policeman was coming along the path, his hands behind his back. The boy got up and wandered away, but not really all that urgently when I think of it now.

Still I thought that was that and I was done with him, but by the time the policeman passed, the boy was back with a few Chinese dumplings that he must have dug from the trash bin near the shack. A long grey barge passed by low in the water accompanied by a newly painted tug, red with blue trim. I waited until the boy had finished eating and then we moved on.

That night we slept under another bridge on cardboard pads among a dozen other wayfarers, all of them locals, most drinking from a shared jug of colorless spirit they passed among them. There was a low fire and just as it had settled into embers two Rastas appeared and squatted there. Before long a small cloud of sweet smelling spliff and laughter tucked up under the bridge supports where we lay. The boy was already asleep but with a knife in his hand, a folding silver box cutter, its blade extended.

So he's not a whore, I thought, or if so, he isn't looking for some omi-polone to latch onto as a protector. That was a relief. Even seeing him lying there, the silver tongue of the blade protruding from his hand, I didn't imagine him a killer.

I woke to find him squatting on the same cardboard where he'd slept and chewing on what looked to be a fairly fresh loaf of bread. He held the loaf in one hand and with the other held a cell phone before him, navigating through a multi-colored maze with one thumb on the keys. When he saw me, he clicked off the phone and twisted one end from the loaf of bread and handed it to me.

"Where did you get that thing?" I asked.

He knew I was asking about the phone. This was before he got the new one from the market.

"I got it from a dead man," he said. "Pretty soon it run out of time same as the man."

A bit of the poet in him then, I thought. Now I wonder.

"What will you do when it dies?"

He looked at me a long time.

"What you think, boss? Lots of people die. So I'll buy another one from another dead man."

"And what were you doing with it?"

"Play," he said. "There is another world there."

"You can bloody well say that again," I said. "There's another world everywhere."

Later that day, tired of hearing him scuffling behind me as we walked but also, I suspect, getting used to having company, I turned to address him.

"Stop dragging your ass back there like a donkey and walk up here like a man!"

Damned if he wasn't staring into the cell phone screen as he walked. Still he yipped with delight.

"You very funny man, boss, ass dragging donkey, what the fuck exactly!"

"Just where the fuck are you going?" I asked.

"Don't know anymore," he said slyly, "now that I'm walking in front."

"Fair enough, boy," I said. "You have a name?"

He laughed again.

"Sure I do, boss, everyone does. Everyone dies, everyone has a name. It's part of the rules of the game."

I took that to mean he wasn't telling just yet, which was okay with me, and that was enough of our chatting for a while. The afternoon was moving on and in truth neither of us knew as yet where we were going that day. There were things to arrange: destination, accommodation, provender, a plan for what would come next.

To be sure Franky—though I didn't as yet know his name just then and can't be sure even now that really is it—was a clever little monkey at least when it came to foodstuffs. He could conjure something to eat out of nothing, whether by stealth or begging or some other use of himself or others, I cannot say. But we'd no sooner set down to rest our legs after a few hours walking than he would scramble off and return with some bruised fruit or a grey hamburger in greasy wrapping, a bretzel dotted with salt or a sagging slice of pizza, its cheese still warm. Sometimes we'd be passing a snack shop and he'd turn in just like that and put a couple of bills up on the high glass counter, gesturing to me as if I were his old man, telling me to order something for us both.

I don't think he knew how to add or subtract. I surely didn't think he knew how to kill except perhaps in games.

Where the money came from, god alone knows, unless that little world inside the screen was more real than anyone would suppose. For a while I figured him for a pickpocket, though I also still considered that he might be peddling his bony little ass to some old toff in a nearby park.

Mind you I kept up my part of the bargain, if there was one. I consider myself an expert in available real estate of a particular sort, able to suss out when a placard advertising a flat to let or a model home signals a space neither watched over nor secured very well. With the boy at my side I likewise became a fair actor at the door of parsonages and such, telling a little melodrama of my fall from fortune and my dear wife's death and how the boy and I were now pilgrims in search of employ heading toward the city where my sister lived.

In this way we enjoyed the occasional real meal and comfortable bed and, once or twice, a free bus ticket to the city where my imaginary sister dwelled. Though we nearly came a cropper this way once as well. When I think of it now, it should have given me a sense that the boy possessed murderous propensities.

It was a Presbyterian manse in a stupid little town with a railway station where no trains came anymore but which was nonetheless surrounded by petunias, with a brass bell on a new rope gleaming yellow outside and its fully restored woodwork polished to a burnish within. For a while I thought we'd stay in the station that night until an old woman shuffled in, apologizing and smelling of violets and disappearing within the shut office. The ticket kiosk clattered open like a roll-top desk and she invited us to sign the guestbook, then offered us tourist brochures, pushing a bowl of lollipops across the counter to the boy.

He looked at me for guidance.

"Don't worry about Daddy," she burbled and gave me a wink. "Take one for today and another for tomorrow, a little sweet never hurt anybody, at least if you brush your teeth."

So we were stuck with the parsonage. I rang the bell and told my usual story to a minister unusually fat for a Presbyterian, at least in my experience. This one was a canny one nonetheless and he asked me where my sister lived. I thrust toward him the cheery little map of the region we'd got from the violet lady at the station with the petunias and pointed to the first name I saw.

"That's here," the parson said smugly.

"I know that," I snapped, nearly ruining everything, but just then the boy stepped out from behind me and took the map in his hand and pointed to a town two towns over. The fat prelate touched the filthy hair on the top of Franky's head and then let his palm slide slowly down along the boy's cheek just a little too fondly.

"You'll need a bath before your supper," he said, gesturing for us to enter. "The both of you," he added from behind us.

After the bath we had sausages and boiled potatoes for supper and then were sent to bed in separate rooms. In the middle of the night I heard yowling and ran to the room where the boy sat up in the bed, the preacher cowering over him in his white cotton nightshirt, his hand bleeding like a stuck pig all over the cotton of the nightshirt and the bedding. The pastor folded his bleeding hand into a pillow like a giant bandage, crying to himself as we ran off, only stopping long enough to help ourselves to what we could carry from the kitchen icebox. On the way out the door I also snatched a half bottle of good single malt from the pantry. As we hurried along the road in the cold on our way out of town, eager to get away before the fat bastard could come up with a story, I tugged at the scotch to warm myself. Once we were far enough away that I thought it safe for us to duck into a boarded-up farmhouse for an hour or two of shuteye, we slept in shifts. The boy went first and I noticed that he did not reopen his folding knife until I woke him when it was his turn to stand guard over us.

He let me sleep until first light and when I woke presented me with the parson's kidney-shaped change purse, a nubby oxford leather thing stuffed with small bills. We had enough to take a bus from the next town and live rather well there for a week.

It was there that he had bought the handsome new cell phone with a dark blue case and a screen like a dark mirror as well as three different SIM cards still in their wrappings from an Arab selling brocante in a booth. Before long the money was gone and we moved on.

Then the wheel spun round again and he disappeared.

Now I faced the question of whether to decide he was gone for good and move on again alone or to remain in this city a day or two in hopes that he would find me. What hopes or whose that common phrase contained I did not know; nor did I know whether this city, once a provincial industrial hub near the border, its factories now empty hulls, was a place to contain them.

Add to this that now I wasn't sure whether those boys had merely been making up the story about the matador and him being wanted for murder or merely boasting. I suppose I wanted to find out the same way someone wants to find out what's on the next level of a game or what someone will say in a story.

Or perhaps I was just lonely and out of hopes for myself, although someone could say, as Rosaria did, that deep inside I must have recognized him.

But that is getting ahead of things.

I knew enough by that time where the boy placed his hopes when the opportunity arose, and so I looked for an internet café of the sort where kinds like him and those boys I'd seen gathered around oversized plasma screens yelping and groaning as they warred together. There were three such places in this run-down town, one run by an Egyptian, another by a Pole, and a third by a woman with enormous breasts and jangling bracelets who in another time and place you would have thought was a Madame. Even here you could not be sure.

In the Egyptian place I spent a coin and searched several spellings for Franky Ali, finding eighty-six hits for that spelling including a page without a picture on a social network and a video of a schoolgirl field hockey team in their changing room, all chastely dressed in white blouses and green plaid jumpers. Other spellings yielded more hits, a half dozen of which were in foreign script, both Asian and Arabic. There was nothing about any murder, although I know now that's because the stories called him by his other name, Franky Lee.

The Polish place smelled of vomit and there was no one there and I did not stay. The proprietor scowled through the window and gave me the finger as I walked off. In the gypsy place, for that was how I figured the Madame, I discovered the group who had been sitting on the curb when Franky disappeared. The same fellow sat at the center, his knees pulled up to his chest, the keyboard sitting on it. Clearly he was the artist among them, the one whose moves they all admired and followed. The others sniggered when they saw me enter but he nodded to me, almost respectfully, and then turned his attentions back to the screen, which had the effect of stilling them. I could not recognize which of the boys it was whose head I had cuffed. Otherwise the place was empty.

The space on the screen was a curious mix of frivolity and menace, a sort of raucous cartoon world that nonetheless had the features of a factory, ramp upon ramp rising up back and forth across the screen among bulbous gears the color of children's poster paints, rotund pistons that huffed and puffed as they rose and fell, and occasional saw blades that unexpectedly flailed across the screen like Brontosaurus tails, lashing away an occasional unwary creature. The latter were neon colored and faintly blob-like but with manga eyes set high in the kind of lozenge-shaped faces that long ago were associated with UFOs. When such a creature would tumble before the lashing blades, it would pop like an old-fashioned photographer's flashbulb, and one of the actual boys would moan, obviously having lost a life.

The Madame swayed her way toward me from behind her counter and stood just over my shoulder watching awhile with me, her enormous breasts brushing lightly against my back. Her perfume had a strong scent of vanilla and baby powder.

"I have some special disks of adult interest," she whispered. "Very nice Czech studies and special interest videos if you like. And there is a private work space away from all this noise."

"Perhaps in a minute," I muttered and she swayed away again.

"You like to see girls sucking on it?" one of the boys said and the others laughed in chorus until the artist shushed them.

"You just missed Franky," he said, still gazing intently at the screen.

One of the neon characters was a master of evasion, moving ever upward, avoiding the hazards whilst shooting it out with the occasional demons who appeared from the shadows of the cartoon factory. These he dispatched coolly, vaporizing them with a shotgun that seemed to dispense shells loaded with phosphorous.

It had to be the artist who proceeded so, clearing the way for the retinue in his wake.

"He was in here?" I asked.

"He was up there." The artist nodded toward the screen. "He's very good, I was glad to have him with me, but then he logged off unexpectedly."

"Can you tell where—" I began to ask but did not know what to ask exactly.

The artist ignored what I was saying in any case. He was in the midst of a demon ambush that it seemed impossible to escape, with an unlikely and enormous serpent slithering upwards through the infrastructure even if he should.

The fee for the special videos was five times that per minute for an internet connection so I made fast work of it. The Madame handed me the CD and a box of tissues. There was lotion in the cubicle.

"I can arrange special instruction for a further fee," she whispered sweetly as she showed me in.

"Perhaps another time," I said, but the interchange and the memory of her smile and how she had pressed lightly against me helped things along.

"Oh my," she said when I came out. "I hope you got your money's worth."

The boys, too, had moved on.

"Do they come here often?" I gestured toward where they had sat.

"Of course," she said. "So you like young boys?"

"Not like that."

"Mmmm," she said, then gave a lusty laugh. "Such strong, sweet creatures, good with their joysticks you could say."

She was still laughing at her own bawdy as I went out into the fading light of late afternoon, looking for what exactly I could not say, unless some reason why this boy, so lately come into my life, now seemed such a part of it now that he was gone.

In this town, white-gloved police patrolled very slowly in observation cars that they drove while standing upright as charioteers within a thick glass turret. Atop this turret an array of panoramic cameras like the eyes of a housefly slowly turned on a small green disk. The police were very polite and nodded to whomever met their eyes. One of these observation cars had just rounded a corner ahead of me near the municipal building as I came out from the gypsy's. From a distance it seemed that another, smaller figure stood like a soldier beside the police officer. I began to run, thinking it might have been Franky. As I reached the corner, however, the observation car had already sped up and I was unable to catch up with it before it was swallowed up into the garage beneath the courthouse next to the municipal building. I wondered whether I should pursue the car, perhaps even file a missing person report. Outside the police garage there was a guardhouse, also made of glass, in which a policewoman stood.

"I would like to file a report," I shouted up to her.

She clicked an intercom.

"Use your telephone," she said and gestured toward a placard next to the booth that instructed those with inquiries or complaints to call a certain number. As for those who had an appointment, the sign instructed to hold their identification before the scanner and await instructions.

The intercom clicked again.

"Please move along, Mr. Dee. You are unknown to the system here."

I had no identification and yet they knew a name for me.

"My name is Franky," I said, "Franky Lee."

She clicked again.

"Very funny, Mr. Dee. Please move along now."

No threat, no smile, just the same polite nod the officers made from the observation cars.

Just down the street—it could hardly be called an avenue—was the small public square that we had been put out of that morning. Even so I decided to risk sitting there again since now they knew who I was and the policewoman could see me from her post. I had to strategize and from there could reconnoiter if the observation car reappeared with its passenger. The same environmental security officer who had told us to move along that morning was still there in the square but this time he nodded politely to me in the way that the police did. He was talking softly into the Bluetooth microphone on his earbuds and I imagined that he was in communication with the policewoman. After a while his conversation ended and he moved through the square pinching spent buds from the hibiscus, dropping them into an earthen colored sack that sat at the hip of his green uniform. It seemed like pleasant work to me.

I sat back on a wrought iron bench and considered my next steps, watching the environmental security officer gather the buds into his sack. Like a worker bee, I thought.

To someone not used to being a wayfarer it might have seemed that my situation was precarious. Sometimes, however, exactly the opposite can be true. Here was my thinking: since they knew who I was, whether from biometrics or an analysis of my online session, and since they had neither acted to detain me nor moved me along as earlier they had from exactly the same place and under the same circumstances save one, all this suggested that they had some need for me. If Franky were in custody or they were after him, they might have needed me to witness or affirm something, maybe even to take him off their hands when they were done with him.

If he was not in their possession, they might have hoped that eventually we might find each other and thus could rid themselves of us both at once without having to go to the trouble of chasing each of us down individually.

Or, and this was most likely, they could very well know exactly where each of us was and organize events such that we would find each other, thinking we had done so on our own rather than like figures on their chessboard. If indeed he had done something horrid, they could in this way determine whether we were accomplices.

In any case it made no sense for me to keep walking now that the light had begun to lapse and the birds had lifted their twilight song. Running after the observation car following so quickly upon my excitements at the Madame's had frankly left me worn down. Perhaps, I thought, I could sleep here after all. Or perhaps life would move on around me and show me what it had in mind for me at least this one day of god's creation.

And so it did. Not long after the environmental officer rounded the far corner of the square opposite my bench, a small electric car pulled up and a plain-looking young woman in a blue shirtwaist dress emerged from it. She wore a small printer on her hip like a railroad conductor and grasped a hand-held keyboard and reader. She was professional but not brusque, holding the lens up before my face.

"Social services," she said and I nodded. "I need to take an observation."

I nodded again as a tiny red beam emerged from the lens and struck somewhere above my eyes where I could not see, most likely at the center of my forehead.

"In good health generally, Mr. Dee, I can see," she said.

She typed something into the hand-held and a slip commenced to print from the machine on her hip.

"Am I being detained?" I asked.

"Oh no," she said and smiled. "Social services. This is your meal voucher." She tore a strip from the printer. "And this your shelter pass." Her smile turned to the best she could offer for a stern expression. "No more than two days."

"I understand," I said, then asked, "Will the boy be there?"

She squinted toward her screen. "I have nothing about any boy," she said, then added, "Don't lose these, they're non-replaceable."

"Aren't we all?" I said merrily.

She waited politely to see if I had more to say, then bowed and turned.

Then she was back in her car and gone off.

"Time to go then," the environmental security officer said.

He had slipped up on me from the other side as I watched the girl in the shirtwaist go off.

"Yes, I know," I said.

"The canteen is due west, toward where the sun is setting," he said. "They can tell you where to find the shelter."

Though I knew very well in what direction the sun set, I said nothing. He had a gentle voice and a surprisingly plump mien for an environmental officer and so I thanked him, wishing him good night.

"Sir?" he said.

I stopped.

"Well, I just wanted to say that I think you're right. We all are indeed, aren't we?" he said in return.

"What's that?" I asked.

"Irreplaceable, or so I'd like to think. Good night, sir."

"Good night," I said.

He left me in a jolly enough mood that I would have waved a hello to the policewoman in the booth had she not been replaced by a tall fellow with bushy muttonchops like an old-time fusilier. This fellow nodded, of course, as I toddled by below him in the bath of security lights that had ascended with the descending sun. I was eastbound, heading away from the sun and the canteen both, hoping that the gypsy's place was still open because I had a hunch about her.

"Ah, Monsieur Véloce!" she greeted me with a laugh. "Your story?"

Business was booming. The boys were back, spread out like lice before the big screen. This time of day, however, another dozen older fellows and one sallow-faced yet dark-complected woman distributed themselves as well at the various stations. It seemed likely, given her good spirits, that Madame was also entertaining others in the private workspaces.

"Your story," I offered in return.

It was the old greeting and marked us as being from another world where the thing of most value was something kept within you and not to be sought at the bottom of these wells of bright light before which her customers sat mesmerized.

"What will it be?" she asked, moving behind the counter. "Another run at dreams? An investigation?"

Hearing this, the sallow-faced woman snuck a glance. I smiled at her. Dark sad eyes sat high on a poxy face. She ran a knuckle below her nostril and looked back down into her screen, its soft light bathing her like a pocked Madonna.

"She works for you?" I asked.

The gypsy shook her head, eyes gleaming, smoothing back a wisp of black hair from her temple with a bangled arm. "You're interested? I could inquire, although there are prettier girls in the holograms."

"An investigation then," I said, but, misunderstanding, she began to move toward where the woman sat.

"No," I said quickly, "I'm looking for something."

"For someone, you mean," she said. "The boy? Little Franky?"

I must have shown my surprise.

"No data-mining involved," she said. "I saw you on the street together before you came in here without him. I heard your conversation with young Candido over there the last time." She gestured toward the game players. "Mere social engineering you see," she said. "Not all investigations require a coin."

"That is a very good thing," I said, "because I am afraid I have come up a bit short for the moment in the matter of specie...." I held out two small coins to show her, of course retaining a larger one in my pocket.

"The cost of one's illusions," she said. "You should have lingered earlier over your disk and gotten the full benefit of your expense."

"You didn't mention holograms then," I said.

"You couldn't afford one then and don't have anything to offer now," she said, and we both laughed because that was the truth of it.

I thought I saw the sallow-faced woman suppress a smile. She had been looking up toward us when I glanced there but quickly averted her eyes toward her screen.

"In any case, it's not what I'm after now," I told the gypsy. "I need some information about the boy."

"You know that you are not alone in seeking him," the gypsy said. "He may be in a certain amount of trouble."

"If you call murder trouble," I said.

"I call murder natural," she replied. "The larva murders the marigold and the butterfly the larva."

"And who's he supposed to have killed?" I asked, a little tired now of this banter.

"Why you, of course," she said quietly, "or at least a part of who you were before you flew away from the husk."

Even as weary as I was of this kind of nonsense, I might have pursued this strange dialogue, but there was a rising sense of excitement in the room coming from the direction of the fauteuil and sofa where the boys gazed up at the plasma screen. Candido's posse gathered closer to where he sat playing alone. They grew silent, almost quivering, as he neared some cataclysmic level, a gateway toward transcendence of one sort or another, the mood infecting the whole place. The men scattered at the various stations looked up from their machines, wasting valuable connect time; even the sallow-faced woman stole glances, and already Madame's great weight was shifting in that direction.

I had business to do and tried to move quickly.

"I don't suppose I could barter—" I said, extending the chit for the canteen before she cut me off.

"A little patience, Monsieur Véloce," she said. "Let's go see."

"An intermezzo everyone," she announced. "Connect charges will be suspended until further notice."

Everyone crowded around the plasma screen, which had now taken on the quality of a tiny theatre, becoming the center of focus for all but three customers, two of the men and the sallow woman remaining at their machines. I was surprised to see that one of the fellows who rose up from his screen was in fact a policeman without his tunic, the uniform shirt, tuxedo-striped white pants, and holstered hand-held and taser giving him away.

It was an icy wilderness wherein crouched a black leopard with eyes of fire and teeth as white as the ice against the ebony fur, licking its—his, the artist Candido's, it was clear—bloody flank and paw, the blood flowing crimson then black into the rime where he paused, a more horrible struggle clearly before him at any instant. Suddenly there was a collective scream, despite everyone's sense of an impending something, as an immense bird of prey, talons outstretched like knives before it, eyes like cruel beads, descended in a shrieking shadow across the screen. I felt the fingers slip into my pocket and instantly gripped the wrist sharply, pressing my own talon deep into the soft channel between the flexor tendons, nail pressing hard against the medial nerve. The woman's body grew limp against my flank but she did not cry out or even whimper. The now partly paralyzed hand was warm through the thin lining of my pocket against my hip. I held her like that, not relieving any of the pressure, as we watched the scene before us. She leaned still more against me, her breath hot and sweet against my face and ear.

"Don't make a sound," I whispered.

She pressed her center against my rump and leg, surely attempting to relieve the pain, but still pleasant in a strange way. Even so I dug into her wrist still harder until she leaned away, finally now making a swallowed whimper. The Madame had witnessed everything. She looked over coolly at the two of us pressed in our own miniature combat but then turned her attention back to the screen.

Candido's retinue had gathered so tightly around him you could not see much more than his bent shoulders and the back of his upright skull.

Yet there was such a sense of calm possession about his figure that the crowd of us that joined the boys leaned in toward him almost despite ourselves as if to offer our protection. It was an epic battle, one where time disappeared into a series of ice caves and iron fortresses, along ridges of volcanoes spewing blood and phosphorous ooze, across leaden seas where gleaming cutters clad in burning metal fired hissing rockets and torpedoes. A giant squid emerged, sloughing off the waters and lashing tentacles that, once severed, flapped off as huge bald vultures, their hides mottled with ghastly purple suppurations. Generation upon generation of armed creatures assailed Candido, some robotic, others blob-like as in the earlier game, anamorphic and malevolent versions of brightly colored children's cartoons. He, too, evolved from level to level, the panther transforming rather awkwardly into a Nubian cliché, a specter that made the gathered audience laugh as if all of them were in on the joke, the Nubian's skin slithering off him like silk to disclose a physique of molded composite like the shell of a racing car, an armor that reflected taser shots back on his combatants. Another time he transformed himself—or was transformed, I do not know, although the murmurs of appreciations from his audience made it seem it was of his doing—into a bent old woman in an abaya. She held a begging bowl before her in one hand and a gnarled olive branch in the other which she used as a cane. In this guise he shuffled through a screen of briary paths through an overwhelming army of faintly comic brutes, something between retro-gladiators and Astérix, who prodded at the old woman teasingly and made rude remarks but let her pass until the very last screen, a tall forest of swaying white lilies with mucous-coated blossoms furling and unfurling in a sinister pulsing, where one of the gladiators stepped out on the path and would not let her pass unless she lowered her veil. The audience held its collective breath.

Little by little throughout this journey, without my quite noticing, the images had migrated from the oversize plasma screens to occupy a holographic projection that curved over the space beyond and above the game players seating area in a half dome. Whether this was something real or a hallucination I could not say, but all of us—save perhaps Candido—gazed upward into a darkness that seemed deeper and more expansive than the room could possibly accommodate, a darkness that danced with the pixels of the scene appearing as if a rainbow in the mist of a fountain of black water. Little by little as well my grip on the sallow woman's wrist relaxed into something almost intimately possessive, a coercive pressure to be sure yet something that almost presaged a caress. I considered shifting my grip to the more natural hand—she'd picked my right pocket with her own right hand, which left her situated at an oblique and behind me—but her left hand now rested on my own left hip and she'd found a more comfortable base of support once I eased the punishing grip into something that merely threatened her with renewing it again. For now then we were married to this position.

It turned out, of course, that the olive branch masked a weapon and Candido easily dispatched the sentry blocking the path, but that was the beginning of his troubles, an overture to the most frightening of his struggles thus far.

The swaying lily forest began to thrash the moment he shot the sentry, the furling and unfurling petals each thrice the size of the old woman on the screen, each frond salivating voraciously in an ooze of translucent gore as meanwhile a harrowing shriek rose from the lily throats in a great whirlwind of sound that seemed to fill the screen and then the whole room where we watched, the noise rising and rising until the old woman had to drop her branch and shield her ears against the overwhelming screams. Some in the room shielded their own ears and a nausea grew within me. The sallow woman removed her free hand from my hip and covered her eyes.

The swarm of lilies sucked up the old woman like a maelstrom, shredding her abaya and then striping her withered flanks and sagging belly and breasts red with blood from the rows of fine, serrated teeth along each enfolding furl. In an instant Candido transformed himself into an enormous snail that the sea tossed from wave to wave until the cathedral spiral of its shell casing shattered, leaving the naked slug prey to the serrated teeth. Just as it seemed he might be turned to bloody mush, Candido deftly transformed into an enormous leathery eel and swam his way free of the deafening sea, slithering into another screen, a space serenely blue for some time until it disclosed itself as the surface of a giant eye, the dark abyss of the pupil coming into view as the giant eye squinted and blinked.

I was bored well before all this, perhaps alone among the crowd. For me there were other stories: the boy to find, somewhere to sleep, and before that something to eat. And, for now at least, I was as much linked to this creature whose wrist I had in a death grip as Candido was to whatever giant upon whose eye he now crawled like a worm.

Just then, as if he had read my thoughts, Candido abruptly signed off from this level of the spectacle and slipped quickly through the crowd. He passed just next to us on his way to the exit, his eyes gazing deeply into mine, an ambiguous smile on his face. As he went out into the night, thin applause from the crowd followed. The spectators made their way back to their solitary screens mumbling their appreciation at the spectacle and sometime in the interim the dark dome disappeared and Madame announced that the connect time would be metered again and that refreshments were available for purchase.

When I turned, the policeman was standing before us. He, too, gazed into my eyes, but with a purpose surely more certain than Candido's had been. The officer cleared his throat, about to say something. Seeing this, the sallow woman extracted our linked hands from my pocket and, all in one move, executed a tango turn into my arms, laughing musically and then kissing me deeply. The policeman considered a moment but then snorted and moved back to where he had draped his tunic across the back of the chair before his screen, glancing back just once at the sweet and unlikely scene the two of us so unexpectedly made.

2

Rosaria swore she was after nothing more than the canteen chit when I caught her hand that evening. "I knew you had no money. I heard you bargaining with Irina."

"For sex!" the gypsy queen said.

The two women laughed complicitly.

"For information," I insisted.

"As you wish, Monsieur Véloce," she said and they laughed again.

In a short time they had become like sisters and before long we were living together in the gypsy, Irina's, small apartment behind the internet café, the three of us in two small rooms, Rosaria's and my narrow bed in an alcove separated by an India print curtain.

Rosaria rose up from the kitchen chair and crossed the room to kiss me deeply again as she had that first evening. She could see that I was perturbed by their joking. After the kiss she pulled me to her, nuzzling my face into the sweet smelling space between her small breasts.

"He takes it nice and slow right now, don't you my lynx?" she mewed.

Irina laughed. "Let me do that," she said. "He'll feel like Candido after a hundred-level session."

"You'd suffocate him," Rosario said, cupping her gypsy sister's enormous breasts with her two hands as if about to juggle cantaloupes.

I sat there foolish, missing only a switch in my hands to become the mock king of the Saturnalia. How had I come to this, I wondered, and yet knew as well as anything it was the boy who was to blame and that all of these troubles he had brought me.

They arrested me the moment I set foot into the street that evening, thinking to put them all behind, the sallow woman and the gypsy queen, the game artist and the boy, this so-called Franky who had brought me to them. Now suddenly everyone had a name: Rosaria, Irina, Candido, and Mr. Dee, the name they gave me that first day through a mistake of the retinal reader.

"Are you sure that isn't it?" Rosaria asked once and I had to admit I wasn't.

"Names haven't been that useful to me," I said.

"Well, this one was," she said, fingering the visatag that hung like a juju on the chain about her neck.

Suddenly, too, everyone not only had a name but a story and thus some place in my affairs almost despite me.

Three of them surrounded me that night, the officer who had been in the café that evening, a policewoman who may or may not have been the sentry whose retinal scanner baptized me, and a swarthy little pug disguised as a wayfarer but whom I did not recognize otherwise. The officer from the café placed a painless taser against the space between my collarbone and right shoulder, leaving me feeling paralyzed yet somehow able to follow their commands, as if I had ceded control of my voluntary movements.

"Please turn and enter the observation car."

"Stand as close as possible to the far side of the reconnaissance capsule."

"Grip the chrome handles at either side and brace yourself."

"Close your eyes and soma."

"Exit soma and aware now, Mr. Dee. Please step down from the capsule and move to the interrogation chair."

"Keep your arms clear of the restraints."

"Awake."

Where am I, I asked them, but it was as if I had said nothing. Their manner suggested that they could hear only what I said in response to their questions, but nothing that I offered of my own volition. It was as if the words stayed in my head.

The pug fellow was the chief interrogator but there were others in the room besides him just outside my view in the darkness, as well as Franky, the gypsy, Candido, and another boy I did not recognize standing just opposite on a platform where I could see them.

There was one other figure, an old man who had been beaten badly, head swollen and blood crusted on his stubbly cheeks, standing on a platform of his own, shoulders slumped, his shirt front bloodstained as well, a mop of disheveled thin grey hair around a bald pate that looked like a tonsure. His parchment eyes were closed at first, giving him the aspect of a suffering saint in some cultish holy card. When I turned my gaze to him his eyes opened imploringly, deep grey-blue shafts like arctic chasms. Then they slowly shut again.

The other four stood silent there, aglow in light, benign smiles upon their faces, their eyes following with interest whatever was said in the room, moving from speaker to speaker. I knew instantly that they all were holograms of some sort, even the sufferer.

"You're awfully smart for a wayfarer," the pug said. "Some of our citizen guests never recognize the investigatory figures as simuls."

"Your story?" I said and nodded to him when they released me to speak.

"We don't use the old language here," he said, unflustered, "and we will appreciate your keeping what you say responsive."

They flooded me then with a sensation that was the memory of pain or its foreboding, but that was not pain exactly. Whether this was induced by a taser sensor in the chair, or a chemical they infused with the IV probe, I could not say. Yet the feeling was profoundly unsettling, much as the moment emerging from a bad dream when you momentarily fear it could slip over you again. Or, I suddenly realized, exactly like the nausea I'd felt grow within me in the midst of the undulating sea of furling and unfurling lilies.

For a moment I was puzzled by this memory but then recalled with some difficulty that it had not been me who was caught among those swaying forms but rather something I had seen on the screen.

I tried to say so but they had not released me to speak.

The Candido simul was suddenly brought forward in some way, perhaps by means of lighting or some other more subtle proprioceptive visual effect. It was speaking although I could not hear what it was saying.

They released me to speak. "I cannot hear what he is saying," I said.

"Of course not," the pug laughed. "He isn't real."

I was aware of others laughing in the room.

"It is enough to say that he and the others have testified against you, even your little accomplice."

The system here was the most advanced tech I had ever seen. Since on the worst of days I am after all nothing more than a petty criminal, such things are not usually wasted upon me. At first I thought they had convinced themselves that I was something more than a mere wayfarer, or, more likely, had spent so much on techs for such a small town that they felt they had to justify the outlay by using it with even minor offenders.

Here is how it is. There are these places, such as this, that think themselves in the future, while there are others—think of the town with the old woman in the tourist bureau with the lollypops and petunias and the plump parson—that occupy an imagined past neither more nor less real than the future. Each has its need for order and its various systems for sustaining it. Each presents an outsider with its own image, and its own image of him as well.

"You are quite a philosopher, aren't you Mr. Dee?" the pug asked as if on cue.

Was he somehow reading my thoughts? No system was that advanced, I knew, nor could any be. It had to be but a good guess, a considered response to what must have seemed to them a lack of the accustomed range of responses under the circumstances, from panic to bewilderment to mindless resistance. Or perhaps they simply monitored my alpha waves, unless the earlier injection had me talking aloud.

"A mere wayfarer," I said. "What am I charged with?"

"Minor offenders, Mr. Dee? Is that what you thought you were?" The pug-faced interrogator grimaced. If they seemed to know my thoughts, they also seemed to be able to search back in them as well.

"You call murder a minor thing? The larva murders the marigold and the butterfly the larva, is that right?"

I struggled to protest but it was as if my jaw were numbed as at a dentist. That was The Madame, I insisted silently.

"We have the tapes," the interrogator said. "Everything you said and did was archived. Everything!" He leered obscenely, suggesting they had surveyed the earlier scene in the private room.

What am I charged with? I tried to say, again the words locked within my head.

"Look again, Mr. Dee!" he shouted at me severely and it was as if iron arms gripped me though no one was near. They turned me toward the hologram of the sufferer whose eyes slowly opened and then closed again.

And Franky? I asked, what is he charged with? But they could not hear me either.

Does that mean I am not real to you as well? I asked.

The simul of the sufferer seemed bathed in quite a different light than that which had illuminated the others, bluer and yet somehow more sharp, bringing the man and his wounds into crisper focus. Deep within I had the sense that I had seen him before and yet this memory was like the language I struggled to utter there, locked.

"Do you recognize his face?"

Suddenly the words were unlocked again. I could speak.

"I'm afraid not."

"He was assaulted by someone who resembles you."

"He resembles me," I said suddenly. It was true, as if once I had dreamed some future self who took the form of this wounded man.

It seemed to me that a look of benevolence came over the sufferer's countenance then, not at all what one would call a smile, rather an easing of the flesh of his cheeks and jowls and forehead, as if, I thought, it were pleasing to be recognized. Suddenly I had the distinct sense that our positions were reversed, that I was looking from his eyes and back at me. It was surprisingly a not uncomfortable feeling.

"I'm sorry," I said.

"Go on please, Mr. Dee."

The pug seemed to think I was beginning a confession. The eyes of the sufferer closed again and the blue light dimmed so that he stood in shadows. We switched back to our previous places, or so it seemed.

"I'm sorry to hear that. I'm sorry I do not recognize him. I'm quite hungry and tired, it's been—"

"Your companion killed this man at a distance by means of a rogue computer program, something quite beyond a virus, Mr. Dee, rather let's say a pestilence."

"You're a pestilence!" I heard myself shouting, not quite certain where this vehemence came from, something quite beyond the anger at false accusation.

They retracted the release to speak, perhaps because I had veered from non-responsiveness to vitriol. However, no sooner had I said this, than I felt a suffusion of good feeling and energy. If sensations had codings, this one was the exact opposite of the profoundly unsettling feeling earlier, the vitriol more like honey to me.

"And this woman?" the pug asked.

The simul of Madame was brought forward.

"I do not know her name," I said.

"Her story?" the pug asked.

From the way he had said it, a little too pleased with himself, giving it the intonation of the old greeting, it was clear that he was being ironical.

"Were you aware that she was the subject of a surveillance action that your presence compromised? Were you aware that your actions put at risk both a uniformed officer and an undercover operative?"

I couldn't talk and wouldn't let them monitor my thoughts. As best I could I put myself in the eyes of the sufferer again, trying to recall that feeling of tumbling out of myself and into him and then back again.

"This person—Irina, as you well know is her name—has told us that you confessed your part in the scheme to murder the old man and assume his identity, that you told her there was no crime in killing off a version of yourself. She says you told her it was like peeling a mask off and under it finding another."

Bullshit, I thought.

"Of course it was bullshit," Irina had laughed when I told her afterward. "They tell themselves these stories and play their little games and before long they believe it is all true, or want to. That is where you come in. They want you to verify their stories for them by giving them credence. If they want to investigate me, I'll strip off all my clothes and prance down nude into the little basement game room where they kept you and they can fill me with whatever probes they wish."

She wiggled as if in the thrill of the probes and Rosaria laughed with her.

But it wasn't bullshit, I knew now. Whether the police were right to think her an agent of some kind or not, it was clear, as clear as my sitting there as an object of these weird sisters' amusement, that she was possessed of certain powers that the authorities did well to fear.

What they had to fear showed itself quite literally, interrupting my interrogation just as the pug was reviewing what they knew of my recent divagations, narrating my life for me as a voice-over for a little video based almost certainly on an intelligence that had pieced a likely trajectory for me from database reports. It was a strange little film to see, my life story truncated into a recent history. It began with a montage of flickery pictures from surveillance three-sixties in other localities. There I was ambling, happy as the fool Irina and Rosaria lately turned me into, along the right of way of an elevated bullet train, a field of sunflowers waving behind me, a small, bald dog I did not remember harrying me, its pocked skin covered in yellow dust. Then a short scene from the fatal day that Franky latched onto me taken from the point of view of a conveyance of some kind floating along the river where I sat chewing the shawarma and gazing toward the water and, as it turned out, the camera. Franky appears at a middle distance coming toward me before I go out of the frame. Then, finally, a split-screen composite shot of me entering the Egyptian, Polish, and gypsy internet cafés, followed by an excerpt from the girl's school video of the field hockey team's changing room. Then there was footage I did not recognize, a maze of backstreets and an attack of some sort, a strange band of creatures around a fire, monstrous black birds swarming like insects in the night, a lake somewhere with a submerged church, and me in a wheelchair, I knew it was me, though my face and eyes were those of the sufferer.

They were trying to frighten me with a past I did not have, and I refused to let my thoughts reveal anything, fought against the fear they were projecting into my eyes.

"Do you have anything to say in your defense?" the interrogator asked me again and again insistently.

Just as I was about to answer, there was a commotion in the shadows and suddenly I could not respond. It was not the same feeling as when they did not release me to speak, but rather a milder form of the state they put me into for transport. It was a consciousness without any personal sense of memory. Or rather it was a replacement for my own memory, such that even now I can recall the splay and flare of lights along the short journey as they transported me from Irina's café to the municipal center that night, even the sensation of being swallowed by the darkness and the gentle whomp as the observation car penetrated the pressurized air of the basement garage, and all that transpired till that moment, and yet none of it seems anything that happened to me, or to anyone real for that matter.

It is the same with the events that followed the commotion in the midst of my interrogation. When I think of it now, it is as if recalling a video program where the character on the screen resembles me.

First the pug descends from what a viewer now realizes was a small oblong platform of the kind that elephants place their front legs upon at a circus.

There is a sense of frustrated conversations and profanity outside the visible area that the viewer cannot quite discern.

One by one, as if the dimming of low energy electric candles, the simuls are extinguished. First Candido, then more slowly Franky and the unknown boy (who was he, I wondered, why had they never asked me about him?), then Irina, a broad smile appearing on the latter's face just before the illumination dims.

The sufferer disappeared quite differently, not fading or dimming, but disappearing in a flash that left me feeling somehow they had embedded him in me like a breath.

Slowly in place of these simuls there appeared three new figures as if in the roles of a folk tale well known in the region: a policewoman all in white closely examining a visatag held in her hand before her, two parallel rows of gold buttons down the front of her double-breasted tunic, a black patent leather belt cinched at her narrow waist; next to her in the center, a sniffling magistrate in a black gown with purple fur along the shoulders and sleeves, and wearing the same sort of earphones and bluetooth microphone that the environmental security officer had sported; and, lastly, beside him, on the opposite side from the policewoman in white, a dwarf in a leather vest and baggy tweed trousers, his face red-complected, his blowzy hair dyed golden and parted in the middle, seemingly an attendant to the magistrate.

As if on another channel the viewer, it is me I realize, can hear the pug interrogator's voice; it is he, I likewise realize, who plays the part of the dwarf, whispering menacingly.

"I tell you, Mr. Dee, if that visatag turns out to be a forgery, not only will you feel things you have never felt before but also I promise you that you will never again feel other things you have come to think your life depends upon. We have a copy of both the visatag flash memory and the circuitry as well and we'll run checksums and diagnostics until we find a flaw. Meanwhile we will trace you through the paths and trails of your memory until we find proof positive of what you and the boy have done. We'll find the old man's ghost in you and we'll drag it out like a lung."

"Ha!" Irina laughed when I told her what the voice had whispered. "Here's a flaw for you!" And she turned and flipped her wide skirt, baring the great crack between the milky moons of her monumental ass. "I'll drag out your dick for you!"

Rosaria laughed and laughed. It was quite a party they were having, celebrating my birth you could say, or rather my retroactive marriage to Rosaria thanks to Irina's decryption scanner and ROM burner.

She had altered the legal visatag so that it included, as Rosaria's legal mate, a Mr. M. Dee, whose image and biometrics matched mine exactly. These, I can only imagine, she had gathered during my private video session that afternoon. The visa authorized both parties to travel as free citizens and/or reside in several hundred listed localities for child welfare purposes, specifically a missing person, a male free citizen thirteen years of age, whose biological parents they were.

In truth Rosaria was looking for her son, Mil, who had disappeared some weeks before.

"Is it—?" I had asked immediately.

"No, not your Franky," Irina said. "Hers is a more innocent fellow, a flower on the dank sea that your Franky bobs along like flotsam."

"Many boys are missing these days," Rosaria said more gently.

"The other boy then?" I said. "The one they did not show me in the way they did the others, was it…."

"Neither of us were there, Mr. Dee, and so we cannot say. You'll have to search for the other boy in your memory just as my dear Rosaria searches these streets."

That we were linked by the altered visatag did not mean that the dear Rosaria and I slept together, of course. That came with time and not entirely at my bidding. That first night after the police released me blinking to the street before the municipal building, I ran off into the darkness before Irina and Rosaria could get to me from where they stood across the avenue. The policeman who released me watched me run off as well. I was bound for the shelter, for a meal and a solitary bed, the chits having been returned to me along with my sole other possessions, the three coins, my unregistered cell phone, and the polished tiny skull of a turtle that I kept in my pocket as a gris-gris. They also handed me the newly laminated visatag that the policewoman in white had held previously. They'd affixed a local nameplate to it with the name Mr. M. Dee and listing my occupation as philosopher, surely a parting joke from the pug interrogator. As I ran, I threw the cell phone away but stopped short of tossing the visatag since I could not be certain whether the shelter would require an identity card for entry.

As it was, it was closed when I got there, a shimmering chromium gate drawn down over the thick aquamarine glass of the building front. Inside I could see the blurred shadows of the evening's residents through the glass, moving through the common room like sea creatures. It was like being late for a dance.

I reached through the gate and banged at the glass.

At first no one could hear me but then one of the shadows passed near enough to sense the disturbance and, pressing her face against the glass within (it was a she, I could see that from her silhouette), mouthed something again and again that, of course, I could not hear.

"No room at the inn?" Irina asked.

She was right behind me, hardly winded after having chased after me.

"Your little wife didn't have the energy, so I sent her home."

"Fuck you," I said.

"That's possible," she said, "but it could lead to jealousy within your new family. And you don't have enough money."

I submitted to her laughter then without protest. It was late and I would settle for sleep if there were to be no supper.

Inside the shelter another figure now smashed his lips and face against the glass. It was the sufferer, his face grossly distorted, and I wanted to cry out.

Irina was standing beside me and we watched the scene as if something in a communal dream.

"You see how crazy they are inside there," she said. "You wouldn't be happy. Come."

She took me back another way so that we were not obliged to pass the municipal building again. In the quarter she took me through the buildings still had darkened doorways and recesses of the old kind and voices sounded from their shadows. Wayfarers and lost men mostly, an occasional unmoored woman. They seemed to know Irina by sight, the way plane spotters know an aircraft by its undercarriage and configuration.

"Give us something," a voice called from a deep shadow.

"What do you want?"

"A tit," the man said, laughing.

"Here's something," she said, and let out a great fart.

The man laughed still harder.

An observation car swung round a corner suddenly and blinded us with a beam. Irina gripped my arm to keep me from fleeing. The car marked us and moved on, the light extinguished.

"You see how it is, now that you are a distinguished citizen," she said, laughing again. "Are not two sparrows sold for a penny?"

And we were back via the back gate of the café where Rosaria sat within before a silver samovar of mint tea. Her red-rimmed eyes showed that she had been crying.

"Yes, many boys are missing," Irina echoed Rosaria that evening after we had tea and pelmeni, the latter washed down with shots of peppery vodka.

Eating finally after all that had happened that day left me drowsy. They wanted to hear all about my adventures and I related them as if reading a story. The two of them were merry at first, but not long after Irina flipped her skirt in defiance to the authorities and their talk of flaws, their moods shifted into something morose as first they considered the charges before me and then spoke about the boy, Mil.

I sat at the table with my head pounding from the vodka and the day and their earnest, insistent voices. The two women sat knee to knee in the ladderback chairs holding hands, while behind them a film of Olympian woman gymnasts played silently on a large flat screen over the sofa, girls of different nationalities in colored leotards tumbling and vaulting a leather horse, chalk on their bare feet. Rosaria told how the man she was living with often beat the boy despite her imprecations, and beat her as well when he thought the boy was sleeping or after he came home from drinking, his clothes smelling of smoke and other women. It became too much for the boy to take, although he, too, lashed out first at his mother, blaming her for "ruining everything," but when she was helpless to change things, he went away. At least that was what she hoped had happened and not something worse. She began to weep again, the grating sound of a small animal in pain. Above her on the screen a girl in organdy cartwheeled diagonally across a blue mat and landed with a grunt, composing her face into a grimacing smile.

I wanted to sleep and then wake to a life without these conversations.

"Why do you think he is here?" I asked snappishly.

Rosaria looked plaintively at me, giving my weary complaint more credence than it was due.

"Why do you think he is not?" she asked.

"I think nothing," I said. "I know nothing. I am not here."

Irina let one hand go, wiped a stray hair away from Rosaria's forehead, then took up her new sister's hands again gently turning back and forth the tiny dark blue ring on her little finger, a circle of blue enamel or some gemstone set with an even more tiny mirror.

"It seems everyone takes you in hand one time or another," I said to Rosaria unkindly.

It surprised me how I was feeling. It was as if I blamed this sallow woman with an unlikely name for my own sorrows, such as they were, as if I indicted her for having trapped me into all these complications, when there was little reason to do so. Still I could not shake a certain animus toward her, perhaps because she of the three of us was so truly hurt. One wrings the neck of the wounded bird.

"Did your son flee because you're a whore and a thief or vice versa?" I asked, doing so almost against myself, as if jeering her.

"I wanted to eat. I kissed you to save you."

"Don't listen to this asswipe," Irina spat. "I should have left him on the street with the rest of the rubbish."

"Turning a frog to a prince," I said, surprising myself.

It was as if with these fairy tale words I suddenly understood something. Both women looked up in surprise themselves. They, like me, could hear a change in my tone.

"I haven't killed anyone," I whispered to myself as much as them. "Neither has Franky."

"Every day we kill who we were the day before," Rosaria whispered back to me.

It was the kind of hocus-pocus nonsense that, had Irina muttered it, would have set my mood back to the anger of a moment before, but from Rosaria it seemed to come from some deep part of the heart where she had been wounded again and again.

"We will have to settle this petit ménage," Irina said. "You can have the sofa," she said to me. "We'll share the bed."

Rosaria looked at me.

"I'll keep her company," I said.

"Ha! What's this, your husbandly duty? Or your stiff prick, Monsieur Véloce?" Irina said. "You'll do what she likes."

Rosaria let go of the gypsy woman's hands and, nodding silently to us, ducked behind the curtain, leaving to us her arrangements.

"I'll sleep on the floor," I muttered to Irina. "I'll leave her to her dreams."

"And if she dreams of a man between her legs?" she asked, but then turned away before I could answer, pulling a thin comforter down from a cupboard.

"Here," she said, "This will all work itself out by the end of tomorrow."

"Thank you," I said.

She looked dumbly at me.

"I mean it," I said. "Thank you for this," I said, lifting the comforter, "and for all of this I thank you."

"The truth is I sleep on this sofa most nights anyway," she said.

I turned to go into the room where Rosaria was getting ready for sleep.

"You will have to be careful," Irina said. "They will pursue you through your memories, although I swear to you they'll find no flow in the visatag. I'm very good at what I do well."

"Thank you," I said again.

In the dark behind the curtain I spread the comforter on the linoleum floor and then lay upon it, pulling an edge over my face and body. In the dark I knew that the woman sat on the edge of the bed for a while without making a sound, then slowly undressed and, with a small creak, lay upon the mattress. In the dark I knew her eyes were open to the ceiling and that she was quietly crying to herself. Then I slept.

Nothing magical happened. I did not dream of the sufferer; I felt no one along the tracks of my memory as I slept. The next day arose before me, and instead of fear about being accused of something I had not done, there was instead what for me was much worse a burden, the smudged memories of all those things I had fled however long ago leaving my land and name behind and becoming a wayfarer: the bright empty pain that accompanies the need to fill the hours, to have opinions, to listen to others, to stay in a place when you wanted to move, to move when you wanted to stay. It felt like there was a raw wound in my brain, the bleeding like something acid suffusing me.

They were both up well before me and I could hear them in the other room, smell the awful smell of burnt egg from a pan on the twin burner, hear the scrape of a spoon against a plate, sense the caramel smell of coffee, hear the fat gypsy woman step over me on her way to the little bathroom, followed by the sizzle of piss upon the water in the commode and then water splashing on her face and arms and tits and belly and the smell of soap and rosewater when she passed through again. Then the two of them laughing once more in the kitchen.

A door slammed and there was no more laughing. No jabber of women's voices. Soon there would be hours ahead to fill and no sense of what it was I was supposed to do or where I was going next, or indeed whether I was going at all.

I heard a soft scuffling and happened to open my eyes as Rosaria stepped over me. I imagined the shadowy nest of fur between her narrow thighs under what seemed a tablecloth wrapped around her as a robe. Her pissing was a softer music, a whisper where the larger woman's was a rush, and suddenly I could feel my own bladder insistent under me and I ached for her to complete her ablutions.

She was humming to herself before the mirror and the sound of one or another implement clinked against the sink. I couldn't stand it any longer and went out to the kitchen, lifting myself a little to be able to piss in the sink. Rosaria discovered me thus when she emerged from behind the curtain, made up like a harlot, her eyes outlined with kohl, mouth like a smashed berry. I was in the midst of an aching piss and couldn't stop. She shielded her eyes but laughed.

"My god, you are big as a donkey," she said, and sputtered with laughter again. "I thought so when you caught my hand in your pocket."

Had I anywhere to go, I would have out of anger. Instead I stormed barefoot through the door into the café. I could hear her running the water in the sink behind me, still laughing.

I moved down the short corridor past the three so-called private work spaces to the front desk. Candido sat there behind the counter on a high stool, his posse nowhere to be seen, no one else in the café as yet.

"Are you looking for my mother?" he asked.

"Your mother?"

Like that she was there, coming through the door from the street, laden with packages. An electric taxi headed off noiselessly.

"Now what's he telling you?" she asked, although to which one of us it was not certain.

She held the door open with her ample rump and Candido scooted out to fetch the packages she had left beside the taxi. He laughed as he passed her.

"He likes to play games," she said without any trace of irony.

"He does things for me in exchange for connect time, watches over the café when I have to do errands."

All this I knew, or could intuit. Why she was telling me these things I did not know.

"I haven't been able to tolerate having a man around."

I nodded. Message noted.

"He's like a son to me."

He was standing next to her as if at the curtain of a little play, a domestic comedy, the two of them beaming, a little irony now inscribing itself upon their visages in this tableau.

I think now that all these things cannot have happened during just one day. I have been outside of time too long to trust my own recollections of the order of things. Mine has been a life in which the way that events unfolded mattered less—not at all, really—than what comes next. Then, as soon as it does, what comes is left behind. Life is like that. One next after another collapsing into itself, a slow motion video of a rosebud flaring and then tightening back into itself like a parasol. Each segment of my life, the rise and fall of sun and cloud and night and dawn, a hard pellet, like rabbit droppings or the deadheaded flowers the fellow in the square gathered up in the sack at his hip. Franky had momentarily interrupted this segmented life, given it the quality of history: the day we escaped the fat bleeding prelate, the evening we saw a snapping turtle with a young duckling in its jaws, the woman who gave us meat pies wrapped in the glossy pages of a fanzine. Still, which one came before the other I could not say with certainty. It is the same now.

Was there a memory of a killing I could not recover?

I searched my memories: I was standing witness before the bar in the basement of the municipal building. I was lying on the floor beneath the sleeping woman, whose exhalations colored the night like honeysuckle. The two women danced about me laughing and shaking their breasts, making a fool of me. The artist pushed through the crowd and met my eyes in passing, he and the woman stood before me, tiny emoticon smiles on their faces, feigning a domestic scene.

Now the gypsy set a small square of polished lacquer before me on one of the tables. I took it into my palm like a bar of black castile and it began to hum, vibrating gently in my hand.

"It recognizes your bioscan, Mr. Dee," she said, turning to busy herself with the rest of the packages. "It replaces the cell phone you threw away so stupidly last night. I had to pay to get that disposed of."

"How?" I said.

"I saw an old friend of yours," Irina said. "The deputy commander of police sends her greetings. She says you were an admirable antagonist throughout your interrogation, setting up such a mental storm they were able to get little from you."

"Who?"

"The pretty girl at the end in the white uniform with the gold buttons, we're old friends. Old friends."

She had by now unloaded most of the packages here and there in the café, Candido helping her. Loaf packs of coffee, a box of sweets set out under a transparent plastic dome, Orangina, and, at the bottom of a sack that Candido held, a stack of the latest special disks with lurid covers featuring drugged blonde girls. These he teased me with briefly, spreading the covers before me like an oversized Tarot deck, before dancing away to secure them in one of the rooms down the corridor.

Irina followed after him, two full sacks of things still in her arms.

"From what the deputy commander tells me you will have lots of help in searching for Franky," Irina said over her shoulder. "It seems he's killed someone."

"So they told me," I said.

"I think you should believe them," she replied chillingly.

"And you still think it was me he killed?" I asked. "Isn't that illogical?"

She merely gazed at me and did not answer and I felt a chill then, perhaps the belated, vagrant draft from when the door was open to the air.

None of this should have mattered to me, since really, as I've said, I had no connection to the boy, neither by blood nor any sequence of events that one could recount as a history. Still I felt stunned. We were in quite another moment now, from a different little play, with a different mise en scène, standing now in the main room of the Madame's apartment, our ménage, where Rosaria stood beaming before the sink and the twin burners that she had just finished polishing into something impressive, the brass valve cocks gleaming, the oblong bowl of the sink glowing like ivory. She was still dressed in the tablecloth, which she wrapped about her like a sari, a long scarf at her waist as a belt, a towel hanging from it as an apron. With her kohl darkened eyes she looked like Devi.

"We are hearing the news," Irina quickly explained to her, adding, "there's nothing about Mil, I'm afraid."

"But little Franky's killed someone for sure," Candido blurted.

They think it is me, I did not say.

Now Rosaria was crying again, why I was not certain; perhaps she felt for all lost boys, and yet it was mildly annoying to me. She rubbed at her eyes with the towel and the kohl smeared absurdly. For no reason at all I suddenly felt possessive, as if these others were taking something, my story, from me. I had a clear vision of Franky's silver knife, the shark's tooth of the razor edge jutting from its metal casing when it was extended.

"How could this happen?" Rosaria asked, but Irina responded to me instead, as if I had asked this question, doing this so naturally that I might have doubted whether I hadn't really asked the question after all.

"Do you know Ynys Gutrin?" Irina asked me, but did not wait for an answer. "Of course you wouldn't. It's a game—"

"The Isle of Glass," Candido interjected.

"Two persons play it," Irina continued. "They vie for the love of a queen."

"Morgan's sister," Candido again.

"Will you stop this, please, and let me speak?"

"They play for money as well," Candido added. "Franky's very good."

Irina sighed and waved him on, beginning to take the things from the bag and put them away, Rosaria helping her as best she could.

"You have to scan your debit card before you play and they bioscan you to be sure you do not cheat. It's very popular among retreatants, a way to increase what you get from your pension."

"That's why these kids play it," Irina took over again. "They are looking to fleece some old fool, most of whom are really playing for the pleasures of the queen."

"It's not a sex game," Candido said.

"Nor did anyone say it was." Irina gestured for him to stay silent. "If you win, there is an interlude like a dream, where you are in the arms of the queen and she tells you stories from your past, weaving in what details they can glean from the bioscan. It's very sweet. Like opium. If you like, the stories can continue, you only have to pay. That's where it is important to wager well."

"And win," Candido said. Irina did not object.

"The old fellow died when Franky pierced his heart with a sword," she said.

"You can't be tried for killing someone in a game," I protested.

The three of them looked at me. It was how it had been whenever it was that the simuls were displayed in the alcove of the interrogation room. All three of them looking toward me benignly, their gazes washing over me, and yet unreal and I the sufferer.

"I know lots of games," I said. "I've never heard of this one. But I know you can't be held responsible for what happens on a screen."

"The old man had a heart attack," Irina said softly. "When they played back the game log, his daughter said he died of love."

Candido laughed aloud. I tried to laugh as well but there was no sound.

"The police say Franky hacked the bioscanner," Irina said. "They say he pushed the old man's pulse rate up until the blood split the seams of his heart. He also emptied the fellow's account before he logged out, and took it all away on flash memory keys."

"Sweet," Candido said.

Irina stared at him so severely that the room took on a chill. He stared her down awhile but then finally wilted before her frozen gaze. He let himself out the back door and went away without saying anything.

"He could have been framed," Rosaria said suddenly. "They can do anything."

It was crazy but once again I suddenly felt close to her. This inexplicable feeling was what people meant when they said such things to one another.

I wanted to touch her face, to wipe the smudges from her eyes and cheeks and touch her lips, and thereafter taste the cherry wax upon my own when I pressed my fingers to them. Yet I knew that was a kind of game as well, a glass island that it would be easy to get lost in.

3

"Do you love?"

"No," I said.

What or who she didn't ask, just do you love and so, were I someone who shared such things, I would have said this was a good question.

I knew—anyone does—that in the game of life one was supposed to return the question in the same form. Do you love. Do you. Are you afraid. Are you. But by this third night too much already had become a series of fixed steps in a game I did not ask to play. Of course I tried to escape this unbidden life as soon as I could, letting myself out the back door not much after Candido had escaped through that same exit, in my case at a moment when Irina had gone to her desk in the café and Rosaria was singing again in the little bathroom. I exited into searing sunlight. The light shocked what memory I retained from the previous night of the winding blackness and several recesses of my odyssey from the shelter to Irina's back door in her care. In the midday glare the brick facades of the warehouses seemed to rise at vertiginous angles and the emptiness of the streets seemed foreboding, as if a place so bereft must surely be under surveillance. Still I made some progress, emulating the strategies of a rat in a maze, pressing against the buildings as if to absorb what little shade the vortices could supply, turning first right then left in alternation when the narrow roads and alleyways forced a choice, progressing in the way of switchbacks or boats tacking against the wind. To become the diagonal in the grid had been my life to then and I was used to it. Briefly I felt free.

The moreso free when, to my great surprise, the alleys spat me out, not in the vicinity of the shelter as I had surmised, but in a place I thought I recognized, a semblance of a meadow, albeit grown up among a field of cinders and broken glass and hundreds of rusty iron fittings the size of women's bracelets, each threaded within as if meant to couple something, all this the detritus of what must have been a manufactory, through which tall grass now grew, yellow and harsh and mixed with nettles and bulbous stems of smelly flowers with the stink of sour laundry. It was, I was sure, the edge of the city, and still there was no one to be seen.

I had to slide down a culvert and crawl back up in order to reach the elevated roadbed beyond the braceleted meadow, the depression deeper than it looked from a distance and, like the counterfeit meadow, carpeted underneath with slag and cinder, bits of which pressed themselves into my palms like a grim mosaic. I heard a car go by on the road above and so waited a moment before pulling myself up the last berm. I was out of breath when at last I crested the culvert and stood before the observation car and the officer who patiently awaited me. From the car that had passed someone stared back at me, having turned full around in his seat; even from a distance he had the countenance of the sufferer.

Of course I thought to run as soon as I saw the officer, away or even back down, but I was cotton-limbed and immobilized, docile before this creature in his dome—he was of Asian ancestry of some kind, with a Mongol skull and placid eyes—suspecting that my interrogators had left me with an interface they could control at whim.

"Your identity card please."

"I have a visatag."

"That will do."

I took the slate grey thing from my pocket; it had the greasy feel of cheap plastic.

"It is much easier if you use the chain supplied with it," the officer said as he scanned it.

"I don't like the feel of a chain about my neck."

"I understand. It's like a noose isn't it?" he said. "Many people don't like it. In that case, I would suggest a woven silk lanyard, Mr. Dee. They are readily available."

"Thank you," I said.

"And your wife?" he asked. "Is she coming along behind you?" He gestured toward the culvert.

"No, she isn't with me."

"I see," he said. "Then I will have to take you back to your temporary residence. Your visatag does not allow you to leave the territory without each other, otherwise you may travel independently within the district as you wish during your stay with us."

"Thank you," I said and he smiled the way they smile at citizens.

"Keep your hands at your sides until you are securely in the vehicle. You'll feel a certain restraint at first."

I already feel it, I meant to say, but either he had switched off my ability to respond or I did not say it aloud and in any case rode silently in the observation dome beside him until he ejected me, gently, on the sidewalk outside the café.

"Good day, Mr. Dee," he said.

Good day, I meant to say, but he was gone and still I could not speak.

Madame was waiting on the sidewalk outside the door of the café. Through the window I could see there was a sparse custom within at this early hour of the day, an old woman wearing an absurd red hat with a wide brim, a satin band, and crimson feathers, two furtive fellows looking at video news and glancing out the window as the observation car disappeared.

"The return of the native," Irina said and went back in, leaving me to follow on my own.

"You could do with a bath," she said when I presented myself within. "Rosaria is out of the bathroom."

"How long have I been gone?" I asked, but she only laughed and went back to working at her terminal, and I went in.

This was worse than being linked to the boy because, unlike my connection with him, I did not know how this would end. With Franky it was always going to be a tragedy, maybe not a murder at a distance via a machine, but something with a certain finality, someone strangling someone, traitorous disloyalty at the wrong moment, self-mutilation, overdose.

As for myself there was little question that I was capable of killing, for I snuffed out versions of myself every day, my life a string of extinguished candles along a series of nameless ridges, like a cemetery when seen from a short distance, a long scar when seen over the whole of it.

With these weird sisters days and nights might repeat themselves like this. The morning hours spent in details of the toilet and housekeeping, afternoons in a useless search for someone who did not wish to be seen, all the while wondering whether the authorities were about to take me in again. Then these hours followed by evenings of their mocking laughter and bawdy, their earnest conversations and shared tears, suppers and vodka and tea, the dark with its rustlings and questions, the fears and suspicions again, weeping and snoring and whistling exhalations and passing gas, tiny moans in the middle of the night, mumbled dream speech in a foreign language, bare feet moving to the bathroom and back, morning like a sharp pain in a dream transforming into a spear of light through the gap where the curtain never quite closed, the gypsy stirring and passing through the grey light like a freighter in a lapsing sea, my bones aching, breath a stink.

"I love," she said.

Who, I should have asked. But her accent annoyed me, the way she pronounced some words midway between two others: son between sown and soon, love between luff and laugh.

I kill love, I thought—then wondered was it true.

Each of the two nights after the first it had been the same ceremony as the first, the springs easing as she sat on the edge of the bed, the rustle as she undressed, the creak as she lay upon the mattress, the soundless crying, the sense of her wide open eyes. The specters slowly making their way through my mind, the pug-faced interrogator, the sufferer, the strange figure at the campfire, descending birds, and sometimes Franky laughing madly.

To the nightly rustle and creak, this third night—if I am correct in the sequence of days and how long it had been—was added an arm and hand dangling beside the bed not far from my ear where I lay turned away from both the bed and her noises, wrapped in the clotted cotton of the thin comforter. It was as if she were fishing me from my pre-sleep before the specters descended again.

The perfume of this flesh was as inviting as its proximity. I imagined the sensation of soft skin, the slight spiraling along the torqued contour of the forearm giving way to the hollow and opposing knob of the elbow, the swell of the upper arm, the deeper valley of the underarm, its soft thatch an echo of that dark hair I had dreamed of seeing that first morning tufted between the girlish thighs under her makeshift sari. I imagined forgetting or being forgotten.

Rosaria says I kissed her trailing finger then, but I do not remember it so. True, I slept that night aware of her flesh and dreamt that someone touched my ear and jaw, a girl from long ago, her face veiled. Yet it wasn't until the fourth night we began to share the bed. I feel as certain of that as I do of any sequence, although when I say so, the two women laugh.

I realize now that perhaps someone somewhere has tracked this sequence quite carefully, that I might be able to consult a surveillance archive and put even the vaguest memories in order. But, even were that so, it is not how a body remembers.

For a while then night became the press against flesh, the occasional grunting emission, unconsciousness, the sensation of her bony elbows and knees at intervals; each night the constant talking in her sleep, her spaniel yelps, the perfumed hair sometimes so damp with fever and fear that I would brush it from her cheeks and whisper nonsense in her apricot ear. My specters came but their voices were muffled, their visages in mist. The evenings that preceded these nights continued as a little domestic comedy with me at the center as a figure of ridicule and affection for these two faux sisters, the one as bad as the other, not just the ridicule and affection but also the two sisters as well.

The mornings and the afternoons, however, were deserts, they weighed on me, soured my stomach, and made my limbs ache. They seemed useless exercises, a figment of a kind of life like the lives of most men and women.

How do you search for someone? There are a hundred such questions that you find yourself with in a life and that no one ever prepares you for, what do you do when someone dies being perhaps the most obvious. How do you survive when you have nothing and nowhere to go is, of course, a like question, but one easier to experience than to explain.

When someone is missing you perhaps imagine that you will spend time in the presence of authorities, who will have regular reports that they share with you, a set of circumstances to explore through further questioning and conversation, theories, perhaps even intimations of outcomes, even the most dire offering a momentary solace. This is an understanding formed by entertainments, which after all are a version of dreams. Instead in the waking world it is clerical work. You file your report. It is helpful if there are scars, "identifying marks" the term of art, a saber slash would be good, a Maori tattoo on the forehead, a garish splash of purple acne across the shoulder and upper chest. A DNA swab, a nest of hair from a brush, is especially helpful.

Rosaria had already done all this.

Then you can wait at home and pretend that life is the same except for this one thing. Or you can stage your own version of what you had hoped from the authorities, talking with neighbors and family and the social workers or priests who have been alerted, like sharks, to your distress.

She had done this as well, or at least as well as someone could who had no such network in this place. People on the street, strangers, asked her about her son.

Or you can march in quadrants, split the city, state, country, or continent into an imaginary grid, walking up and down each street and alley, each *sentier et chemin*, promenading within it like a provincial politician running for the local assembly on a platform of having shaken as many hands as possible.

It was this part of her search for her son into which I was inducted, a census worker in an empty city, looking for one particular living inhabitant.

These days, of course, you can accomplish this kind of search promenade via a simul, view as we did at least once each morning the vagrant waves of the missing on a terminal screen. It was, I admit, a shock to me to find out that it had come to this.

We would sit on three high stools of chrome and leather at the counter before Madame's monitor: Rosaria, Irina, and me. Once or twice Candido joined us, standing in the interstice between the women, grinning to me whenever I caught him looking down Rosaria's bodice. Before us was the census of the missing.

"It's like Doppler radar," I said the first time I saw it. "Storms marching across the screen."

"More like the swirl of leaves," Irina said. "Storms do not reverse themselves as erratically or bounce off of each other and merge."

"*Un caleidoscopio*," Rosaria said. "A kaleidoscope," she said and we nodded, exactly.

All the missing were monitored by virtue of their emanations, whether cellular signals, hacked bio-restraints, implanted or nanotech medi-monitors, debit cards, rumored top-secret black technologies, or, more prosaically, reported sightings by citizens or authorities. Inevitably intercommunications and coincidents among the missing disclosed that a group of them had coalesced into a sort of pack. Subsequently as each pack formed and was identified, it was assigned its own color, actually a matrix of pixels, Candido explained, that stayed with them by inheritance and intermixed when they shifted packs.

"Like wolves and rabbits, toads or wasps, right whales and the sunset moth," Irina said. "We have been following them for decades, people too, through data mining and social computing."

The boy Mil showed up as a bright red pin with interspersed violet; he was moving within a loose pack of maybe twenty kids, the whole thing having a faintly yellowish underglow to mark their boundaries. They were far from here.

"It's crazy, why do we stay?" I protested, although in truth I had no appetite to uproot, at least not as long as I was shackled to this situation.

Madame clicked and selected a historical view over the past forty eight hours, zeroing in on Mil's red-violet pack. They moved like pollen in the wind, thinning as they flitted through this city, dispersing, pooling again. It was hard to keep Mil's bright pin in focus midst this swirl of lights.

"Where are we?"

She looked at me and clicked again, zooming in, a bright blue rectangle marking the café as she stepped through the forty-eight hour history again. The bright pin centered itself in the rectangle an instant and moved on.

"He was here."

"We can see where he's been, not where he is or will be, although there are predictive algorithms that can suggest where we should search," Irina explained as if I were a schoolboy.

"Not so much search as prepare ourselves to be were he to be there," Rosaria said. It was obvious she had been schooled in this language, which seemed to me as much a religious mumbo-jumbo as any other.

"Can't we just sit here and monitor the movement of the pack until it seems to be swinging through this sector?" I asked.

"None of this is really happening," Madame said. "Not in the way that you can bounce a ball and reach out into the air to where it will fall. These are just pictures of events."

"And they are all boys, these packs?" I asked another day.

"The representations treat them separately. It is rare that a single girl will travel with a pack of boys and even if the whole gang is mated, whether permanently or flexibly, it is useful to represent it as if the girls form a tribe of their own."

Candido was looking at the screen with us.

"It helps monitor the sex trade to keep them separate," he said. "And in some places the boys are forced to be soldiers."

"Girls too." Rosaria said.

"Girls too," Candido affirmed. "Soldiers and whores, boys and girls, spare parts."

"Franky?" I asked.

Candido touched the screen and chose a new view. "His current position," he said.

A bright orange pin with a greenish glow appeared inside the bright blue rectangle where Mil's pin had been.

"Here?" I said.

Candido snorted.

"Franky's good, he probably pulled out his medi and shoved it up your ass while you were sleeping! They'll think you swallowed him."

Rosaria could not keep from laughing, though she saw how it annoyed me.

Candido clicked another view. A small blue-green wave like a ragged edge of surf swayed to and fro across the territory. He selected a bright silver pin in the midst of the wave then plucked out a tiny cell phone from his ear like a jewel. "Look," he said. It was glowing the same silver color.

"So it is not only the missing?" I asked but no one answered me.

"You are here as well," Candido said. "They would not want to lose you now, although this—," he said, pulling the visatag from my shirt on its silken string, "this has a sort of built-in parallax diffuser in its circuitry that my mother and I are very proud of. You always seem a little off from where you really are and sometimes the locator signal takes a wild ride that makes whoever's monitoring think its their equipment that's at fault."

"That's what Franky has as well," I said. It was half a question.

"You are very smart for a dead man, Mr. Dee," Candido said, not laughing.

The thought came into my mind then that I was perhaps another sort of prisoner, left into the custody of this circus and yet no less monitored, no less under suspicion. In this light Irina's access to the police headquarters and her and Candido's ability to burn these complex circuits and to make their way through fantastic spaces at will, both virtual and actual, might suggest that they were another sort of jailor, and my time with them a much more subtle interrogation, one that guised itself as freedom.

Nonetheless that was how we looked for Mil. We would check the representations each morning and then go out where he might be likely to be at some time or another, "preparing ourselves to be" in Rosaria's sentimental phrase, yet also knowing he too could be sending false coordinates. It was like torture to me. We walked the city like Adam and Eve thrust from the garden wearing rotting leaves and smelling of grave soil. Afternoons she left me to myself and went to her work.

"What work?"

"I gather small things and sell them," she said. "There are markets that appear and disappear where people come to see."

I knew she was lying. Another time she told me that her sister deposited credits to her debit card to help her find Mil.

"Why would she do that?" I asked. "There's nothing in it for her to have another mouth to feed. If she wants, I'll send her Franky when I find him."

It was a crazy thing to say. I had no interest in finding Franky, short of curiosity that is, seeing how it would end, although in truth I had no real hope that I would ever know whether he had killed the old man. I was much less eager to be in proximity to him now that he was being hunted and it could conceivably be dangerous to be around him if they targeted him with drones.

Each day I feared Rosaria would cry again but generally she kept her tears for herself and the night while during the day she was stoic, an engine of mindless routine, making her rounds, going to her job, back by supper.

"I could gather small things as well," I said.

"You already do," she said, with neither irony nor bemusement.

Why I was not required to contribute to the ménage was a mystery to me. I had settled into a lazy kind of entitlement that I resented. It was a step toward being contained. Or maybe precisely the experience of it, my soft jail.

"I'm your fucking monkey!" I complained one night as they sat in the kitchen, Rosaria sprawled in Irina's ample lap, exhausted after dancing a polka together.

Irina stretched across and stroked through my trousers.

"Fucking monkey or the organ grinder?" she said, sputtering with laughter. "I hear the two of you at night."

"I'm soundless." Rosaria seemed offended.

"You sound like a concertina," I said. "A concertina in the hands of a monkey."

This made them both laugh and I felt oddly pleased.

I knew I was not dead, although how free I was wasn't clear.

One evening Candido and his posse staged another spectacle of the sort I had witnessed the first night, this one however in a different game world. I did not stay for it because it bored me, knowing too well that it would proceed and end the same as before, only through a different landscape. If I needed fantasy there were more private ways. That I was alone in this opinion I knew from the gathering excitement among the customers, including, I noticed, a policeman again, although not the one from the first night, and not in fact a policeman but a policewoman I had never seen before, this one ugly as a rat, pear-shaped and with such big hips that they made her waddle. She noted when I left and smiled at me through the window; Madame, too, marked my exit, but in her case with some unaccountable annoyance, as if I were demeaning the product. Night was falling quickly as I made my way past the light-flooded façade of the municipal building to the small square, half hoping someone would hail me there, even that the authorities would take me in again, that some event would overtake me, perhaps the world itself set spinning with such centrifugal force that it would spit me out of this life.

Instead I slipped into a stupor, settling onto a bench just beyond the hazy arc of illumination from the avenue and municipal building, falling into the pungent, overwhelming odor of the hibiscus as if it were a pool. Alone fantasy was possible. In this case I imagined Rosaria's sweet small breast in my mouth, the nipple stirring, myself stirring as well, the way her limbs clamped around my hips as she shuddered. An adrenal chill shot through me and I became aware of dark shapes moving everywhere through the darkness of the park. At first I imagined they were giant black insects, their pincers clicking slowly against each other in the shadows. Almost instantly I realized these were not insects but birds and that I recognized them from somewhere, the clicking coming from a flock of grape-black starlings, each the size of a skull, foraging among the lawns and hibiscus bushes, roosting on the fences, wires, and high branches, hundreds of them, thousands even, yet all of them silent except for the clicking, without their usual squawks and shrieks. They were not afraid of approaching closely and yet did not bother me, neither pecking nor screeching, just moving dark in the darkness, their oily feathers gathering a sheen of light perhaps from the moon.

There, deeper in the park on the next bench, was Franky, in such a shadow I could hardly make him out from the darkness surrounding. He fed the starlings something from his pockets, casting it out before him like grain.

"Hey boss," he whispered. "You okay?"

"Should you be here?" I whispered back and gestured toward the arc of light and the municipal building.

"Like nose in face front," he laughed. "They never find it."

It was loud enough that a pair of the starlings screeched and lofted.

"Ssssh," I chided. Why, I don't know, maybe fearing to be captured with him, maybe fearing a drone descending in a whistle through the darkness.

The starlings settled again, foraging.

"You miss me, boss?"

I hissed with swallowed laughter at the absurdity of the question.

"I didn't do it," he said, his voice cracking with emotion. "You gotta believe me, Boss. You're the one who can prove it—you're the one with his memory. You got to free me, Boss, you got to save me."

"And who will save me?" I asked

But he was gone and the birds were as well.

Suddenly the park was bright as day, as aglare as the warehouse alleys had been when I slipped away and tried to run. The air was acrid with phosphorous from the descending flares and another more carbon-like odor from the arcs of the helicopter spotlights, like a light burning out in a theater, a gunpowder smell. I could see the paths clearly, the little shed where the environmental officer kept his tools, the hibiscus blooms like the faces of babies.

"You are becoming quite a nuisance, Mr. Dee," said a voice on a loudspeaker upon one of the noiseless helicopters. "You are disturbing the wild life, please go home."

I have no home, I tried to say, but then felt myself rising despite myself, and shuffled off toward Madame's where the show was just ending, Candido coming out the door trailed by his *équipe*.

"Did you enjoy the show?" he asked.

"I didn't—"

"Oh yes, you did," he cut me off. "You did, my darling. I saw you there among the birds."

And they laughed and went off. I imagined the band of them appearing on far-offs screens as a wave running along an undersea ridge.

There was a good deal of chatter again among the patrons following that evening's spectacle. Rosaria was steering a tray of coca in tall glasses among the tables where patrons lifted them from the tray and tucked coins in her apron, this one an actual red construction, two small pockets at either side of a large central pocket that was stuffed with little bags of snacks, sunflower seeds and dried fruit rolled into the shape of cigars. Madame was at her counter with three men lined up before her, perhaps awaiting one of the rooms. Down the corridor toward the apartment, the waddling policewoman emerged from one of the rooms, tucking her blouse into the waistband of her uniform pants, her face flushed in blotches, her brown eyes in a swoon. She smelled of sweat and lavender.

Perhaps Candido was offering me a mad truth, I thought, and this is all a show for me. It made no sense that the copters could locate me in the park and descend upon me, yet not have discovered Franky. What I was seeing was the spectacle of my own fears. Now this policewoman presented me with a parody of my pathetic fantasies, a combination of sexuality and authority witnessed furtively, a glimpse at a woman's most vulnerable moment. One's own mother or the tarted-up aunt everyone has, her black beauty mark like a tiny spider just below crimson painted lips, a powdery crease descending into her lacy décolletage, her flirty laugh like a choking crone.

Right then and there, as if it were something I had been contemplating for some time, I knew that only I could truly investigate this killing that Franky was accused of. If the earlier apparition of Franky in the square had been but a projection of my fears, I would face them. That surely was what he or it meant by saying I alone was the one who could offer proof, I alone was the one who could be a savior.

I'd begin my investigation when Rosaria went off to do her mysterious work the following afternoon. I knew this would bring me into some danger since they suspected me of somehow being his accomplice, or at least were saying as much in hopes that I would lead them to him. Still it was something I had to risk, even if it put him—or me—into danger. It wasn't so much his having appeared in the park that led me to this decision as a sense I had that I would not be able to get my life back until I did.

When Madame and Rosaria came back to the rooms that night they were neither of them as lively as usual nor as inclined to poke fun at me. It was if they held a grudge against me or perhaps were weary of my resistance. Nonetheless they entertained themselves like children, making tea, lingering over the samovar whispering and giggling together like sparrows, and now and again glancing back at me. Me, they brought an icy vodka scented with some herb, probably rosemary, then took their tea to the sofa across the room and sat brushing each other's hair. Rosaria brushed Madame's in a small fury, whipping it into storms of black; then Irina, her own hair as burnished as the starlings, slowly ran her fingers through the hair of the Devi-manqué Rosaria, following these caresses with the slow pull of a languishing brush. I left them like that and went in to lay on my back on the small bed, my mind turning over the events of that evening. When Rosaria finally slipped in behind the curtain and undressed, I pressed against her so hard that she reached back and grasped where I swelled, pulling me deeper toward her. I pushed her up on her knees, her face down in the pillow and entered from the posterior, something she liked, yet for the first time since we had become lovers, taking the darker entry. "No," she whimpered, but then relaxed her sphincter and I entered easily and exploded in an instant, she, too, unwound in an exhausted moan. "My little flower, my little flower," I whispered in her ear and then slept as if at the bottom of a dark well, a dreamless place where for a while I was free of both specters and the day-to-day. Tomorrow would bring an adventure, hopefully the last, and I could return to a sort of eternal uneventfulness.

I suspected that it would not be difficult to find the address of the rooming house where the authorities claimed the old man had been murdered, although I planned to stop at the internet café of the Egyptian so that the gypsy would not discover what I was up to in my search. Even so she suspected something.

"I hope you are not getting any ideas," she said as Rosaria and I headed out to the day's sectors.

"I thought ideas were my vocation as a philosoph."

"Your vocation seems to be putting the horse in the stable," she laughed. "But she seems to like it enough."

"So much that we're eloping," I replied, and Rosaria blushed.

"You'll miss your wedding cake," Madame leered. "It's covered in cream."

Then, just as we were leaving, she shifted her tone to something more insistent. "Seriously," she said, "do not underestimate their powers. You are nothing to them. Like those little lost dots on the screen, you are mere dust. They'll sweep you away in an instant."

On the sidewalk Rosaria was crying, whether for her or me or all the lost boys I could not say. Little by little as we walked the crying stopped and she became a zombie of purpose.

That day by chance we were searching, if you could call it that, in a park-like quarter where the houses were a checkerboard of bleached cubes between green squares of the same size, an area which as it turned out was not far from where the old man's rooming house had been. Rosaria was quiet, I assumed because of the previous night.

But what does a man know? I thought. Yet I could not leave it like that.

"What will you do now?" I asked.

"Search," she said, "of course."

"No, I mean after all this."

"After what?"

"After you find him."

She stopped in the middle of the *chemin*. "I haven't thought that far. What would you say I should do?"

"Tell him that you have been searching the world for him."

It was an unsatisfying response, I knew.

"Tell him it is not a game. That you wish him well. That you would like him to come with you, but if he does not want to, you want to kiss him before sending him off."

It was me she kissed instead then, it was a surprise, a wet kiss on the tip of my nose like you would a dog, but tender nonetheless. "Thank you," she whispered in my ear. I struggled to be free of the embrace but she held me there another instant, still whispering. "Please," she said, "please listen to what Irina says and be careful. I do not want to lose you as well."

I have been lost for a long time, I wanted to say, but instead moved on ahead and we walked up and down the grid of green until it was time for her to leave for her supposed work, another morning behind us.

"Aren't you going back?" she asked.

"No, I think I'll stay here," I said. "This district is as pleasant as it gets in this strange town. I think I saw a place where I could get a Sambusac for lunch."

"You'll need money," she said, and without thinking reached down between her breasts to where the small coin sack hung from its twisted silken cord, counting out three coins, one platinum. "For a drink," she said.

"I could suckle a nursing mother's nipples for this much," I said.

It made her laugh despite herself. I held the coin before me and kissed it to thank her.

"It's round and coppery as someone's nipple," I said.

"In your dreams, perhaps, but not mine, mine are black as raisins."

"I'm after dreams," I offered.

"Don Quixote," she said.

I watched her move slowly back along the *chemin*, her narrow hips swaying.

The old man's room was empty, already cleaned and ready to let, which made it simple to get access from the landlord once I had found the address searching on the terminal in the Arab café while my Sambusacs were warming on the griddle. I had one of each, chickpea, meat and onion, and pungent halloumi cheese. Two other customers ate at the counter with me, looking down at their plates. As I stood to leave they spat on the floor behind me grunting what I took to be curses and sharing low laughter. They suspected me of something.

The landlord did as well.

"It's too small for a couple," he said.

"I'm alone," I answered.

"I thought you had a wife," he said. Whether he could somehow read my visatag or had seen Rosaria and me along the streets, I couldn't tell.

"No, no wife."

"I thought you were a veteran of the war, the way you walk," he said.

"Isn't everyone?" I asked.

He smiled broadly. "You are right about that, brother. And that is why the rent is to be paid in advance in specie. I've been burned too often by stolen debits. The commode is down the hall and we keep it clean. You can use the sink if the night is too long, but that, too, is to be clean. And no cooking is allowed."

I nodded but didn't say anything. This seemed to make him uncomfortable.

"I'll leave you to look about," he said.

Still I said nothing.

"I suppose you know that someone died here, is that what it is?"

"Someone has died everywhere," I said.

"True enough, brother," he said. "Don't be long."

"I want to see the light," I said.

He seemed puzzled and glanced toward the switch.

"From the windows," I explained. "I want to see how it would be to live in such light."

"A philosopher," he said, a lucky guess I supposed.

There was nothing at all to be seen except the light, the place was clean, he was right about that much. The brightly painted white table had a single green chair, the paint chipped just slightly at the bottom of its legs. There was another, stuffed chair that smelled slightly of camphor and an animal of some sort. The window looked out on a concrete channel where the gutters drained into the street, dry now in the sunshine. I had a sense that I had been here before.

Feelings were not enough to go on. I had hoped to find something palpable, not so much a clue as some evidence of a lingering presence, something that could help me gauge the old man's final circumstances. Along the edges of the floorboards against the base molding there was a skim of residue from the mop, hardly a crust. In the little cupboard under the sink there was a hot plate, which either made the landlord a liar or perhaps showed him to be someone more liberal and accommodating than he wanted to seem at first. When I moved the hot plate, I discovered a bent and desiccated filter from a Chinese cigarette with a faint ring of lipstick at the end, something whoever cleaned the room had missed. The police, too, had missed it, one supposed; that is, had they ever looked.

There was one other thing that everyone alike had missed, and which I likewise would have missed had I not sunk my head into my arms at the table staring down at the floorboards, perhaps hoping to see some lingering evidence of where the old man bled and slumped, perhaps merely weary after a meaningless morning and a fruitless search and thus soothed by the hypnotic rhythm of the floorboards so perfectly spaced at intervals.

Midst these measured boards there was no mar or stain to mark where he might have fallen. However something glinted in the narrow gap between two floorboards, caught by the light that flooded in from the window after I pushed the canvas curtains back along the carbon rod. A filament memory stick, the thinnest needle of shining metal, not much thicker than a horse's hair, not much longer than a fingernail, was lodged between two floorboards and nearly invisible. I worked to flip it up on end using a toothpick that I had luckily taken with me from the Arab café. The memory needle was so sharp at each end that I had to hold it gingerly between my thumb and forefinger so as not to pierce them, thin and sharp enough also that it easily buried itself beneath a fatty bit of flesh at my waist when I heard the landlord coming back again and feared that he might discover it if he had me scanned.

4

It was not the landlord. Instead a fairly tall woman, handsome but not pretty in a tailored midnight blue wool suit with chalk blue pinstripes, stood in the hallway just outside the door when I reached it. She had the look of an official of some kind, but not a social worker or a detective, at least in my eyes. Her dark eyes moved with great animation back and forth before me as if she were scanning me into some hidden device through her pupils.

"I'm sorry," I said. "Are you thinking of renting this place as well?"

"No," she said and pressed past me into the room, turning completely sideways in an awkward fashion to pass me in a slide step as if to be certain that we had no physical contact.

"You're a policewoman then?" I asked and she laughed aloud.

"My god, no! Those useless bastards, all smiles and soft words, but violent hearts."

She was scanning the room in much the same way she had scanned me, her eyes not so much darting as tracking carefully at successive levels before her.

"You have the window coverings open," she said. "I'm surprised this place didn't melt away after suddenly being flooded with light after all these years."

She turned about on her heels in a way that reminded me of the turrets atop the observation cars.

"You are blind," I said, suddenly realizing.

"In a fashion, yes," she said. "I have the latest optics."

So she was scanning me.

"And you are the guardian of the boy who killed my father, I believe."

"Those are very fine optics," I said.

A smile formed on her face, a kinder smile than one would have supposed might have come under the circumstances.

"So is that what you propose to do for me as well?" she asked.

"What's that?"

"Take the place of my father now that he is gone."

"The boy they accuse latched onto me some time ago, but I haven't seen him in days, and I'm not his guardian and surely not a father to him."

The smile retracted as fast as it had come. "That's a lie," she said quietly.

"Which part?"

She ignored my question and moved to the window.

"They are waiting for you," she said.

"I'm not surprised," I said. "I seem to have become a hobby for the authorities."

"Not the authorities," she said, turning back toward me, scanning me again, perhaps trying to read my reactions. "Two dark men in sandals and long shirts with little caps."

"Taliban," I said. "I dined with them today."

"I'll see you out," she said. "They will dare not attack while you are with me. It would bring down heaven upon them."

"And will you stay with me forever?" I asked.

"Long enough to get you back to your quarter," she said.

There was a different smile on her face, droll and self-aware, and a twinkle of light in the scanning eyes.

"After that you can pray for my intercession," she added.

She had a charming laugh.

"Our lady of the camellias," I said, then added, "I don't think that Franky killed your father."

"Now you've told two lies in one afternoon." She smiled again and reached for my arm.

"So if you are not a policewoman, what are you?"

"You could think of me as someone in service of the truth," she said, "a sort of prosecutor, if you will."

"So am I on trial?"

She let go of my arm and turned to face me, standing before me for a long time without replying, her eyes tracking over me as she had at first. I began to feel deeply uncomfortable, as if her abilities were not reserved to optics but rather some deeper kind of probing, forming a picture of who I was beyond the image of myself I presented to her. In time she replied, as if reporting the outcome of the scanning.

"Oh yes," she said, speaking the words slowly, "oh yes, please, make no mistake. You are on trial in ways you cannot yet imagine and by forces beyond your ken."

Then she took my arm again, doing so in a way that made clear it would be fruitless to ask anything more of her just then.

The landlord was nowhere to be seen as we went out, nor were there any dark men lurking around the building. We strolled slowly through the quarter emerging via a path between low buildings just opposite the square near the municipal building.

"I will leave you here," she said.

"Do you have a name?" I asked.

"Do you?"

"You may be the first person hereabouts who did not seem to know it already."

"I don't believe in electronics," she said rather earnestly if paradoxically. "My father and I argued about such things and that's why he moved to this wretched room. If he had not—"

"But your eyes," I said.

"They are not my doing. I didn't lose them myself and didn't replace them."

She stopped at the edge of tears.

"My name is Alex," I said.

It surprised me, coming suddenly to my mind like that, and yet I felt sure that it was not a third lie for that day, but rather that my true name had come back to me from wherever it had been lost.

"Good afternoon then, Alex." She turned and moved away almost robotically, as if levitating a few centimeters above the sidewalks like a maglev train.

"And you?" I called after her. "What is your name?"

"I thought you knew it from the news reports," she said.

She smiled back over her shoulder, still moving effortlessly away,

"Camille," she said, pronouncing it the French way, without the L's.

"Au revoir, Camille," I said.

"Au revoir, Monsieur Day," she said.

I was to see her soon enough and in several guises, but before that came the question of how to examine the contents of the needle memory without Madame or the authorities finding out. Now that I knew her as well, I might, of course, have considered whether to share what I found in the memory stick with Camille, but she had made clear that she had no interest in electronics and, for then at least, I didn't know where to find her again.

Since Rosaria, too, had shown little interest in techs since that first night when she was less caught up with watching the spectacle than picking my pocket, I didn't concern myself over what she might think of my having found the memory stick. Still she shared everything but her body with Irina, and maybe even that for all I knew, and so I would have to be careful that she didn't give me away.

In truth I knew that Rosaria would find the needle almost instantly if it were still there beneath my flesh the next time we slept together. Hers were gifted hands, the tactile equivalent of Camille's scanning optics.

I could surely ask Candido where one could find a memory reader but I couldn't trust him either. Were he and his mother actually in service to the authorities, even possessing the memory stick would be damning evidence.

Somewhere I knew there would be listings for establishments other than Madame's, the Egyptian's, or the Polish fellow's if one searched the directories for memory readers, but which establishment to choose was another problem. A commerce station or some neighborhood place might offer memory readers as a service to their clientele, the way the Sambusac café had its old terminal. Yet where to store this needle in the interim?

I was passing through the square again and, as always, it was empty. Not even the environmental officer was in sight.

Like nose in face front, I thought.

Three small birch trees, almost saplings, stood at the edge of the path just beyond the environmental officer's tool shed. I squatted before them and squeezed the flesh on either side of the embedded needle the way one expresses pus from a carbuncle and pulled the needle out painlessly with my other hand. Quickly I inserted it under the tight paper of the mottled white bark at the base of the birch, then rose to see if anyone had seen.

The environmental officer was watching me from the doorway of his little shed. I nodded to him and he to me, and then I left the square thinking finally you have to trust someone.

At Madame's nothing was the same. She was not at the counter and there in her place was another boy, not Candido, perhaps one of his pack although I confess I have little sense of their faces. The room seemed airless, although there were no customers save an old woman before a monitor against the wall. The whole place smelled sour as yeast, the odor emanating from her.

"I'm—" I said to the boy at the counter.

"I know who you are," he said, waving impatiently. He swam through translucent water in some game world, the water at that instant turning dank, maroon with his blood after a creature had sunk its teeth into him. He scowled as if I were to blame and I went on past him to the rooms to see if perhaps Madame or Rosaria were there. The rooms were also empty.

Where the India print hung to separate the bed from the main space a new suit of clothes hung upon a copper colored hanger on the bar. Upon it were a man's trousers and a tunic-like shirt in coordinated colors, the trousers what they called taupe and the tunic a greyer shade yet enough brown to blend perfectly. Both were expensive, as were the ankle high boots that sat under them, kangaroo skin I believed, though I had no reason to think so. A belt of the same leather was tucked in one boot, while in the other there was a pair of brown cashmere socks with a note pinned to it.

4 U MOAN AMUR RZRIA the note read.

It hadn't struck me that, though she spoke so well, and seemingly in several languages, Rosaria might not know how to write. With correction algorithms and voice recognition it was a skill increasingly lost. Yet someone's own name was usually remembered. Not only did she speak well, but she seemed to know the characters from old stories and other such lore, even poems beyond the ones that children sang. Perhaps this was a joke of sorts, a note in textese to mark where we were and what brought us together.

I could not remember when I last received a gift beyond some paltry thing. The gifts I could remember were like when Franky twisted off the end of his loaf of bread, little gestures, half unlikely, and always suspect. I'd been given nothing so grand as this since the time I had a true name and a full story, if no longer an actual family. The ensemble hanging there like an Easter outfit briefly lifted from my shoulders what had been an ever increasing weight, one exacerbated by the encounter with the woman who called herself Camille; a feeling that I was increasingly caught in others' complications like a gnat who had veered by chance into a spider's web, a trap unmeant for such a minor creature, one who offered little substance to prey upon, my being so caught up a mere accident, one that derived totally from the logic of the weave of gluey strands and not from any design that took a puny creature such as me into account, let alone had aims upon him. And yet my life was on the line, or at least some version of what I had become was under question or, if I believed Camille, on trial.

Perhaps this present was meant to outfit the defendant, I thought.

The clothing fit perfectly, the boots as light as my own feet. I was a new man. I would not have been surprised had I been able to fly.

I folded the outfit carefully and lay it out upon the bed, then scrubbed over my whole body carefully in the bathroom as if to be worthy of such a new mien. I took the occasion to wash out my former clothing and set the pieces out to dry upon the copper hanger, hanging it from the hook above the sink. From Madame's highboy I chose the pair of her panties with least decoration, a dark ruby red with a mahogany waistband, to serve while my own underwear were drying, then dressed again in the new outfit.

A proper chevalier, I thought, so giddy with these new sensations that I might have feared that Camille had somehow drugged me.

Mine was the ecstasy of a gnat drunk with the spider's liqueur.

Just then I thought I heard Rosaria in the corridor outside the rooms and I went out to thank her.

There was no one there but the smelly old woman who had been sitting at the terminal.

"Please, sir," she said and held out a hand as if for a coin.

"Fucking bitch!" The boy grabbed her from behind by an arm and spun her violently. "I told you we have no bathrooms for customers."

The old woman yowled in pain. "Let her go, damn it!" I shouted.

I led her by the hand back to the rooms and left her in the bathroom while I waited at the table in the main room. An awful stench enveloped the space and trailed with her as she emerged, as if she had shat out a corpse.

"Bless you," she said, and held out her hand again, this time with a coin in it.

"No, no," I said. "Go please."

"You are a saint," she said, tucking the coin back in a pocket at her waist. "May Jesus and Saint Lazare bless you! May your old mother greet you in heaven."

I had no mother, I thought, but the old woman was gone, letting herself out the back door, heading out to the alleys and warehouses as if she had been here before. Once she had disappeared about a corner I propped the door open, then opened the door to the corridor as well thinking to air the place out before venturing to see how the old woman had left the commode.

Again I heard a voice that sounded like Rosaria and I went out into the corridor to hear where it had come from. There was a slight rustling and a scuffle of what sounded like bare feet behind one of the doors to the private rooms.

"Sweet Jesu, Sweet Jesu," she chanted from within.

I pushed the door open and marked a dim tableau bathed in the blue light from a holo projector. The vision was an obscene holy card. Rosaria knelt with her back to the door before the naked Candido, whose head was back and whose eyes were closed, his hands pressed against his side, fists clenched, the vision of a saint in ecstasy. Rosaria's upper body blocked my view of the boy's belly, genitals, and legs.

His eyes snapped open when he heard the door swing open; they were gleaming black things.

"You are not seeing what you believe you are seeing, Mr. Dee," he said calmly, his features limned blue with the light. "You can't trust your senses in any of this."

The kneeling woman wore a simple blue wrap-around cotton shift tied at the waist. It might have been the uniform of a chambermaid or a pilgrim's habit but in the blue light it took on a cloud-like radiance. When the door swung open, she bent her head downward and clasped her hands before her motionless body. As she turned toward the door I ran off, rushing back out through the rooms and the open door into the alleys where the old woman had gone.

This time I would succeed in escaping, I thought, this time I would be a wayfarer again, this time I would fly, this time I will remember nothing. If there was a trial, I would be found innocent on account of not having existed.

Quickly then, I lost myself in the alleys as the afternoon dwindled, turning this way and that until the light began to fail and I knew I had to find a place to rest and think through my next steps before I escaped this place that had trapped me into a litany of names, events, and alien visions. I had no sense where I might find shelter among what, during that first night that Madame had brought me from the shelter to her place along these same alleys, had seemed a metropolis of deep doorways and recesses with men shouting from them. Most such entryways were as yet uninhabited in the lapsing light of early evening. No wayfarer, I knew well, would settle into a spot before dark, for there was too much yet to accomplish in twilight, the possibility of begging, or thieving, something, meals from shelters and the odd good citizen, drink, capsules, a discarded overcoat that might make good bedding. There were what I suspected to be capsule dealers here and there in the shadows down the narrow alleys. A whore wearing a filthy pink tutu and paratrooper boots staggered toward me, breasts showing through a net top, her face painted like a harlequin.

"Hello Captain," she called to me. "Here's a hand job for you if you're nice."

She was drunk on something, glue or homebrew or maybe a capsule from a previous patron. She lifted the shirt of her tutu and showed her crotch. I pushed on past her.

"Or would you rather have a rub," she shouted after me. Then: "Come back you cheap bastard!"

I can be forgiven for thinking her more honest than Rosaria, although in truth I was already uncertain about what I had seen, even though I gave Candido's self-serving words no credence. It was possible that I had mistaken another kneeling woman for Rosaria or misunderstood the whole scene, since it all happened that fast, although in my mind's eye I saw her turn to me as I fled, her eyes damp with tears yet her expression contemptuously serene. I also considered the locale. For those who could pay the fee, special rooms could be fitted out with projections of holos that suited someone's fantasy. These, however, were nothing I could afford, nor anything that I had need of since the night that Rosaria first clove to me.

Too much had happened for one day—the white cubes, the kiss on my nose, Camille and the memory needle, the old woman giving birth to a stillborn child, the cavalier—a person couldn't trust his own sensations. Three birches stood in a grove somewhere, two men spat on the floor of a resto and laughed.

It was a mistake to occupy myself with such distractions and images at dusk. It was the hour when wise creatures sought shelter and looked out for themselves. It was the hour when vultures descended in shadows. I knew all this, knew as much too late, at the moment the pipe first whacked me in the center of my shoulders, stunning me and making me vomit a thin stream of bile on my new kangaroo skin boots. The second thump rattled my skull in a dark flash and with a sound that echoed like an electric shock in my teeth. It was the last I remembered until I woke, my head aching like a drum, the taste of blood in my mouth.

"*Hola, compadre*, you awake now," a voice said.

I forced my eyelids open. They too, it turned out, were blood-crusted although I found out in time that the band who had found me in the alley had done their best to clean me up after they dragged me into their vaulted abode. The sight that welcomed me back to consciousness from what I remembered as a dream of crows could as well have been a continuation of a dream. Indeed I had a sense that I had seen the scene before my eyes once before. Four Peruvians from a pan flute band occupied the chamber before me, their alpaca blankets and hats set aside, three of them standing by a small charcoal brazier over which one of them squatted, roasting what seemed like a skinned cat. Beyond them an oily torch was stuck blazing in a pile of bauxite sand illuminating a brick vault that rose up in the shape of a huge bottle, the brick narrowing into a chimney high above where the shadow overtook the torchlight. A single star shone in the middle of the dark disk at the top of the neck toward which rose a twine of thin smoke from the charcoal and the thicker rope of tarry smoke from the torch.

I tried to sit up but my head screamed as the flash of black returned and I fell back into it, knocking myself out against the concrete floor.

I woke again in what from the light coming down through the chimney seemed morning. Four of them squatted around the brazier where one had been before I hit my head again, three men in loose white shirts and a woman in a wide embroidered skirt, her legs swaddled in colored cloths. They were sharing a breakfast of porridge but when they saw me stirring, the youngest of the men detached himself from the group and knelt at my side.

I forced what sound I could from my acrid lips to let him know I was burning with thirst, but began choking before I could form any words. Another of the four was at my back holding me by my shoulders, careful to keep me from falling back lest I knock myself out again. The woman appeared above me, a row of gold-capped teeth gleaming behind a wide smile. She held a gourd of sweet water to my lips and I sucked greedily but then spat blood on the concrete next to me. She wiped at my mouth with a soft cloth and offered the water again. One of the men spit a mash of fruit of some kind into his palm and held his hand before my mouth, feeding me the way that birds do their fledglings. I'm not ashamed to say that I took this sweet pap in without a second thought. I drank some more water and signaled that I wished to lie back again.

When I woke next I could not tell what time it was from the light, but I was alone, or so I thought until I heard the sweet, low notes of the flute echoing. They had left the youngest one behind with me.

I was covered with one of their alpaca blankets and wearing only my borrowed underwear, the gypsy's ruby panties. If, as the saying goes, clothes make the man, in the eyes of this band mine must have made me seem a figure from their stories, the Horrible Bird fallen to earth, a creature worthy of care. Or so said Manco, he who had been left to tend me and who through these days became both my nurse and teacher. His mother Mayra, the woman who had squatted at the fire, played the tambourine, collected donations, and sold the recordings when the band moved through the city. Her boyfriend Wenceslao played the zampoña, a broader version of the same flute that Manco was playing when I awoke. Miguel Angel played the guitar. All this Manco told me in a rush that first morning.

I say first morning although I have no sense really of how long it had been when I woke the second time and heard him playing the pipes. These four lived in the banked furnace of a deserted bottle kiln deep in the warrens of the old industrial district. Each day they went back out to play music and raise money and, they hoped, find the way to the underground city. Each day they left Manco behind to look after me and he related various stories in a gentle voice while I lay there, in the first days alternating between fevers and chills, and for however many days thereafter unable either to raise myself up enough to eat or drink by myself. I do not know how many days passed that way, except that there were many stories, some fading in and out of my consciousness like dreams.

Again and again one particular dream would swirl through my head like a delirium. I was in the dock of a tribunal behind a narrow cage of iron bars just wide enough for my shoulders, the bars reaching way up into the air above me, so high you couldn't see the end of them. High on a dais before me the judges sat; most of them I did not recognize, although I had a sense that Camille was among them as well as one or more of the policemen from when I was first interrogated here. Always I was trying to explain, to plead for myself, and always these far-off magistrates seemed to be talking among themselves and laughing, not listening to my pleadings.

And then I would suddenly be awake, as if I had torn myself from the dream like a sheet from a book. Almost always Manco would be there, softly telling his stories.

On the so-called first day Manco told me that they had been moving from city to city and country to country for as long as he could remember.

"Your father?" I asked. But there was something wrong with my tongue, it was thick as a folded cloth in my dry mouth. I had not yet seen my face and so did not know the extent of what had become of me.

Speaking even this much made me terribly weary and I began to sweat, shivering in the blanket.

"Sssh, ssh," he calmed me. "*Tómelo con calma, compadre.*"

At a certain point the others would come back, suddenly there, surrounding me like mountains, looking down upon me, chattering in a language I did not recognize by name.

"*Allillanchu?*"

"*Allillanmi, allillantagmi.*" Then gesturing to me. "*Allillanmi kashian.*"

They would nod gravely.

"*¿Cómo te fue?*" Manco asked.

"*Karun purina pisiqtaq k'oqao.*"

Sometimes the woman would squat next to me and take my hand, murmuring,

"*Aylluykikuna kanchu? ¿Tienes familia? Maypin wasiiki? ¿Dónde está su casa?*"

"He doesn't understand, Mamay," Manco would explain.

In truth I did understand some of these things, and not just the Spanish, because in long hours while I was drifting in and out of sleep, Manco would amuse himself by tutoring me in these phrases, even writing them with his finger in the skim of sand upon the floor of the kiln.

"If you learn these, you can talk to the jaguars, *compadre*," he would say and laugh. Other times he would play the pipes and then sing a song about the moon, singing *Luna, lunera, cascabelera.*

When finally the swelling released and I got back my voice, I tried to tell him that I needed to retrieve the memory needle from the base of the middle of the three white trees. He thought it was a fine story and urged me to tell more when I could speak a little better. For his part he told me the story of the hidden city and why they sought it, a story that had less to do with myth than history.

According to the tale, one of the cities in this region had been a secret military base in the time between long-ago wars, the freezing period Manco called it, probably a better phrase than the so-called cold war that printed histories remembered it as. Only half the city was open to citizens and absolutely no part of it was open to strangers, who were executed upon sight if they strayed there. The other half of the city was restricted to military but a former sailor told K'ak'a, Manco's uncle Miguel Angel, that below this part of the city yet another city sat like a shadow of the first, only real, a duplicate world meant to house the rulers and the armies if there were a final war. Wide avenues of white-painted buildings were laid out in a grid under intense electric lights that cycled through the colors of the day above, first purple then pink then yellow then white before darkening slowly again through violet and peach and then settling into a soft glow where soldiers and their girls could walk under a dim twinkling meant to mimic stars. Now, according to K'ak'a the city was open to anyone who could find it and those who lived there were rich and happy and generous to strangers who found their way there.

"Eldorado?" I said.

"Guatavita," Manco corrected.

Since K'ak'a first heard this story, their band had moved from town to town trying to find the entry to Guatavita, seeking it as some seek heaven.

"I hope we never do find it," the young man told me earnestly. "I would miss the mountains and the sea."

"Why?" I asked.

"They give shape to the sky," he said. "And besides that I want to fall in love."

He said this as if the two things were connected in a way that made it seem that perhaps they were.

As the days went by it was clear that Manco was becoming as restless nursing me as I was being there within this brick bottle edifice. I wanted to get away, although depending on how clear my mind was, I wasn't certain from time to time what I was escaping or why. Yet at other times the memories returned as vivid as the light above and with them a strange feeling of loss mixed with pain. A combination of my recurring dream and my own real memories made me feel that I had to get back to the world outside in order to defend myself. I felt that somewhere, perhaps in a version of K'ak'a's Guatavita, I really was on trial.

It seemed that I was also on trial here, or that at least my remaining there was increasingly in question. For on certain evenings after the others came back Manco would quarrel with the two older men, raising his voice to them in a way he never did with his mother. I imagined he was telling them he was tired of being trapped inside with me while the sky shaped the city beyond and love awaited somewhere.

One evening, not long after one of these encounters, Manco and his uncle squatted next to me where I sat propped against the wall and smothered in blankets.

"Tell Miguel Angel the tale of how the great bird took your memory and placed it in a silver needle buried beneath a tree," Manco said.

"Yes, please señor Qusqu, I would be honored to hear your story," his uncle said, offering me a drinking gourd with a clear liquid that smelled of strong spirits.

I drank some of the liquor and my head seemed to clear for the first time since the attack.

"Perhaps I will write you a song," the uncle explained.

"It isn't my memory," I said. "It belongs to a spirit, someone whose heart came apart at the seams on account of love."

"Perhaps you will write the song," K'ak'a said. "Tell me."

"But I haven't seen its images as yet," I protested. "When you found me I was about to retrieve this needle before leaving the city altogether."

"Because your friend, *el Viejo*, is dead, you are sorrow."

"Sorry," Manco corrected him. "It's better to say sad."

"I am sorrow is a song," I said, and the uncle nodded.

He pondered awhile and then said, "Maybe is better to tell what you think these memories hold." He squatted in silence a moment. "Better for a story or a song," he said. "It isn't good to look at memory directly."

He looked toward the sky at the top of the bottle chimney and made a gesture as if shielding his eyes.

"*Como el sol,*" he said.

"Like the sun," I repeated.

Manco shifted his weight uneasily, as if impatient that this momentary alliance of older men was keeping him from something.

"You think there may be a clue to the golden city in those memories," I said. "That's it, isn't it?"

"Sometimes an old man has seen everything," Manco replied.

"*Un viejo hombre es a veces ciego,*" his uncle said and offered me the gourd again. When I declined, he touched my shoulder gently and then rose and went to the fire.

An old man is sometimes blind.

Manco stared after him with more sadness than annoyance and when K'ak'a took up his guitar and strummed it quietly beside the fire, the boy joined him on his pipes. His mother stirred the fire and the profile of her face was bronze in the light. It was the end of my life as a certain someone, I knew that even then.

I began to tell Manco that I wanted to go with them when they left this place. The idea clearly troubled him.

"You need," he said and showed me his forearm where a thin red tile was embedded in the skin, a kind of identity chip in some places.

"But I have," I said and reached for my visatag, but the chain on my neck was empty.

Manco looked away sadly.

"No, no." I tried to push up and stand but was still too rocky for that even after all these days. "It must be with my clothes," I said, pointing to where they hung from, pressed and clean, above my shoes like a scarecrow.

"There was nothing, *compadre*. Maybe they took it, *los reptiles*."

The reptiles. I had been attacked by reptiles; it was as good an explanation as any.

I knew then I would have to get back to Madame's and seek her help or I would never get out of this town. But first I had to be able to stand.

"I would like to shave," I said to Manco.

He looked at me uncomprehendingly.

"*Una razor*," I said.

"I know," he said. "*Una navaja, una razor*. I don't think you should...."

I tried to stand again and toppled over sideways. My legs had lost all their strength over these days.

"Wait," he said, "I will get."

He returned with a large black enamel basin filled with clear water, and a razor of a kind I had not seen in years, its handle made of an antler. He set the bowl aside on the floor and helped me arrange myself, sitting Indian style as they used to say, then he carefully set the basin in the diamond cleft between my bent legs. A splash of warm water spilled over my thigh not unpleasantly. I looked down at the water rocking in the basin and there was a stranger there. It was so shocking I let out an involuntarily yelp and Manco steadied me.

As the water in the basin slowly ceased its rocking and settled into a still mirror I saw a face like a monkey, one lip cleft over the other in a gap over a broken tooth, a broad nose smashed against the face, pinkish-grey patches of smooth scar tissue where my thin beard grew around it, one eye also with an extra lid of scar, the black terrified eyes of a stranger.

In panic I managed somehow to get to my feet but staggered against the brick barrel of the wall, pulling myself along it against the vertigo and the feeling that my legs were collapsing under me, trying desperately to get to a glass of some kind, a true mirror where my real self would appear. I was without my borrowed underwear, I realized, although how long they had been gone was a mystery to me. I pulled myself along the wall like an upright crab as Manco implored "*señor, señor,*" he, too, moving crabwise next to me, steadying me against a fall. I somehow formed the idea that there was a mirror in the pocket of my new trousers and I pulled myself toward them circling the round walls of the room, looking back at the nest of blankets where I had lain for god knows how long.

As I came nearer to where the clothing hung Manco seemed to comprehend what I was up to and abandoned me to my own balance and ran ahead to gather them in his arm.

"You want to dress, I dress you. You want to shave your hairs, I shave you. You want to know what happened to your face, I tell you."

I grabbed the trousers from him and searched the pockets, they were empty but for the skull of a small turtle that I vaguely seemed to remember. What I could not remember just then was what I had looked like before this.

"All gone," I said and my voice sounded like a sob.

"They stole everything but the skull, *compadre*. I think it scared them."

"No, I mean me," I said. "I am all gone."

There was quite a scene later that evening when the band returned and found me sitting like a mummy king upon a pile of fire bricks stacked, arms and back, like an easy chair, the bricks covered over with two of the alpaca blankets, wearing my once new outfit and boots. The polished gris-gris skull hung on the chain around my neck like an amulet, and my head was crowned in a finely woven white straw fedora with a copper colored band and a disk of gold foil like the sun at the center of the band above my forehead. The hat which covered much of the stripes and patches of scar tissue where my hair once had grown had been his father's, Manca told me, a man known as a great wizard in his village.

"My mother, too, is a bruja," he said. "It was she who kept you from the kingdom of the dead, she who healed you with poultices of leaves, herbs she found and some she brought with her. Without her, you would be dead."

That part of me was dead in any case I did not say to him, nor did I think I had to.

"You were badly beaten, *compadre*," he said softly.

"How long was it then until I woke that first time and then hurt my head again?"

"Weeks, my friend," he said. "I cannot count them. I stayed here with you while my family went away to other cities and played and then came back, even then thinking they might find you dead. You woke the second day they were back. We stayed because of that. But also because K'ak'a still believes the underground city is near."

It was K'ak'a who reacted first to the sight of me seated there, berating Manco in a mix of Spanish and their language both, until Manco's mother intervened, touching each of them under their chins, calming them. Even so K'ak'a broke away and went out into the night, something that in my experience, as much as I could trust it, none of them had done before. Manco's mother called after him but he was gone. She and her boyfriend moved off a ways to confide in each other while Manco slumped to a crouch where he and K'ak'a had been arguing. His mother and her boyfriend gazed back toward me from time to time as they talked, then she broke away and knelt next to Manco, as if to ask him something. They, too, looked over to me.

I felt then I could sit there forever, indeed like a mummy, in my taupe outfit and my foolish hat. I could not then imagine any other life given my circumstance.

Manco's mother bent over, fiddling in one of their packs looking for something. She emerged with a small, embroidered sack closed with a silver string and brought it over to me, untying the string as she came. Inside was a small mirror set in a lapis lazuli frame with a mother of pearl back.

"Manco says you want to see yourself, my friend," she said. "We did what we could. It is better to live."

The monkey man glared back at me a little sadly, the funny little hat propped upon his skull, two of his teeth I now realized crowned with crumpled metal, possibly aluminum, but with a seed pearl in the face of each.

Just then K'ak'a returned and knelt where I sat with the mirror in my lap, Manco's mother beside me. Manco came over to see what was going on.

K'ak'a held out his brown hand, palm up, before me, in it a small silver needle.

"Your memory, señor," he said. "It was where you said, although one of the three trees is gone."

5

At first I thought Manco and his band were taking me with them after all. It took me another two or three days to regain real strength once I had, in horror, tested my legs. I ate voraciously during that time and, for the first time most likely, became a burden on this small family, eating whatever they brought back as well as whatever I could find that they had stashed away in their packs. An ugly bird needs strength to fly, I thought.

They indulged me in this, taking small portions of the stews and porridge that they subsisted upon, breaking the sandwiches they brought back from their playing into disproportionate pieces, giving me the breast and leg from a roast chicken, and offering squares of bitter chocolate. When I was not eating, I chewed the leaves Manco's mother had given me, rubbing the copious saliva over my scars in the way she had showed me.

In the evenings, whenever they played music together, I took up Manco's mother's tambourine while she played a small concertina. At times I kept a small beat that to me sounded like falling water; other times the rhythm brought me memories of sleigh bells and the sensation of snow from a place and time I could not recall exactly.

Taking part in the music soothed me and I was hoping they would see that I could pull my weight, at least until we were free of this place and I could earn enough to get myself a new black market identity.

The night before they left I sensed they were leaving because of the way Manco's mother moved about the space and how she attended to their packs and instruments. That night also they fixed me a great plate of foods of all kinds while each of them ate almost nothing. K'ak'a kept passing the gourd of clear liquor. Then when we went off to sleep it was not Manco but his mother's boyfriend who lay down in his blankets next to me.

He and I had never spoken directly. I assumed that he spoke only their language and that, as an outsider of sorts, he kept to himself, bound up with Manco's mother in their blankets at night and by her side as they moved from city to city.

I heard his voice for the first time in the early morning.

"*Vaya! Vaya!*" he whispered in my ear.

His breath smelled of violets and chocolate.

The circle of sky above the bottle chimney was still pitch black and the torch fire splashed tongues of light against the brick walls.

He was holding the little hat with the gold foil disk and gesturing for me to put it on. I stood quickly thinking something must have happened to make them leave before morning. Still I thought they were taking me with them.

The boyfriend helped me wrap the alpaca blanket around me in their fashion and then fastened it at the waist with a rope dyed indigo. He pushed the hat down farther on my head and gave me a package covered in a small blanket and wrapped with the same rope.

"*Vaya! Vaya!*" he said again and gestured toward the low arched door where they came and went.

By then I realized that the others were still in their blankets, although I could see from the way the torch fire caught them that their eyes were open. Something about the situation was so strange that I resisted slightly before the low door.

"Where are we going?" I asked and tried to turn back.

He pushed me back down without a word, his arms so strong that it felt as if he could break me in two if he wanted to. The hat slipped off as I ducked but he had it in hand as he came out of the cubbyhole behind me. He pushed the hat down upon my head again and whispered, "*Vaya,*" pointing forward. Thereafter he walked keeping a step behind me with a hand on my shoulder and steering me wordlessly through the winding alleys upon which the pre-dawn light fell like thin milk.

We walked quite a while like this until we emerged into a neighborhood I thought I recognized, moving along a street with various storefronts and toward a taller glass-walled building cladding and mullions of green copper. We went around behind this building to a loading dock where he pushed a button and a bell rang softly just on the other side of the door. After a time the door lifted up just high enough for us to duck under and then silently went down again.

I thought then that he was taking me to die.

It is strange to me even now to think that under these circumstances I nonetheless felt no further urge to run away. Indeed I felt nothing at all except resignation coupled with a longing to recall what my face had looked like in my prior life. As we stood waiting for the freight elevator to descend, I found myself trying to remember the litany of names of those I had met since Franky began to follow me however long ago. For the first time in a very long time, I tried to recall the faces of my parents and tried as well to remember whether I once had a wife. The elevator jolted to a stop and ended my reverie.

A tall, pale man dressed all in black was standing there to greet us and he looked so much like the old images of death that I began to laugh helplessly. This seemed to distress my companion.

"*Vaya*," he said sharply, though there was nowhere to go.

"Hello, Mr. Beckmesser," Death said, and I laughed still more.

If his roster indicated that I was coming to join him, he had me marked as the wrong candidate, although in truth at that moment I could not remember what other name to give him.

The three of us entered the elevator and it began to ascend again. I counted two, three, four floors but then thought I had missed one. Although I still felt an unearthly calm, I sensed that I was trembling between them. The elevator jolted when we stopped and I nearly fell but they each caught an arm and supported me between them as we went down the darkened hallway and through a door to where there was a pod shaped dentist's chair, a chaise lounge upholstered in green leather. A large plasma screen hung on an arm from a wall bracket, Candido's face perfectly framed there.

"Yes, that's him," his voice said and I began to resist, knowing something was terribly wrong here, but the two of them were so strong they easily overpowered me, pushing me back in the chair and securing me with the restraints.

Candido's face was replaced on the screen by a winter scene of snow softly falling along a river valley through which a pewter river flowed, a glint of sunlight breaking through the snow clouds painted over far pines. It was very relaxing.

"The capsule please, Pacha?" Death addressed the boyfriend. The latter extracted a small leather bag from his belt and took out a small crabapple.

Death grinned. "That's very clever of you, amigo," he said. "The perfect carrier."

He turned the apple in his hand until he found the blemish, then extracted the memory needle.

In an instant I knew what they were doing. What they had in mind for me was a kind of death, erasing what little self I had left and overlaying another's memory.

"No!" I groaned. "No, no, it's not me! That's not my memory!" But they had restrained my head and jaw and the words gagged me just as they had when I emerged from my coma however many days before this second death.

The pale man inserted the needle in the memory reader and its contents streamed through a high speed montage of random images, colors, irising and exploding lights, and face upon face, place upon place, screen upon screen in a dizzying cascade before me.

I must have passed out then, mesmerized by Beckmesser's phantasmagoria, before Pacha and Father Death applied the electrodes to my scar-mottled skull, not erasing but inserting the old man's memories and fantasies among my own. If I had been found guilty of being an accomplice in murdering someone, my punishment was to live forever an accomplice to his memories.

I found myself outside the building on the street, alone in morning light. From the passers-by and traffic it seemed perhaps eight o'clock. A police vehicle went by but it was not one of the observation cars and, in fact, seemed faintly retro, the officer's uniform different. He did not smile at me the way they do.

I realized why I had recognized this district. It was not far from Madame's along an avenue I had been on several times before. However it was almost impossible to imagine going there after all that had happened. Instead I went back behind the copper building to the loading dock and rang the bell, which seemed much louder than before, but no one came. I tried the door but it would not move.

I was aware of the weight of Beckmesser upon me, his memories pressed against my own but not replacing them, rather lying as if layers of a stream, different currents at different depths, not quite in synch, one sometimes still and languid while the other rushed, then the other slowing; at times the two were almost in tandem, not synched but rather as if in harmony, yet the eddies along their edges interfering as if in a moiré pattern in a way that made my head ache.

These were, of course, not the whole of his memories, but rather what had passed through his mind when he linked to the machine, whether playing his games or viewing other scenes of his own or others' making. Often these were accompanied by his voice, a raspy, low whisper that nonetheless had a certain kindness. Sometimes what he said was addressed to a beautiful young woman named Carmine, whom I recognized as someone I had met before but with a different name. From time to time she would lean forward and reach toward him, as if stroking his cheek, and I was flooded with tenderness and longing. Other times I struggled through the layers of his memories like an out-of-breath swimmer attempting to rise from an underwater cave toward a deceptive horizon, one that marked but another depth, with yet another sky beckoning above. At first this process of moving between Beckmesser's encapsulated memory and that of my own was painful, but in time I learned how to look through these interfering memories as if through conjoined lenses sliding in and out of focus, floating from one layer to the other when necessary.

I could not get to Carmine that first day.

However, given my disguise, I thought perhaps I could reconnoiter the café and perhaps even confront Candido about all this.

Just then, however, a young girl startled me by running up behind me.

"Excuse me, sir," she said. "You forgot your package."

She held out a package tied in a small blanket with an indigo rope. Neither where I had gotten it nor where I had left it was clear to me.

One of the child's piercing blue eyes was crowned with a half-circle scar like a second, phantom eyebrow.

"How did you hurt yourself?" I asked and she examined her hands before her, as if looking for what I meant.

"No, no," I said, and took the package from her. "There's nothing there. I meant your forehead, above your brow."

"A star kissed me," she said. "That's what my mother told me."

Now I held the packet before me just as she did.

"Do you have a doll for me in your package?" she asked.

"I don't know," I said and I set the wrapped blanket down on the path between us and began to fiddle with the knotted rope to look at what was in it. As I reached for the package I noticed a small red tile the color of terra cotta beneath the skin on the underside of my right forearm just above the wrist. Dim markings on the face of the chip appeared through the translucence of my skin.

I had once known someone with a similar identity chip.

I turned to the girl but she was gone.

I worked to untie the indigo ropes but the knots were tight and intricate and the sun was rising to mid-morning height and so I decided to move on, first shedding the blanket I still wore tied around me as a coat.

"You have to stay warm, Papa," said a voice that I recognized from Beckmesser's memories.

It was good advice to either of us, I knew, and I might regret not having a warm blanket by that evening, but I was already weighed down by too much and it felt good to be out in the world in just this cotton tunic and pants drawn loosely about my waist and the package slung over my shoulder.

When I rounded the corner of the street where Madame's café was located, I thought at first that I had made a mistake in having discarded my disguise. But then I recalled what had happened to my face and knew that disguise would no longer be a concern when I next saw Madame and the woman whose name I could not remember. Yet because the apparition of Candido had so easily identified me and since also the girl with the scar had not seemed repulsed by my simian appearance, it made me wonder. I approached the window of a darkened storefront and used it as a mirror. The same ape-like creature appeared in the glass complete with the pinkish patches of scar that I had first seen in the enamel bowl that the boy held out for me. Franky, I thought, that was his name. Why would I remember that, as well as how to get to Madame's café, and not the name of the woman I had slept with or where I had seen Carmine before?

Where was the hat? I wondered, unable to think where I had lost it.

Someone was laughing behind me. Candido. I recognized the sound of his laughter and had not forgotten his name.

Of course there was no one there, neither in the reflection within the window nor even when I turned. My mind—these minds—were playing tricks on me.

It was then that I realized that this particular empty storefront was exactly where Madame's café had been.

This was crazy. How long had they been gone, I wondered, how could they disappear so quickly, and without a trace? I pressed my face against the glass in hopes of seeing something I would recognize, perhaps one of the narrow scraps of colored pasteboard they gave you when you rented a machine (how did I remember that?), or one of the purple paper napkins that Rosaria handed patrons when they purchased something from her as she passed among them hawking refreshments after a spectacle.

Rosaria! There, that was something.

Inside the storefront was empty and spare, not a scrap to be seen. I had begun to violently rattle the door handle, why I was not certain, when two men grabbed me and pushed me against the window of the entryway, the thump of my body against it echoing dully within.

Policemen, two of them, in the same older uniforms.

"Do not resist or we will spray," one said, holding a small aerosol before my face.

How quaint, I thought, I have not seen those for years, not since bio-restraints replaced them.

Once there were dreams packaged in such canisters, Beckmesser's memory insisted. There were aerosols of such sweet fragrances, cocoa and bacon, licorice, a woman's shoulder, a meadow of lavender, the odors along a train track.

"Daddy, please," Camille said.

Camille or Carmine?

"Stop your mumbling," one of the policemen was saying. He was reading the identity chip with a handheld reader twice the size of the current versions. Surely these guys were auxiliary police or maybe private security.

"I'm sorry, Mr. Beckmesser," the policeman said after he had made his readings, the two of them freeing me. "Were you having trouble with your keys, sir?"

"Trouble?" I asked.

"This building is yours," he explained. "We thought you were a traveler breaking in."

Traveler was what they sometimes called wayfarers.

"My keys," I said and began to pat about my own waist. There were no pockets in the tunic or the pants. I fumbled with the rope on the package again.

The policeman was very gentle. "Allow me," he said and he took my right forearm and turned it outward so that the red tile pressed against the small reader on the lock plate.

We heard the tumblers drop and the handle turned easily.

"Your story, sir," the policeman said.

"We're very sorry," the other one said.

"Your story," I said.

They were about to get back into the police car parked just beyond the small group of onlookers that had formed on the sidewalk. I recognized the face of a young boy in the crowd. The policeman turned back toward me.

"Do you have anyone, sir?" he asked quietly.

"Anyone?"

"Does someone look after you? You seem a little confused if I may say."

"My daughter," I said. "I have a daughter."

"Would you like us to call her?"

"No, no," I said, "I'll use the machines within. Thank you."

It was the wrong thing to say, I knew. I saw how they looked at me. The place was empty. Someone in the crowd on the sidewalk laughed.

"Move on, all of you," the other policeman said. "You'll all be old soon enough."

"We will call her for you," the younger policeman said and they were off in the old-fashioned cruiser trailing a scent of burnt wiring like the first-generation maglevs.

Inside there was no sign of what once had been. The floors were carefully swept without any marks upon them to disclose where the tables had been, nor was there evidence of the power strips or the networking fibers. I had a memory of having searched a floor of another kind than this, that one not polished concrete but plastic fiber decking made to look like old wood. A window looked out upon a nearby spillway or canal but it was dry. A needle memory had lodged itself in the space between two of the simulated planks and I tried to fish it out but my fingers trembled and I had no tool to extract it. I would tell Camille. Or was it Carmine?

A tweezers.

None of this had happened, I knew.

Or perhaps someone had said that.

"A knot in time is not a not," somebody, a fool, once said. *His* name was Franky, the other had been someone else.

The floor was not discolored or marred where Madame's counter had been and the doorways along the hall opened to equally empty rooms, although a bed frame with no mattress leaned against the wall within the last of them.

Rosaria was in the room where Madame had lived.

In fact she wasn't. That was a mistake, merely something I called up in memory, a glitch. Nor was there the hot plate or the cupboards, no table or chairs, no bed within the alcove. Not the hanging cloth, nor even any bar to hang it upon. There was a sink, although it seemed smaller than I remembered, and another still smaller sink inside the small bathroom where the water was running in the commode. Within the commode the pink corpse of a baby floated, its skin wrinkled and shrunken.

No. It was a doll. An old woman had left it there.

I opened the back door. It looked out on an alley which led to the loading dock of the copper-clad building. There was a young boy standing on the platform in the sun.

Beckmesser was in love with someone in another world, a queen, Elinor by name. The sound of that word made my breath catch and my heart race. Or were those the words to a song? The boy on the platform was waving something over his head; it looked like a banner on the end of a spear, although he may have caught a large fish, an eel, or perhaps he flew a small kite at the end of a string fastened to a stick.

I was aware that for some time everything had been happening much too neatly, as if according to an external order, one event following upon another neatly in sequence as if in a series of screens, yet the sequence of them without the ennui or the emptiness of life, no patches in the road where the sun steamed up and weeds choked in tufts of tar between concrete squares, no waiting, no remembering, no tooth aching until you could wriggle it free of the sagging gums and then the coppery taste of blood, no dead bird drab on a sidewalk. None of the wreck and debris of life appearing. Thirst, the feeling of confusion when you woke in a basement somewhere, someone searching through your things thinking you were asleep but thankfully not hurting.

Oh Daddy, she—Carmine, I think, or perhaps they were the same—said.

Elinor touched his brow. Her fingers were cool, with the texture of the softest lambskin gloves. Where is your crown, my lord? she asked.

I slept on the floor in the middle of the room, the tied-up packet of the blanket under my head for a pillow.

When I woke there was really someone, not an image I had projected, but someone. I could see the shaft of light searching along the walls and floor along the perimeter of the room, sliding down to a corner, then coming toward me on a diagonal path, bathing my face.

"My god, I'm sorry, I thought someone had broken in, are you all right?"

It was not a policeman but some kind of guard nonetheless, dressed all in dark green and with an embroidered patch upon one shoulder. He had a gentle voice and a plump face and, like most of those who appeared before me now, seemed like someone one of us, Beckmesser or I, recognized.

"Do you know who I am?" I asked, still lying on the floor.

"Of course," he said. "We work for you, Mr. Beck."

"And who is Mr. Dee?" I asked.

The fellow rubbed his chin like some character in a video, his face only half-lit from the flashlight that he had averted toward the ceiling.

"I can't say that I know," he said. "Would you like me to drive you back to your house? Or to a doctor?"

For many reasons, I wanted no more complication, no house, no life within it, no set of new names to learn, no faces to recognize. I believed I was well, just serving a sentence, caught up in a sequence not entirely of my making.

"No, I'll stay here for now," I said. "I'm feeling better now. I was very tired and then I had some soup."

I could taste the soup in my memory, it was fragrant with rosemary and a broth made of lamb bones. But when had I eaten?

Two men spat on the floor and then chased after me. I ran and ran.

"I would feel better if I could take you somewhere," he said.

I thought for a moment.

"Is the town square still there?" I asked. "Around the corner across from the municipal building."

Even in the half-light the concern in his expression was evident.

"You are better off in here than in that damn place this time of night. No telling what goes on there in the night. I'd feel better if I take you home, sir."

"No, I'll stay here," I said, then added, "I'm expecting someone, a possible tenant early in the morning."

Did I remember this?

"At least let me get you set up," he said and went away, the light following with him. Somewhere there was a far thrum like a stringed instrument. He reappeared.

"Got that old cot down in the storeroom," he said. "There's no mattress but I brought something from the car to cover the springs."

He offered his hand to help me up and I took it. His hand was large and strong but the palm and fingers were cool as powder. We went hand in hand to the other room where he had spread a large green raincoat the color of his uniform upon the springs. He had brought along the packet I was using as a pillow.

"Do you have my hat?" I asked.

"Your daughter won't be happy, Mister B," he said. "You sure this is what you want to do?"

"My daughter?" I said.

"Camilla," he said.

"I don't think you need to tell her."

"Maybe not, but she knows things even so."

He set the pillow package at the head of the cot.

"You be okay?" he asked.

"If I'm not, it won't be your fault," I said. "No one would really miss me."

He snorted.

"We are all irreplaceable, or so I'd like to think. Good night, sir."

As I saw it, the question before me was to disentangle myself from whatever was not me and to let events take their own sequence if that was how it was to be. In one part of me I made my way along the dark street outside, first checking that I could unlock the door and get back in again with a wave of the identity chip if need be, then walking slowly around the corner past the municipal building, which to my surprise was no longer bathed in light nor fitted out with the glass guardhouse where a hussar with a handlebar moustache once held court. The square, too, had fallen into disrepair in such a short time, the paths no more than dirt and cinder tracks, both the benches and the small shed gone. Figures moved through the shadows and in one corner of the park two of them held down another while a third violated him or her, the victim moaning, the attacker grunting.

"What are you looking at ape man?" A voice shouted.

"Want to be next?" Another called out and laughed.

I had a revolver in my hand; where it came from I was not sure.

I fired a shot into the sky thinking it would bring the authorities. The bullet disappeared into the night in a modest blue flare from the end of the barrel. There must have been a loud report, however, because my ears rang and the attackers ran off.

Cautiously I moved toward where the victim lay but there was no one there, merely a depression in the tall grass much as when deer lay down to bed themselves.

There had been no deer for years.

Elinor loved them. "The hart and hind are each other's hunter," she said awkwardly.

"Is anybody here?" I called out softly, not wanting to attract more hoodlums.

No one replied.

I made my way back undisturbed and the tumblers opened when I waved the chip before the lock plate. Only then did I realize that I had not looked where the three birch trees had once grown.

Two, someone said. Only two remained.

All the while, of course, another part of me lay there while these events went on elsewhere in space or time of someone's making, perhaps my own. I was aware that dreamers walked for hours in distant kingdoms and, more aptly, that certain medications—ironically devised to bring surcease or sleep—often had an opposite effect in the corporeal world, sending sleepwalkers off unbeknownst to themselves, although where the mind resided was unclear. These were matters I knew I could discuss with others should such opportunities ever present themselves again. Franky and his sister, both offspring of philosophers themselves, would be interested in such matters. They, however, had long ago emigrated.

What could I mean by that?

The sleeping thoughts of the part of me who refrained from the already related nighttime adventure consisted of these lists and logical conundrums. Four wooden boxes, say, each of their four sides a different color, each of the four boxes possessing the identical colors in sequence (the color of the bottoms unknown to me), had to be arranged in such a way that a series of colored balls could be bounced so as to land within them one after another in such a way that they would open up a dream. The dream began with the sky itself opening still further, as if dawn were the massive shell of a crustacean from a lost eon, its covering carapace various shades of grey but its ruffled lip opening to a quiet dazzle of pink and orange and bright lavender, widening still farther and farther into a dizzying swirl of cream and yellow. A knocking echoed in the abyss, the boxes shattered, the colored balls rolled away. Nothing in this was causal, rather governed by a different logic.

The knocking continued, followed by the dull resounding of a fist banging on glass.

By the time I realized these sounds proceeded from the world above the dreams, the knocking had ceased. Still I rose up from the cot, keeping the green wool greatcoat wrapped around me and, rubbing my eyes open, went into the room with the sink and urinated against its square sides. My urine smelled of herbs and sulphur. I had seen a horse piss once upon a rock in a way that the water sprayed back in a rainbow over its flank. The woman I was with laughed and said, "My god, it's as big as yours!" After it was done she wanted to sneak up to gather the crystals that she was sure would remain in the soil.

"Citrines," she said. "That is the name of them. They can cure many ailments."

The water did not stop flowing from the horse.

Rosaria laughed and clapped her hands as if it were magic.

I ran water to flush away the smell of herbs and then splashed some of it upon my face. I wished for a mirror, then I remembered there was one in the packet I used for a pillow.

Someone was knocking on the back door now, so I waited.

"Herr Beckmesser? Herr Beckmesser?" a woman's voice called.

I opened the door and my tenant was standing there, her son at her side, holding her hand.

The boy's obsidian eyes were dangerous, I knew, and so I took care not to look into them, averting my eyes like the ranger had averted his beam during the night.

Yet he knew who I was and could identify me if asked.

The woman was Carmine, I was certain.

"No," the woman said. "My name is Irene."

"Did I say that aloud?" I asked.

"I'm not sure now," she said. "I thought you did. Perhaps I was hearing something."

"I'm a little lost," I explained, "like a river that has split into two streams."

"I understand," she said. "It happens to all of us. We have been wandering, my son and I, for years."

I was waiting for the town bells to ring to signal the hour.

"Excuse me," the woman said, "can we come in? My son is restless."

I looked down at the boy, still careful to avoid the dangerous eyes, and only then noticed that the woman was barefoot, her feet broad and brown beneath a broad patterned skirt, the toe nails colored carefully in silver polish.

"Can I bring you shoes?" I asked and, as soon as I did, I knew that was not the right thing to say.

Still they both laughed and it relieved the tension of the moment, so much so that I risked looking at the boy, who seemed five or six years old and with sweet face and mischievous grin, his skin olive, bushy brows and thick hair black as his eyes, which shone with light within. I knew him once.

"Say hello, Andy," the woman prompted the boy.

"Come in, come in," I said, although they were within the room by then.

"I didn't think that was his name," I said.

The boy had my little hat with the gold foil disk in his hand.

"Thank god you found it," I said and tried to wrest it from him. He started to cry.

"Oh let the nice man see your hat," the woman said. "He's only joking."

He handed the hat to me and it sat on my head like a little cup before sliding off and rolling to the corner of the room, the boy chasing after it delightedly.

"I had such a hat when I was small," I explained to the woman.

The boy ran back with the hat and urged me to put it on. It rolled off again and he laughed and ran after it.

"Enough Andy!" the woman said. "We have business to do. Go explore this place. See if you can find a bird."

I knew there wouldn't be one but then had a sense that a forest grew within the large space where Madame once had her café, a green and verdant place with parrots and toucans and small Asian finches in many colors. It was a waking dream, I knew. Still I could smell the damp perfume of the jungle.

"I have the money," she said and turned away, delicately reaching down within her blouse and pulling a small embroidered sack closed with a silver string from the space between her ample breasts.

"I will have to pay the first month in specie," she said, "because we have no credits as yet. I promise we'll have the next month a week before it is due."

"Where will I go?" I asked.

For a while during this time the things I spoke often surprised me, arising as if specters from a deep pool, silver fish that spoke like troubadours, the rough discourse of carp.

The embroidered sack was still warm from her body and with a spice scent of perfume.

"Were you hoping to open a business here?" the woman asked.

"No, I mean, where will I live?"

She laughed like flowing water.

"I'm so sorry," she said. "I could see you slept here. Thank you for taking the trouble. I'm sorry we had to come by so early but Andy doesn't sleep and I will still have to work while we fix this place up before we open."

The boy was back, I realized, squatting in a far corner and looking at us.

"Do you want to kiss her?" he asked.

"*Taci!*" she said. "Stop that silliness or I won't take you with me."

"A man paid twenty *reales* to kiss her just once," the boy said impishly and she made as if to chase after him and he squealed with laughter.

I looked in my hand where I had poured the coins from the sack, pennies and florints and the new issue ducats that I had not seen for years.

"It's all there," she said. "But of course you may count it again if you like."

The coins, too, were still warm.

The boy was pulling brightly colored feathers from a sack before him, which I realized, when I looked more closely, was in fact my blanket packet that he had somehow been able to untie. Besides the feathers there were dried leaves of a kind I recognized, the polished skull of some small creature, and a small mirror framed in lapis lazuli. There was also a holo in a plastic covered folio with a lurid cover of naked women and men, limbs intertwined in an orgy.

"I am so sorry!" I exclaimed and snatched the folio from the boy, who laughed.

"They are having a party, aren't they?" he asked.

His mother was blushing.

"The place is yours," I said. "What sort of shop do you have in mind?"

I was attempting to conceal the holo as best I could, holding it tightly to my hip.

"A small exhibition space," she said. "A theatre of illusions, more like a café."

"Do you have any money?" I asked and she seemed confused, gesturing toward the sack I still held in my other hand where I had gathered back the coins.

"I—" she said. "We thought…."

I extracted a new ducat from the sack, holding the holo between my legs while I did so. "No, I mean something for the day," I said. "You'll need breakfast before your work, the boy—"

"No, no, we are taken care of," she said.

She seemed to realize well before I did what I was asking.

"Would you like to come with us for a while?" she asked. "I know a gypsy place nearby if you would like to have a pastry and strong coffee."

She turned to the boy and remonstrated him in a language I did not recognize and he began to repack the leaves and feathers into the blanket. The woman, Irene, reached gingerly between my legs where I still held the holo and handed it to the boy who nested it within the carefully folded blanket without a further word, placing it next to the small mirror, then tying up the whole packet again.

6

I was snatched away before we could reach the gypsies that morning. On the street before the empty shop someone waited in the shadows. It was the girl with the phantom half-circle eyebrow and she held a polished silver bowl before her, the morning sun splashing up in reflection from the surface of the liquid within in rocking patches of light.

"Would you like a drink, father?" she asked, holding the bowl up toward me.

In the surface of the water I saw that my face and skull were as they had been once, perhaps a little younger than when I first came to this city, but someone I recognized.

"I have your doll," I said and turned back toward the empty shop to get it.

Irene and her son looked distressed. I had a sense that they were waiting for me to answer some question.

"I'm sorry," I said, "did you need something?"

"I asked about the keys," Irene said. "How we will get back within?"

"I was distracted," I said. "I—" I turned toward the girl as if to explain but she was gone and with her the image of my healing.

"I have no keys," I said. "The lock plate is programmed…." I held up my arm to show the identity chip.

"Here." A woman beside me held out a burnished disk, a programmed key. "My father is a little confused these days. If he's leased the store to you, we will, of course, honor that agreement, but he needs his rest."

She was holding me in an embrace that also seemed a restraint, a soft arm around me, just above my waist, affectionate and yet with just enough force that I knew I could not escape her. In any case she was accompanied by the same stout fellow who had arrived during the night all dressed in green and with his beam of light, who now stood at my other side, still in this makeshift uniform, holding my blanket packet firmly under one arm, gripping my arm with the other.

I knew enough by now to recognize that this wasn't me at all but rather that a memory of Beckmesser's had come to the foreground overtaking what I was experiencing in the present. Yet this was the first time in a day or two that I could remember these two streams converging so. The new tenant, Irene, knew me as Beckmesser, and the handsome woman beside me—Camille, Carmine, Camilla—appeared so often in his memory that I knew she was his daughter.

My daughter.

"We're taking him home," she said, offering her hand to the woman. "I will come to see you again after you've moved in and begun your business. What is your name, may I ask?"

"Elinor," the new tenant lied. "This is my son, Francisco."

No, I objected, no, she is lying, she's a bruja and she's lying, but I was unable to speak on account of some sort of tranquilizer that was already spreading through my veins like warm honey from the place where the man in green had injected me.

They kept me drugged for some time, my daughter and the officer, in a place I recognized from the memories: broad green lawns leading down to a small sapphire pond from a low white stucco house with topiary trees before it. I could walk the lawns in freedom or, if I wished, the man in the green uniform would wheel me in an old-fashioned bentwood chair with a wicker back and seat and wood-spoked wheels with gutta percha tires. To be this kind of captive in a place of such great beauty and familiarity was not as troubling as it might have seemed, especially since—perhaps benefiting from the sedative they gave me—I became much more adept at navigating between the two streams of memory that flowed through me, Beckmesser's and my own. Increasingly I could turn from one to the other as if shifting between video transmissions.

And yet, at least before she lied to my daughter, I had been looking forward to talking further with the bruja Irene, for I had some sense that I could have asked her questions, and confirmed my gathering certainties, without arousing her suspicion or turning solicitude to anxiety. I was not so naïve as to be unaware of what was happening to me, not just caught in a knot of time as someone had said, but caught between a full life in progress and a fragmentary and edited montage of one that had been for some time snuffed and for months before that had been led in fantasy.

I knew that figures in one scene overlaid themselves in another like the morphing toys of children or the more sophisticated versions cosmeticians and surgeons wielded to display futures to their patrons. Even my own appearance oscillated within a long band of parallel times, so much so that I could not be confident that I would recognize myself in a mirror or the surface of the sapphire pond just beyond these lawns when the man in green rowed me upon it.

There used to be a game when I was very young, one not played on a screen but rather on an actual table, a game not unlike the logic dreams that sometimes assailed my sleep, where you shook a canister of brightly colored sticks and spilled them on the green felt of the table and then tried to extract as many of them as you could before the resulting pile collapsed and you had to begin again. It was like that for me during those days. I would begin to trace something, the differences between Carmine and Camille for instance, how the one was a shade of deep red and the other a variety of white flower, the camellia, known as japonica, of which Camilla was only a variant, but which could as likely be pinkish to red, purple, or peppermint in color, as well as the many people, real or imagined, who had referred to someone by these names, and the various young women, all of them perhaps one to whom they had referred, when suddenly I would be lost again, confused about what I had set out to do in such a reverie and what it would matter in any case should I remember.

Other times I would try to match up the different little boys and girls with their names, again getting caught up in something of a horticultural puzzle, as if their faces were flowers and garden beds their occasions—someone in a schoolgirl jumper, someone else in a white tunic with gold buttons, a cartwheeling girl in organdy, one with a half-circle scar, another in a shirtwaist, a pretty little baby named Maria Elena, all of them mapped on a screen like migrating wrens—and then midway in the process suddenly not be certain which of us had seen them or whether they were real. Of the boys, Manco and Andy and Franky and Candido and a group of urchins whose names I did not know but whose faces flickered in my stream of memories, I was more certain; to me they were as real as a part of me, though cut off, like the tip of thumb I'd lopped off in an accident—when?—or the broken teeth replaced by pearls wrapped in crimped aluminum.

The boys, too, could be mapped somehow, I knew.

If I make this sound distressing, it was not. The weather was fair, the lawns were green, and sometimes my daughter would come and sit by my side on a white bench and sing to me a song she called the flower duet, the echo of her voice lingering over the water like a mist. I knew none of it was real, but I, too, wanted to linger before moving on to wherever my life had taken me in the interim, or, more exactly, to whatever I had been sentenced to.

To be sure, under the flowers were such shadows, lurking there the way dark dreams slide back and forth beneath the surface of even the brightest day. To the extent that I could collate what had happened to someone known as "me," the creature whose face I had seen in the silver bowl the girl held out before me outside the shop, I could begin to map something that took on the quality of an adjudication of some sort in the form of a series of gateways. Each time I passed through one gate an instance of me was left behind, adhering to the successive gates like gel transparencies in the form and image of me but fleshless. The sensation was quite like when an animation is slowed down to mimic how movies used to be, the succession of see-through selves freshly damp and clinging to each portal.

I knew also that there was something I had to do, something I had been sentenced to in a sense. Part of it, I knew, involved solving my own murder, or the murder of the man whose life I occupied in these illusions, though the most salient of these I could seldom summon and never sustain; the elusive Elinor—the real one, not the lying bruja with her demon son—did not often deign to appear.

There was, I realized, a sordid explanation. The occurrences within Ynys Gutrin were a commercial proposition and belonged to whatever entertainment combine fashioned and distributed them and not to the player participants. All that Beckmesser could remember was himself remembering and not what had "happened" in any present sense. Dreams of dreams were thin clouds and cast thinner shadows on the lawns beneath.

I wondered, though, whether I could talk Camille into letting her father play something that pleased him and thus experience this world for myself, perhaps even encounter Elinor. I thought it might help me determine who had murdered him, or if such a thing had happened at all.

"We have none of those worlds here," she had protested the first time I brought it up. "Isn't this world pleasant enough?"

"But no more real," I said.

"Oh Daddy," she sighed, "Papa!"

We sat for a while in silence, fireflies were rising from the lawn at dusk.

"Don't start with that stuff about wanting to have a place of your own again, please," she said, her voice weary and worried. "You can hardly manage a day alone by yourself. Really, you would have frozen to death had Cedric not found you sleeping on that shop floor."

How could I have frozen to death in summer, I wondered. Unless, of course, it was much longer ago than I remembered. There were so many fireflies rising against the far hill that they seemed a shimmering curtain of light. Now and again one flared over the water of the pond, his own reflection answering him.

"Is Cedric your husband?" I asked. "I think I do not like him and that is why I want to move out."

I had plucked this knowledge from the flow of Beckmesser's memory.

She sighed again. "You're hopeless," she said, "or I am. You know full well that Cedric is the groundskeeper and Marco thinks the world of you. He loves you like a son."

"Like Franky," I said. "He latches on."

"You're living in his house, Papa."

"No," I said. "I am living in your house, the one he stole from you."

The dark was rising from the lawns around us like the mist that now rose from the pond; it was the antimony hour, the sky still blue grey holding the last light like a cup of cider.

"Oh Daddy," she said, "sometimes the things you say are so beautiful I can cry about what's happening to you. A cup of cider is just so perfect...."

Apparently I had said this aloud or at least she seemed to think I had.

Even the cider light dimmed and we went up, Camille walking arm in arm beside me.

"I'll have Cedric look for your Ynys Gutrin," she said patting my arm. "But you have to promise me that you won't spend too much time or too many credits upon it. It upsets Marco."

He took my house and now he wants my money, I thought, but did not say. I had no image of this Marco that I could summon and I wasn't sure exactly what wealth, if any, I myself possessed or where it would have come from.

I began to worry that I was losing track of time, not in the routine way that someone like me could not keep track of days, but rather that time itself was a scarce substance, not just slipping through a narrow passage like sand through the hourglasses of stories, but rather evaporating, dissipating like an entropic mist rising from the surface of the pond, never to be refreshed or replaced. I thought that somewhere in that mist another part of me was running out of options while I was deserting him to himself. There in that mist was the real prison. Meanwhile out here, whatever that could mean, I had so much to do to get out of the places I was within, layer on layer of time slipping under my feet, walking up an endless sand dune. Meanwhile that other someone literally seemed to be a runner, in and out of time, jogging along a distant ridge at dawn while I bedded down in twilight.

This feeling was amplified when I awoke one morning in the darkened room that looked down on the stream that flowed toward the sapphire pond to find Cedric sitting there in the upholstered armchair beside the bed, his mouth half-open, snoring lightly, each snore fading into a whistle.

He woke when I woke and, like a robot, immediately launched into talk, the snoring stopped like a cork with his words.

"You're something else, man," he laughed. "I mean I spent all of the last three days or so trying to find some game called Ynys Gutrin, goin' in and out more stores and bazaars and market stalls, searching more network game boutiques and online stores than you can imagine, only to find what you want is something they ain't even released yet, in fact just started developing! Damn thing won't be available for years and the folks who told me what they knew said it was top secret. Man, you're something else, you really is. My own real life garden going to weeds while I'm out searching for something that ain't even been announced and only been halfway thought of! How do you know these things? Really, old man, I'd like to know. I'd be rich as you if I knew as much."

He was fond of Beckmesser; it was clear in how he laughed.

"I dream them," I said. "My dreams go forward and my life goes back."

"You are something else," he chuckled.

I am, I thought, it was accurate to say so. Something caught up in time like a leaf spinning in a stream. Some of what I remembered had not yet happened and some of it had never been, while the me who-I-was and the me who-I-am converged and split like grafts on an apricot tree. I tried to remember what it was that I had realized not long before about how life was occurring in too neat a sequence and what I had thought it meant for me. I decided at very least to test that hypothesis, figuring that the same wave that had brought me from the café to the brick bottle cave to the copper-fronted glass building to this place, might catch me up again and toss me forward in time, or the illusion of an exit, like the cinder ditch at the edge of the city where once, long before, I had almost escaped all this.

So I decided to wait through summer, but then Marco came back from his conference and I was forced to make a move. Again I woke one morning with someone in my room and at first thought it was Cedric again. Yet as soon as I felt the cold smear of the alcohol wipe followed by the cool chrome of the bioscan probe upon my forehead, I knew it was not Cedric.

"Don't squirm, Papi." Marco's voice resonated soothingly in the dark in the fashion that is called a good bedside manner, yet the way he said "Papi" marked a certain disdain.

"Who are you?" I protested.

"You know who I am," the voice insisted.

"Daddy, it's Marco," Camille said from the shadows. "He's home from his conference and I asked him to look in on you."

"And so you've entered my sleep, the both of you?"

"You're wide awake," Marco said brusquely and turned on the overhead light.

"Can you leave us a minute?" he asked Camille.

"He's my own father," she said.

"There are procedures I need to do without his having any distractions." He was as brusque with her as he had been with me.

"All right darling," she said, "I'll leave you two together." Then she touched my forehead and it was the soothing touch of a true camellia.

It was me she called darling.

"I have to pee," I said to Marco.

I was surprised to see that he was a stunted little fellow, handsome enough but with a block for a head, albeit covered in carefully barbered dark curly hair over shoulders a little too broad for a man of such height and arms that hung down almost to his knees trailing long, soft fingers. He was wearing a well tailored suit of tight summer-weight silk tweed nearly the color of the pond beyond.

He handed me the plastic urinal with a bent neck and broad handle, a gold cufflink flashing on his wrist. This was a well tailored fellow of some means and yet the *Bête* to *La Belle* Camille at least in my eyes. There was something of the pug about him that made me think I had seen him before in some other guise, something from my own rather than Beckmesser's memories. The folds of his lip and his hooded eyes made me think of someone else whom I could not place.

Perhaps myself, I realized, the way I had seemed when Manco first showed me my face after the beating.

Manco and Marco. Separated by a letter.

That might mean something.

The urine that fizzled into the container smelled of lacquer and molasses.

"Sit up please!" he said, pulling me up roughly.

He pinched at either side of my eyelid as if to pop out my eyes.

"Ouch!" I shouted. "What are you doing?"

"I wanted to see if you are wearing lenses. I was hoping to dislodge them."

"Why?"

"You are not who you are," he interrupted me. "I don't know what you have done with Camille's father or what you are hoping to get away with, but I can assure you that Cedric is just outside that door if you dare to try anything."

He was washing his hand with an alcohol solution and the room smelled like a clinic.

"Are you a doctor then?" I asked.

"Wouldn't you know that?"

"I've been confused," I said. "That's why she wanted you to see me."

"I'm going to give you an injection that will make you sleep for some time but will not harm you. I want you immobilized while I run further tests and we decide what to do with you."

It was then that I began to struggle, although Camille later said that our voices had been growing louder before she and Cedric rushed in and found us grappling.

"Stop that right now, both of you!" she shouted. "Get him, Cedric," she ordered.

It was Marco she meant to restrain. She sat upon the edge of the bed and held me, her tears already flowing.

"What in the world am I going to do with the two of you? The men I love best in this world and you can't get along!"

"He is not who you think," Marco said. "He's an imposter, maybe a simul here to cause us harm. If they have kidnapped your father or worse, they may now want one of us."

Cedric looked confused about what he should do. He let go of the doctor, who smoothed the sleeves of his suit where the other man had gripped him. Camille continued to hold me.

"You've been working too hard, Marco," she said softly. "I shouldn't have asked you to do this after such a long flight."

"I'll run the DNA swab and you'll see," he said. "It will bear out the biometrics. For now let me give him this injection to restrain him just long enough to convince you."

"No," she said firmly, and reached for the auto-injector. "He's had enough drugs pumped into him these last few days. Perhaps that's what you are seeing in your tests."

Marco pulled his hand away from her as if to do it nonetheless, but Cedric gently restrained him and the doctor let the injector drop to the floor where a circle of dark liquid seeped into the carpet.

"I'll get his imprint without the swab. I can run the tests on his piss," he said and reached for the plastic urinal.

Cedric, however, anticipated this coup and poured the stuff into the soil around the huge potted ficus in the corner of the room, keeping the urinal in his grasp until the doctor stormed out of the room.

"Thank you, Cedric," Camille said calmly. "He's overwrought about what's happened to Daddy, and he misses me when he's been away. I'll calm him down."

She left me alone with Cedric who slumped into a chair.

"We got to get you out of here, my friend," he said. "I know the doctor's right and you ain't who you say you are and if he tested this jar he'd find out as much. But I also know you don't mean anyone no harm. Even that first night when I found you on the floor of the vacant shop, I knew there was something that didn't match up. You look like who you are but something about you reminds me of someone I saw in a dream."

"We met in the future," I said. "You were working as a greenskeeper."

As soon as I said this I felt a recurrence of the feeling that life was occurring in too neat a sequence. Perhaps he had been my warder even then, this greenskeeper, perhaps the whole city or an elaborate prison constructed of illusions of your own making.

"Maybe I was," Cedric said. "Stranger things happen. We can worry about all that once we figure how to get you out of here, Alex."

"What did you call me?"

"I thought you just said that was your name."

I tried to think who it was I had been with once before when I surprised myself by saying that was my name.

"I keep waiting for the scene to change," I said.

"Nothing going to change without you doing something about it, my friend. Me and you," Cedric said.

"I need to get somewhere in the future," I said. "I think I can find the way there if you get us back to the shop."

"We all get somewhere in the future eventually, my friend," Cedric laughed, "even if it's that last black abyss that no one comes out of."

I did not say that it was that abyss of Beckmesser's that I hoped to find. In truth I wondered whether I could once again find the checkerboard quarter where Beckmesser had lived, let alone find my way to any future beyond the one I was living into day by day albeit in gaps and stutters that elided whole patches of time.

"You're going to need some resources, my friend, or Camilla will reel you in again soon as you use your credits. She worries about him, despite that husband of hers."

For the longest time I thought Cedric was from the islands because of the lilting way he talked and how his full face was nut brown, but his bushy eyebrows and slick black hair made him seem as if he were from somewhere else. In the following days I enticed bits of his story from him, but like all men there were parts he held onto. He came from an island across the world on the other end of Ram Setu, an archipelago of some sort which according to him the gods used to walk upon long ago along with their monkey army. He had run away from home after his father died and his mother remarried a cruel man who wanted her to beg.

Something in how he said this gave me the sense that he meant the man wanted his mother to become a prostitute, but I didn't ask if that was what he meant. In any case this history seemed part of why he took up my side against Marco in this confrontation, although I also knew it might simply have been out of affection for Camille—his Camilla—to whom he was clearly devoted.

Or, of course, that story, too, could be an illusion, part of the crystal penitentiary my dreams spun like silkworms.

In any case using Camille's money to get away was out of the question, though she had entrusted Cedric with the passwords for her credits and the combination for the vault where she kept monetary flash memory as well as some specie and jewelry and the gold bracelets that Marco had given her for their wedding.

The mention of flash memory recalled a memory so vivid I could feel the blunt keys in my hand.

"Somewhere there are nine keys of flash memory on a key ring," I said. "Each a terabyte of valuation that I converted over the years."

"Bearer memory and not pass-worded?" he asked.

I nodded.

"And not encrypted?"

I nodded again, although in truth I was no longer certain why I had mentioned these keys and what more I knew about them. And surely not where they were or whose.

"Is that all you know?" Cedric questioned me, as if I were holding back some key information.

I searched the intertwined layers of memories, my own and Beckmesser's. I saw skulls, three small skulls.

"Each key is stamped with a signet," I said. "Three small skulls, two above and one below."

Cedric laughed aloud and slapped me heartily on my back.

"Get in the wheelchair, my friend. We'll take a stroll down to the pond and I'll show you something," he said.

It was chilly outside and the lawn was dappled with yellow leaves and green grenades of black walnut fruit from the row of trees that ran up to the house from the dock. How could it be autumn, I wondered, when only yesterday the fireflies had lifted from the lawns at twilight. Cedric tucked a blanket around me to keep the chill out, the same alpaca blanket that Manco had once tied into a packet for me.

"My things?" I asked. "My mirror?"

Cedric patted his small leather backpack.

"Everything safe, my friend," he said and patted it again. "We're going sailing."

He was clearly excited about something.

The flat bottomed-boat Cedric called a dhony although I think it was properly called a dory. It was large enough to almost never rock and with a sharp prow that tracked true in the water whether he rowed or, as he sometimes did, stood and pushed it using the oar as a boat pole. Instead of the bentwood wheelchair, we took a smaller folding one of black titanium down to the dock where he stowed it between us on the boat. The truth be told I could not recall why they had begun wheeling me around at all since, as best I knew, I could walk perfectly well. From the dock we could see Camille waving. She was bundled up in a white parka with a knit hat like the Peruvians wore. Marco was nowhere to be seen.

I felt that before long I would not see her again for years, at least in Beckmesser's story, and it made me a little sad to see her waving so forlornly in the clear October light, although I knew full well that given how erratically time was behaving I might see her again somewhere in an instant.

Cedric rowed most of the way out to the sunken chapel but then stopped and extracted the plastic urinal from the backpack and filled it with water from the lake, then let it sink slowly into the lake until we could not see it anymore.

He remained standing, poling the boat slowly as we neared what he wanted to show me. Only a small marble cupola showed above the surface of the water and so from the house and lawn it looked like a knobby island made of bone. Cedric approached it carefully while I peered down into the water at the shadowy walls of the submerged church, the boat tipping slightly as we each leaned over.

"Inside the Chhatri is a shelf," he said. He meant the cupola, and he reached in under one of the windows.

"And above the shelf is an iron hook cemented in the marble."

I sat back on my bench and the boat leveled.

"No, please, my friend. Lean over again, it is a little awkward to find it."

When I looked down again koi fish were swimming through the reflection, red and white and yellow patterned creatures breaking up the lost visage of Beckmesser's face.

"And on the hook, if I am correct, are the keys to your freedom," Cedric said, his arm wet up to the shoulder by now.

"Ye lo!" he said and held out the ring of key-shaped flash memory chips.

I reached for the ring but he held it back and instead sat on the opposite bench addressing me gravely.

"I want you to understand some things, my friend. I'm not planning to be your sidekick or to call you sahib or anything of the sort. If I go with you now I may very well lose the best position I have ever had since I left home. Worse, I may lose the love of only the first woman I have cared about since my mother. Why I am doing all this I really do not know. Perhaps you and I are bound to each other by something out of our own control. That may be but I also know that if I do not follow through your story with you, it will not end well. If you are right and these keys hold a fortune in bearer memory, then they belong to me as well as to you since each of us found them in the depths of something not our own. Me while diving to explore the chapel below where they hung in the vestry as if they belonged to a long-ago priest, you diving into whatever strange torrent of mixed memories you occupy. Without you, I would not have recognized what these might be. Without me, you would have never found them. Even so, we still, neither of us, do not know whether the flash memory still functions or whether its valuation isn't encrypted after all."

It was quite a wonderful little speech and I had a sense that I had heard it before, seen this whole scene among Beckmesser's memories.

"I understand," I said. "Five for you and four for me, that's fair."

"Four each and one for the two of us, sahib," he said, dangling the keys over the edge of the gunwale with one hand and reaching to shake my hand with the other.

I began to laugh. "Okay, my friend," I said.

"Good thing you got the joke," he said and dropped the keys, snatching them neatly out of the air just at the last second with the same hand that dropped them just before they sunk.

 He rowed us slowly so as not to arouse suspicion, rowing to the opposite shore from the house where a narrow paved road wound sinuously through a pine forest. He pushed me along the road in a half-trot, the leather backpack of my treasures, now including the flash memory keys, on my lap. After a number of turns a paved drive led back into a shed in the trees where a small vehicle, more cart than car yet still enclosed and with a small heater, sat covered with a tarp and plugged into a recharger.

"This cart is mine and no one else's," he said. "I built it from a kit. The doctor will have no grounds to complain that we've taken something from them."

"Let's leave the wheelchair then," I said.

"You're sure, my friend?"

"Sure," I said. "Once we reach the future I expect to be able to fly."

Cedric looked at me curiously as if to discern whether I was serious.

"Truly, sahib," I said, and he laughed in relief.

On the way into the city he told me the story of how he had come there, having worked for Camilla for years before she met the doctor.

"This was while your—I mean, Beckmesser's—wife was still living with him at the house and before he flooded the valley."

"Because she died?" I asked.

"No wonder you fooled Camilla," he said. "You know enough from time to time to even fool me, though nothing will fool the doctor's instruments. With his biometrics he's become a very powerful figure in the government."

Suddenly he seemed to think of something.

"Still," he said, "I'm not sure if it is correct to say Beckmesser did it *because* she died. To me, there is no way of knowing whether what anyone does is because of something else or just the order of things."

"Still, he loved her."

"Of course."

"There is no way of knowing whether what anyone does is because of love," I countered.

"No wonder they thought Beckmesser a philosophical fellow."

They thought me so as well, a philosoph I thought, though did not say, suddenly recalling the occupation they had long ago programmed on my visatag.

Long ago, that is, or yet to come.

Cedric had started working for Camille when she was a young woman living in a new development that had sprung up in the city. There he helped her with a little garden that led from the rear of her apartment and did other chores. The layout of the development reminded him of villages on the island where he grew up, four apartments in each low white building, two up, two down, the buildings set amidst what then were bare patches of mud, the footprints of the bare plots equal to the area of the building foundations, the patches meant to become lawns as soon as turf was laid down.

"Problem was they had built it on a toxic dump and all the turf kept dying. All the birds had flown away and yet the young people thought nothing of this. She wanted me to help her grow a garden in the terrace behind her rear apartment. I kept telling her to leave, though I managed to get Hostas to grow in raised beds. Hostas grow in great jungles, wild as the sea, where I was born."

"I think that apartment complex is exactly the place where I want to go," I said. "I've seen it before, I think. Not there exactly, but in a building quite near the white houses where Beckmesser will live out his life."

"So it will be a sort of slow suicide for you going back there again then, is that it, Alex?" he asked.

It was a question for which I had no answer, neither practical nor philosophic. Being anywhere is a kind of slow suicide when you think on it.

Cedric drove on, continuing the story.

Camilla did not stay in the garden apartment for long once she met the doctor whom she fell in love with, a dark haired man with a strange magnetism about him, not her type at all, or so it had seemed to Cedric, and yet someone who brought arms full of flowers to her dressing room following her performances to woo her.

"She was a singer then?" I asked.

"She is a singer now and was then, yes. A nightingale, the sweetest ever, which was why I agreed to work as her personal assistant. "

Cedric had been wary of Marco from the first, thinking that his very courtesy seemed a mask.

"Like Monostatos, in the opera," he said, "a villain in disguise."

I looked closely at him then to see if his own face disclosed such a mask.

The electric car hummed along a road on the periphery of the city that bordered a thriving industrial district spewing colorless fumes that filled the small cabin of the car. Cedric reached beneath his seat and extracted two surgical masks, handing one of them to me. Outside my window there was a deep culvert, almost a ravine, which led to a series of warehouses on the other side. We passed a parked police vehicle and Cedric waved at the officer, who gazed blankly back upon us.

"Nothing can live here, the earth is saturated with metals and when the sky inverts the air is yellow-green," Cedric explained. "If they ever close these places, it will be decades before people can inhabit here again. Yet every night the travelers bed down in these ravines now that the police have begun to chase them away from the underpasses and doorways elsewhere. This city is dying."

Just then I saw a figure crawling up over the berm along the culvert, a terrified looking fellow with sallow skin and wary eyes, seemingly out of breath.

"Stop!" I shouted. "Please!"

It was me I saw, of course, a phantom of me crawling up prematurely from the miasma of time, perhaps a specter of my imagination and yet no less frightening to me, no less in need of someone to help him.

"We can't," Cedric said softly. "The police already have him. They keep trying to crawl out like tortoises and the police keep throwing them back. There is no escaping the advance of time."

And so the wheel spun round once more again, past the double zeros, and left me where I began, or rather where some form of who I am began to veer away from all I knew and led me ever toward the end.

7

In coming days I thought a great deal about what Cedric had said about the tortoises in time. To be sure he was right and there was no escaping and yet it seemed to me that time itself advanced along a path that was like the bed of a treadmill, its great loop so tightly woven that it was almost impossible to spot where one edge of it was carefully bound to another. You could be thrown back and the advance would catch you up like a magnet but you could not leap forward, only watch as the great tongue you walked upon emerged relentlessly ever and again from its opening, moving back behind you.

Our place on the loop of time presented problems for us from the first. We had found the district easily enough, having stopped first at a credits station to test one of the keys. The valuation was, as I had expected, unencrypted and beyond either of our imaginations, such a grand amount that we were wary to extract too much of it either in specie or smaller transaction card denominations, afraid the system itself would mark the anomalous value were we to withdraw it all at once.

"Jesus!" Cedric said. "You sure you want to find a rooming house, my friend? You could buy a half dozen mansions with how much is on this card."

I was sure where I needed to live but the problem lay in that great loop of the treadmill, for the landlord I had once met was not yet the owner of the house where Beckmesser had died, and the current owner, an old woman, was not at all eager to encounter two strangers, especially two as strange as we.

"I'll call the police," she said through the space of a chained door before we were able to say anything.

Cedric reached into the pack and pulled something out that made her jump back. It was an old cell phone, the size of a scrub brush, the first phone of any sort that I had seen, I realized, since the man called Pacha brought me to the copper clad building where Death lived.

"I'll call them for you," Cedric said and punched in numbers, handing her the phone through the opening.

"I don't know how to use this," she said and surprisingly slipped the chain, letting us into the vestibule.

"You don't know who you can trust these days," she said, "what with the travelers creeping about at night and the strange kinds moving into all these new places they are building like rabbit warrens."

"Am I a strange kind?" Cedric asked sharply.

The woman met his gaze directly.

"Well, I mean, you are, aren't you?" she said. "Can you blame an old woman for fearing what she does?"

"I had a mother once. Perhaps I still do somewhere," Cedric said.

"Poor man," the woman sighed. "Please sit down, the both of you."

She gestured toward two stiff chairs, then addressed Cedric.

"Did she leave you?" she asked.

"No," he said, "I left her. I did not like what someone else was making her do, and she wouldn't change for me."

"All sons feel this after a certain age," she said. "My own wants me to move away from here and to make this place a rooming house."

We sat awhile in silence.

"What was her name?" she asked Cedric.

"Rosaria," he replied.

"Damn it! Not you!" I cried out. "You're lying."

I jumped up from my chair and retreated toward the door. The old woman's eyes glowed with fear.

"Please, my friend," Cedric said quietly. "We are unnecessarily alarming this lady who has shown us such courtesy."

I'd had enough of overlay and complication, of aliases and multiples, of eddy and counterflow, of punctuated and labile time. I wanted respite, I wanted certainties, something, or someone, to count on, some one thing to stand still.

"How could I be lying about my own mother's name?"

"What did you say?" I demanded.

"Roshenara," he said. "It is a very common name where I am from."

"That wasn't what you said!" I turned back to the woman. "Tell him," I demanded.

"Eleanor," she said. "My name is Eleanor. Would you like tea?"

Somewhere a phone was ringing, a persistent, electronic tone like the Japanese tunes of early game arcades. Cedric extracted the bulky cell phone from his pack again, the conversation staccato:

"What is it? Yes. No, I haven't? What? How did you find us? When? Damn. How? That's impossible. And she's asking for me? You are the doctor, I'll have to trust you, but the question is can she?"

Cedric clicked the phone off and stood there looking stricken.

"Your mother?" I asked.

It was logical, of course, given our conversation in the old woman's parlor, but when I think it over not very likely.

"I'll tell you outside," he said. "We should let this kind lady be. My friend and I are looking for rooms to rent," he explained to her. "We were led to think you had them here."

"Was it my son who told you this?" she asked.

"A man in a story," I said and she nodded her head as if that explained something.

"I won't give all this up," she said. "To him it is property but to me it is a story, my own story, my own history. Children shouldn't want to profit from the mere passage of time."

Cedric waited impatiently by the door.

"Thanks for inviting us in," I said. "And thanks for the offer of tea."

"Tea is important," she said. "The ceremony of it."

I took her hand and kissed it, why I did not know. The back of her hand smelled of talcum and was dry as paper. She touched the side of my temple with the same hand when I straightened up after the kiss.

"There is a blue house at the corner, Alex, it's there my son lives. He has several properties where he rents rooms and apartments. Tell him you were talking to me on the street and I told you to come."

"When did you tell her your name?" Cedric asked when we were back on the street.

"Did I?" I asked. "Well, it must have been when you were on the phone."

"There's been an accident," Cedric said, "although I don't know whether to trust Marco. It may just be a ruse to get us to come back. Camilla has hurt her eyes, badly it seems, a freak accident with a laser he was using to survey near the pond. Somehow she didn't see the beam and walked across it while looking into her compact mirror."

"Surveying for what?" I asked.

"Who knows," Cedric said. "Sunken treasure maybe. Who knows if anything is true?"

"It sounds unlikely," I said. "Like something from an animation video. But why would he hurt her?"

"To keep her," Cedric said. "She was close to leaving him, I think. With you gone, he might not think he could hold her."

"Did she even use a compact?" I asked. "I thought they were only in antique shops or stories."

"Oh that part is true enough," he said. "She's very vain like most performers and she's always looking at herself in one mirror or another. Her compact was something you gave her—Beckmesser did—as a gift for her first recital."

"Backed with lapis lazuli?" I asked.

"See how it is? You know everything. You have the benefits of two lives."

"And so get to die twice," I said. "What will we do?"

"What can we? We've left. If she's well again, she will find us. If not, there's nothing either of us can do. We'll go visit the son."

I was confused.

"Her son?"

"You know she has no children," he snapped. "Nor can she have any. I meant the fellow in the blue house that the old lady told us about. Her son. We'll see about renting a room."

"And Camille?"

"Once we're established, I'll see what I can find out. There are ways into that house that only I know."

No one answered the door at the blue house and we had nowhere to go and so we decided to wait. We sat on the wooden stairs that led to the vestibule wherein we could see an old-fashioned umbrella stand and an unmanned monitor for a surveillance cam in which we could see multiples of ourselves peering in and receding. Even after we had turned our backs to the vestibule to sit on the stairs, I knew that the procession of us remained on the screen within as well, phantoms only a few feet from our presences.

Somehow it made me uneasy to know this and I tried to explain to Cedric as we waited.

"You don't need a screen to show you that we are all phantoms, my friend," he said. "What we show the world hides as much as it discloses."

"So does that mean that the true self, whatever that may be, roams empty halls within us as well?" I asked. "That would make it as much an adversary as an ally, wouldn't it?"

"All these questions about a simple multiple image! You *are* a philosoph," he said, not without irony.

"Did I tell you they called me that?" I asked.

"At a certain point what's told or known merge, like your phantoms and presences," he said.

"Fair enough," I said, "but they meant that as a joke. They gave me that occupation on my visatag to mock me."

"Or to mock philosophers," he said. "And what, pray tell, is a visatag."

"A kind of computerized identity papers. What were you given when you came here?"

"What I paid for," he said in a tone that made it clear this was not something he wanted to pursue.

Fair enough, I thought. We each of us draw a line around our shadows upon the ground and keep the rest at depth. Despite the matter with his mother's name and the confusion with Rosaria, I had at some point already determined to trust him, sidekick sahib or no. If he were my warder in a dream of my own making, then it would be an image of myself that I trusted; and if some other forces had installed me in his care—even were he one of them—for now, from what I could tell, he meant me no harm.

So as we sat there I told him as much as I could recall of my story, but especially the difficulties which I believed faced me should I attempt to prove Franky's innocence. Some of these were not unlike the logic puzzles of my dreams. For instance, it might be possible that I could live forward into the era I had left behind, doing so day by day without benefit of any of the slippages or passages in time that had thrown me forward or shot me back over what for me still felt as if it were my recent past. Yet were I to get there—and in truth I did not know whether that was a matter of days or years—my own doubleness would still have left me trapped. Beckmesser's collage of memories would have come to its end and yet I could not rewind the events that had overtaken me before I assumed his memories. I could not undo going out that back door at Madame's and into the alleys where I was beaten and wrested from time. Nor, though I did not mention this to Cedric since the matter of Rosaria's name was still too sensitive to me, and the episode too horrific, could I erase the events that had sent me out.

"What you are talking about in my country we call Vaikuntapaali, a child's game but one played by sages, the ladder of life," Cedric said.

"You cast the shells and sometimes climb up and other times slide down the serpent's back."

"Chutes and Ladders."

"Yes, exactly. The point is you always eventually get to the end and, while it may be useful to declare that someone who gets there first is the winner, in truth it is what happens within you along the path that matters. Mathematically the game is a Markov chain, future states depend only on the present state, and are independent of past states. It is what mathematicians call a drunkard's walk."

"That may very well be," I said, "but I am the one who is lost."

"You've missed the point of the game," Cedric said. "We are all lost."

I had a memory then of being a child at a time and place I hardly ever recalled, out in the late summer night at the hour when the lingering light has turned dull silver just ahead of the darkness and the street lights flickered as if uncertain about whether to come on, the echoes of other children's voices and the barking of neighborhood dogs muffled as if within a well. I was hiding, in the midst of playing a game like hide and seek but one that involved two armies each trying to capture the other's token from where it sat upon a stone. Any soldier could capture another from the other's army and those captured had to sit in silence like a mute chorus behind the stone with the token. If you made a run for the token you could see the excitement in the eyes of your captured comrades, some of them even rising to their feet as if to cheer you on, yet covering their mouths with their hands lest they make a sound, for the game was lost as soon as someone heard a captive even peep. This night, however, I was far from the stone and hiding alone, listening for the whispers of the soldiers in the opposite army, holding my breath until my lungs hurt and I had to gulp for air, my heart beating audibly within my chest, my arms aching from the scratches of brambles and thorns from places where I had hidden, almost drunk with the sickly sweetness of the honeysuckle that grew along the fence behind which I hid and along which, on the opposite side, one of the other soldiers moved, his sneakers visible beneath the slats of the fence.

This memory could have been a dream for someone else but for me it was real, somewhere I had been when I had a name and family, a place in time and somewhere to live, the smell of bread and the sour scent of my mother's perspiration, night crickets and the Perseids overhead, the slant stars flaring and then snuffing as they descended into the great ocean that circles the earth overhead. It was there I lived still.

"You again," a voice said and pulled me from this reverie.

The owner of the blue house had come back. I cannot say that I recognized him as the landlord I had met once looking for evidences of Beckmesser's existence. Nor did I know which of us he thought he had seen before.

"You *are* both veterans, aren't you?" he asked.

"Of a sort," Cedric said. "I served in her majesty's light infantry."

"And you?" The man gestured toward me.

"Air force," I said.

It was one of those things that just came to me.

"Suborbital, of course," I added.

Cedric smiled.

"And now you are homosexuals," the man said. It was not a question.

"Would that make our chances better or worse?" Cedric asked impishly.

"Your mother sent us here," I said softly.

"I don't care where you stick it in," the man said. "Homosexuals make the best tenants: tidy, prompt, not so noisy."

"Better then," Cedric affirmed.

"Better than what?" the man retorted.

So now we were to be lost in a land of riddles, I thought, weary once again—weary still—of this game of endless complications that, rather than lifelike, seemed merely a version of the essential emptiness of the day to day, thinly tricked up with verbal cul-de-sacs and facsimile interactions. There had been a time once, not long before in some way of reckoning, when I might have found a nightly squat, or even a congenial space to spend a day or two, perhaps even one of this fellow's own properties, without all this riddling and interrogation. I was beyond care then, beyond mourning.

That I thought this shocked me.

Mourning whom? Mourning what? What had brought that word to mind beyond mere homophonia I could not say. Morning and mourning were long connected in history at both large and small scales. One wakes to loss and the light shifts forever.

I watched Cedric and the landlord talk as if they were figures behind thick glass, mouths moving like guppies, one laughing, the other ruminating and then turning back to open the door and disappearing within, emerging with a set of keys connected by a twisted wire to a wooden paddle painted with the head of a duck. I could hear nothing, my hearing dialing down as if someone were lowering the volume of an audiopod; then my eyes dimming in much the same slow dissolve; the sensation in my arms and fingers following behind them into a numbness akin to silence or darkness. I thought I was dying at that instant and yet felt paralyzed, unable to call out to them.

In some part of me I expected to wake to find Manco squatting before the brazier and the throat of the brick chimney rising to a pale blue coin of morning sky above me. Or not to wake at all, although how to cast that eventuality as an expectation was not clear to me. What would the sensation of not waking be? The white scar upon a white page after a mark has been erased perhaps, or how the same water folds into water again and again at the brink of a falls.

Instead I was sitting in a green chair across a white table. Cedric was attempting to call someone on his oversized cell phone. He dialed again and again, muttering "damn" between each call.

"I'm sorry," I said. "I must have dozed off."

Cedric looked curiously at me.

"Anything but," he said. "I thought for a while you would not shut up. You know how the story goes? 'Mine host, don't be, I beg, too stern,' etcetera. The story of your lost love, the story of your poor daughter, the story of a parson and the lady of camellias, I thought you would ruin everything, but our friend seemed to like your stories well enough to allow us to let this manse."

"I remember nothing, " I confessed. "How long ago?"

"He just now left. You've been here, and yapping, the whole time, even now."

Been somewhere but not here, I thought, perhaps beneath the Perseids or before a wall of fireflies, but neither in this mind of mine nor Beckmesser's either. Drunks and sleepers, I knew, had such episodes, relieved from memories and the unfolding moments both.

It might offer a way out, although you would have to wander through a mansion of black doorways until you found the one that folded you back within time. Meanwhile you would risk going through a door where you would lose everything, even your fear of losing it all.

"First you need to solve your mystery," Cedric said.

"How much of that did I say aloud?" I asked.

"How would I know?" Cedric replied. "I heard what you said but how much else you had to say I have no way of knowing. The point is you are still yapping, you haven't stopped for the last half hour."

He stopped dialing and banged the phone against the table. "Fucking phone!" he said as the back shell of it tumbled free and the battery spun on the table.

Cedric reached within its open carapace and extracted a small green chip with a tiny blinking LED. He held it delicately between his thumb and forefinger.

"Someone is tracking us," he whispered, though now there was no reason to do so since the chip could only function within the receiver.

"The doctor?" I asked.

"Or your friend El Camino," he suggested.

"I don't know what you are talking about."

"Jesus! Are you sleepwalking? Or just out of your mind," he laughed. "Minds, plural, I suppose. Jesus indeed. You told the landlord and me a long story about this boy with the powers of a shaman, ending with an elaborate ceremony where he appeared as an apparition before women kneeling in prayer. A miracle worker, the way you told it."

"Or Satan."

He shook this off. "It's all the same," he said. "Kali, Shiva, Bhavatarini."

"Are you sure that was the name, El Camino? Could it have been Candido?"

"All the same," he said again.

"Perhaps, but could you tell me what I said?" I asked. "There may very well be something in it all that will help me find a way out."

"I'll try, my friend," he said, then smashed the chip against the table with the side of his palm, smashing again and again until the LED stopped blinking and a crack opened along the green edge of its miniature world.

"I will try in time, but for now I have things to do. We'll need some provisions while we stay here, and before that I want to see what I can find out about what's happened to Camilla. Do you think you will be all right alone for awhile?"

"I've been alone for years," I said.

"Which one of you is speaking?" he asked gently. "Or is it both?"

There was no need to answer.

"Here," Cedric said, setting one of the flash memory keys before me on the table as well as a small electronic device with a tiny, two-line screen.

"What's that thing?" I asked.

"In case we get separated or something happens," he said. "It's a pager, surely you've seen one before."

"Not in years."

Cedric shrugged his shoulders dramatically. "Years or days, for you who knows? Think of it as a thread through the labyrinth. High above the world a condor circles, a high-flying satellite called Gurula, doing nothing but listening for the peeps from these electronic titmice, most of them long abandoned. The company whose rocket put it into orbit is long since gone and no one in the wide world below any longer cares about it. Except of course for the few of us who retain these things. It's as free a channel as you can find in this sea."

"Thank you," I said.

"Be careful, my friend," he cautioned as he left.

What I intended to be was not careful as much as to be free of cares, if not careless. I sat at the white table, staring at the opposite wall, trying to recover a sense of time within me, letting myself flow with Beckmesser's memories when they came, not trying too hard to force my own to float up from the muck of confusion in which they were sunk. I was neither asleep nor in the drugged sort of enforced amnesia that I was coming to suspect had overcome me earlier like a truth serum when I babbled to Cedric and the landlord. Instead this was a pleasant interlude, like smoking dope or sitting in the spell of a pill, the light of the passing hours marking itself like a map upon the wall before me in gradients of brightness and shadow that fell in turn across the slantwise equatorial of the rib of repaired plaster, a white seam upon a white wall, which marked a crack in that opposite wall like old scar tissue, the crack itself evidence of the settling of the house and world into themselves over the course of time. The sensation, this visual silence, so soothed me that for a goodly time no memories interspersed, only the slow rocking of light upon the lunar surface, this Lacus Oblivionis. It was as if I were held in my mother's arms.

Then Rosaria was there with me, sitting in the green chair along the side of the table to my right, her knee pressing softly against mine, her small hands folded on the table before her, calmly turning a set of aquamarine and silver prayer beads between her fingers, her sad, dark eyes watching me swim ashore from far along some horizon.

It was, of course, a shock and I cried out despite myself. I reached for the pager but she took my hand away gently before I could press the button.

"*Nu vă faceţi griji*," she said. "Don't worry, darling?"

"What are you doing here?"

"Still looking for Mil, of course."

"How did you get here?'

"I followed you, my dearest."

"Back through time?"

She made a gesture of dismissal. "A mother does what she has to," she said.

She rose from her chair and moved to my side, putting her arms around me, my head against her small breast. The touch, the warmth of her was real, the saffron scent of her flesh filled me. I began to weep.

"You are still hurt," she said.

"A mother does what she has to," I spat the phrase back at her, trying to wrest myself away.

"He told you," she said. "You do not know what you were seeing. It was not happening."

She released me a little from the bond of her embrace, turning my face to meet her eyes. "In any case, what makes you bitter hasn't happened yet, at least where we find ourselves now at this instant in time. This you cannot deny." She smiled benignly. "You've been there to the storefront. You've seen that there is nothing there as yet. What will happen will happen, what will not, will not."

"You were whoring those afternoons," I said. "When you went away."

She sat back in the chair without saying anything, yet not before first kissing my cheek. She met my steely eyes with softness.

"You think you understand everything," she said. "You think grief is a land you traverse alone."

I knew then that she had once been my wife.

"I was alone," I said. "Alone I carried the coffin. Alone I walked to the grave because you were still bleeding and you could not join me. I remember the weight of the white box in my arms, the white enamel surface like obscene frosting, grasping it at both ends with the little silk handles of twisted white rope, afraid the baby would jostle within the satin blankets. The undertaker wanted to walk with me but I would not let him. We would walk this path alone, Maria Elena and me. I whispered to her that we loved her, her mother and me, I whispered your name to her like a litany, Maria Elena Carmen Rosaria de las, whispered to her the whole while until I set her down within the white box in the ground and someone came out from the trees and began to shovel the clay upon it."

In memory the face of the gravedigger seemed Cedric's. And there was something else I was not remembering.

Rosaria wept softly yet ground her small fists into her eyes violently as if to rub them from her face.

"Please," I said, and touched her cheek. "Please don't hurt yourself."

Slowly I began to be overcome with feeling as if my hearing were dialing down as it had earlier, my eyes dimming despite me, my arms starting to numb. I feared losing her if I fell into the same chute.

"You have to help me!" I said, taking her hands in mine. "They've given me something to take my feelings away. It's like they are turning a dial. You need to help me."

At the moment that I asked her help she was there for me, squeezing my hand so tightly I could feel the ring upon her little finger press into my flesh like a thorn. She was holding me above the surface of an abyss as if saving a man from drowning, wrestling to hold onto me against the tug of the undertow, fighting with a ferocity of spirit that flowed through her arms into my own limbs and heart. Though she and the white room both appeared through a dim white veil as if through a scrim, for that moment the awful power of this amnestic wave could not snatch me away from the present moment.

In the way that a drowning man knows the course of his life with an unparalleled clarity, I, too, suddenly knew that the same person or force that was doing this to me had also caused Beckmesser's death.

It was as if Rosaria had looped back here to show me this. Again I felt myself slip away, yet not now into the blankness but rather into the sleep of infants in limbo, feeling myself float slowly down like a leaf gliding back and forth to the bottom of a dark pool, all the while gazing back up at Rosaria until the depths eclipsed her ivory face. Within this pool I was safe and no longer alone, I knew. Although I expected to wake to find her gone again, and myself perhaps jolted forward or back into time again, I knew there was a way out now if I could only find it again, a line through the labyrinth.

He thought she would be gone when he awoke but she lingered there, *Elinor le Douce, reine des royaumes de l'extérieur*, Elinor the Mild, Queen of the Outer Kingdoms, a gauzy veil, blue as a fair sky, framing her fair face, her soft eyes gazing down upon him from the gilt chair.

He was reaching to kiss her hand when the ivory knight appeared upon the scene, his buckle and gauntlets clanking carelessly, visored head proudly propped up by the gorget with its foppish yellow gold decoration, his foolish ivory greaves looking like cricket pads.

"That you, boss?"

The knight's voice was muffled by the visor, but boyish and familiar.

"Franky?"

He felt the sting as an electric shock along his spine when the knight stunned him with a blow of the flat of the broadsword, his eyes dimming and his arms growing weak.

It was happening again. "Please, you need to help me," he said to Rosaria.

To Elinor.

The boy was laughing at him.

"Are you going to weep or play, old man?"

"I don't know who you are."

"Look in the mirror. I'm who you are, you are who I am."

The mirror, he knew, was in a sack made from a small blanket folded and tied with a strong cord the indigo color of certain midnights, the mirror also framed with precious stone the color of the sky at dusk. Yet where it was now he did not know.

He did not know where he was.

The mirror was a pool within a silver bowl, a monkey-faced fellow grimacing up from it.

The laughing boy struck him again, the flat of the sword ringing dully against the shoulder armor yet numbing his arms with the force of the blows.

Why don't you kill me then? he thought. Why keep me shuddering like a worm in the husk of this strange self?

The boy transformed to a dwarf in armor.

"You're squirming again, Papi," he sneered.

He was slipping into the dark pool again when suddenly the lights flared like lightning.

"What's happening to you, my friend?"

Strong arms under mine were pulling me up from behind like a second trying to get a boxer to his feet after the bell had sounded. It had been night for some time.

"Has Camilla been here?" Cedric asked. "This place smells of perfume."

"A dream," I said.

"You have very vivid dreams, my friend," he said, handing me a handkerchief of gauzy linen that had fallen to the floor, its hem embroidered with flowering herbs. I sniffed it but it gave forth only the dry scent of ironed cotton.

"There is something going on in the city," he reported. "Troops moving through in covered carriers, silent policemen at the intersections gazing at traffic. I went by the storefront but the windows are covered three quarters of the way up with year-old newspapers. A slimy little fellow came out of the door while I was there, locking it behind him. 'The circus will be open a week from Wednesday,' he said."

I tried to recall how long it had been since I knew what day of the week it was or when that mattered.

"But Camille?" I asked. "The house?"

"As I told you, something was happening in the city. I was wary of taking the usual routes but the road along the periphery that you and I took to get here the other day was jammed today with official traffic. I left the electric lorry at the outskirts of the park and hiked through the trails to the eastern edge of the pond where the brown leaves still clung to a tangle of undergrowth. I watched the house for an hour or more but saw no sign of anyone moving about. Even as the daylight faded, no lights shone within the house. Four deer grazed near the shore of the pond in the gathering darkness. Just as I was about to leave, Marco's car pulled up along the drive and he helped her out and into a wheelchair. She was wearing a tall fur hat and a fur coat that reached her ankles but even from the distance I could see that her eyes were bandaged. Despite all this, even from behind the bandages and at such a great distance, I had the strongest sense that she was looking at me, her gaze like a force scanning the horizon until she found me. She was telling me that all would be well, telling me to take care and wait to hear from her."

"Telling you how?" I asked.

"It was the strangest thing. Telling me with her vision, its emanation carrying through the bandages and over the darkening pond. Once I had received this communication, heard from her lost eyes so to speak, I made my way back along the dim paths, found the lorry, and came right back here. As I pulled up here I thought I saw the form of a woman leaving through the shadows. I thought she had somehow come here ahead of me. That's how strange the force of her vision had been."

Hearing Cedric's tale and trying to piece together what had happened to Camille with Rosaria's surprising appearance—she, too, wandering in time—I began to form a notion that, just as Cedric's pager network, he said, was a part of a still functioning yet forgotten, if not abandoned, network, perhaps these particular mirrors backed in lapis, both that which Manco's mother gave me and that which Beckmesser gave his daughter, were themselves equally powerful devices upon an unknown network. This offered some of an explanation—a motive—for the absurd coincidence of light that Marco told Cedric had led to Camille's loss of sight, although it turned the so-called accident to something more malignant. In some way I supposed that such a network of mirrors could explain the force that Cedric felt as well as whatever it was that fought to overcome my sensations, and indeed my embodied consciousness, at intervals, that dark pull which Rosaria had been able to save me from as if tugging against a whirlpool for possession of my body.

The dwarf doctor was behind all this somehow, I thought, though whether the troop movements and general alert in the city had any bearing upon our own events wasn't clear to me. Nor could I recall that Rosaria possessed such a lapis-backed mirror.

I was considering whether I should share these suspicions with Cedric when of a sudden the sapping feeling once again began to come over me, once again my hearing fading and the dying light of the room dimming and flickering in my eyes as if somewhere out on the quiet streets beyond a malevolent vehicle cruised slowly and played beams of blackness back and forth from a great inverted spotlight, penetrating the walls of the dwellings before it with a concentration of entropic force. This time, however, I was unable to cry out—for Rosaria, for Camille, for Elinor, even for Cedric—my throat constricting as if I had been poisoned and my arms tingling with the gaining numbness. The mirror, I thought, the mirror, if I could only hold the mirror.

8

The ivory knight was sitting upon a stump, his helmet at his side and his back to the rider at a clearing beside a waterfall. They would come now to a final reckoning perhaps, the rider thought, or at least each glimpse the other face to face once before the end, whenever that might arrive. Just at that moment, however, his great grey steed stumbled on the mossy stone of the creek bed below the falls along which they approached the clearing, the horse's hooves no more than clicking the stones slightly as he righted himself, without whinny or neigh, a well-trained warhorse, a veteran of many campaigns. Still the ivory knight heard them approaching.

"Will you strike an unarmed foe without warning?" the ivory knight asked, not turning, his back still toward the approaching rider. "Will you attack from behind unchivalrously?"

"Show yourself, knight, and be recognized," the rider challenged him. "In that much thereafter we will be equally armed."

"And if you fall before the horror of my visage, will I then be justified in striking you?" the ivory knight asked.

His laughter rang among the stones beyond the clearing.

He held the polished buckler before him and in its mirrored surface the rider saw his own face.

"Can we imagine the past or only the future?" I asked.

Cedric considered the question for a time, giving it full weight before responding.

"I imagine the former is called memory, my friend," he said.

"You imagine."

"I meant no irony," he said. "But, yes, I expect that memory is perhaps a variety of imagination."

"And imagination a kind of memory then?" I asked.

"In a symmetrical universe, yes," Cedric said. "It is known as the conservation of parity."

Conservation was much on our minds. We had been there seven days since the city had been shut down. I knew because I counted them by lining the small white stones I'd snatched from the gravel path outside the door into a row upon the windowsill. Seven, the number of days in a week, but since nether of us knew on which day the week's retreat had begun, I gave these days names of my choosing: shoe day, raspberry day, dry day, the day of poison rain, dove day, groaning day, the morning of tea with sugar.

Shoe day because I had lost a shoe, the left one, running back from the road to escape the hose trucks before we knew that the city was shut down. Our intent at first was to visit the storefront and see if we could discover what the slimy fellow had meant by the circus and what exactly had become of the bruja tenant and her son. We got as far as the landlord's blue house when the hose truck swung around the corner without warning, a recorded message blaring over and over again from its loudspeaker, and a figure like a firefighter in armor manning the hose cannon.

"The department of community safety has ordered a curfew until further notice. Please stay within your dwellings to maintain public order. The department of community safety has ordered a curfew until further notice. Please stay within your dwellings to maintain public order."

"Run!" Cedric called out.

"The department of community safety has ordered a curfew until further notice. Please stay within your dwellings to maintain public order," the voice droned, but I was stunned, unable to move.

The hose hit our feet at about the same time Cedric's hands pressed against my back, propelling me out of my paralysis. The force of the water cannon spewed the white stones upon the scraggy grass of the rooming house. My shoes were soaked and I ran out of one of them but when I stopped to fetch it, Cedric pushed me forward again.

"These things can break bones, my friend, and if they knock you down it could kill you."

But the cannon ceased well before we reached the door and the truck went on proclaiming its message of public order. From our window later that afternoon, I could see the dog that ran away with my shoe, a scrawny thing, limping on one of its back legs.

We were in for trouble should the curfew last long since Cedric had been unable to provision us on account of the mobilization. What we had to eat between us were only the leavings of what Cedric had brought in his bag that first day: a cellophane pack of mint hard candies, two rolls of fruit leather, shards of a cookie mixed with lint. Among the remnants from my blanket sack that he had stuck away, we discovered the sheaf of dried leaves and, miraculously, a kind of jerky or pemmican I did not remember ever having.

"But this you do remember?" Cedric asked, holding up the pornographic holo.

"Remember having, yes," I said. "But none of the sort of adventures it recounts, nor really whether I have ever viewed any of it."

"Ah, a religious observance," Cedric laughed. "The ecstasies of the angels and saints."

Saints ourselves, or at least hermits, we spent much of the rest of that day in fasting, having only a mint candy each, drinking water from the sink, and gazing out the window, counting each time the hose trucks passed, seeing the dog run away with my shoe, and once spying a thin, dark woman in a raincoat and ballet slippers hurrying along the sidewalk, holding a shawl wrapped round her head and shoulders and looking down at the walkway. She was so beautiful to me that I thought of her for hours, how she rushed upon delicate feet along the sidewalk despite the danger.

The lights stayed on most of that day without interruption and Cedric monitored official transmissions on a little radio he wore in his ear but there was no news really save the recurring bulletin saying that the department of community safety had ordered a curfew until further notice and another recurring announcement, accompanied by suitably sentimental music, Cedric said, reminding listeners that it was Kinswoman's Day and to be sure to wish your aunts and cousins the happiest of seasons.

"So then it is a Sunday today?" I asked.

"Not necessarily. The feast can fall on any day, depending on the inferior conjunction of Venus, when the planet comes closest to the earth."

Perhaps then the young ballerina was hurrying to a celebration.

"They could be lying," Cedric said. "By declaring it a festival day the public would be less disturbed by the curfew, at least those with their kinswoman living with them."

"Or those with memories of them," I said.

"Again, a philosoph!"

Yet it was not as a philosoph, but rather as an explorer, that Cedric interrogated me that day. At first he questioned me idly, as if merely to pass the time and fill in blanks, but increasingly, I realized, his questioning sought to fix me in some system of coordinates, for which, if not time or space, then narrative would do.

Your story, the old greeting, I thought, like the knight's empty hand offered as a token of benevolence.

I tried to recall the events as well as I could, beginning with when Franky appeared. Cedric interposed immediately. "You had no family?"

"No kinswomen to speak of," I said, evading memory and him.

For a long time I tried to recall just what I had been eating that long-ago day as I gazed out upon the river watching the barges while Franky wandered off in search of food and came back with the dumplings he shared among us both. It was funny, the dumplings I could recall exactly, the dark half circles of oil they left on the paper in the shape of a kiss, but I could not for the life of me remember what I had been eating and had not shared with him.

The life of me exactly, I thought.

"Do you remember what year that was?" Cedric asked.

"The third, I think," I said, "since I became a wayfarer."

"And did you keep track of that with stones as well?" he asked, pointing to the two white pebbles on the windowsill.

"Two is right, isn't it?" I asked. "What day is this?"

"Kinswoman's day plus one, Venus heading outward into space," he said. "You fell into one of those swoons of yours then woke up babbling about dumplings."

I began to wonder if he was telling me the truth.

"I think you swooned from hunger," he said. "I have half a mind to go out to look for something, even to beg some ration from our landlord, though the radio still says the curfew remains in effect."

"But why is that?"

"Why?" he asked. "There is a curfew because there is a curfew. I suspect our friend, Doctor Marco, has some hand in this. I wouldn't rule out a conjunction between public and private events, a way to keep Camilla and her story contained."

This, of course, was what I had speculated earlier and rejected as too simple an explanation. Now I wondered whether Cedric fed my own thoughts back to me as my warder, another of those instances of too neat a sequence.

Despite these suspicions, I didn't want Cedric to go out but I had no way to say that. I was afraid that a swoon would come again, one I might not return from, my sentence becoming something much worse than an endless repetition of simple sequences, especially since this attack had set upon me without the intervening symptoms of the dimming and loss of feeling.

"Surely you had a mother," Cedric was saying for some reason.

"And a wife," I answered, for the same reason.

He studied me with a steely gaze behind which, nonetheless, there was a sad sort of empathy. Or so I read his eyes.

"And babies?" he asked, but I did not answer.

One, I thought, a porcelain figure encased in a white enamel box, sunk in the dark throat of the earth like a lozenge.

The ivory knight thrust at the rider with his thin contus, catching him where the gauntlet met his wrist, the blow no more at first than a burning sting, until the blood began to flow into the cuff like wine into a goblet.

Cedric was gone for the remainder of that Kinswoman's Day plus one and into the next morning. I counted the stones on the sill twice that day before I slept and again when I woke, auditing the passing of time. Twice also during the night I signaled him through the pager, once when I woke sweating from a dream and again when the first light illuminated the dun overcast the next morning, yet wherever the forgotten satellite soared Cedric seemed to elude its call.

Therefore the day I called raspberry day, the second by my reckoning, found me alone under a deadening overcast. I was left without lights most of the day although they flickered on once or twice midway in the morning and again once in the mid-afternoon when a power surge caused the overhead bulb to explode into a shower of silver glass and glimmering powder, leaving the room smelling of burnt grass. The rest of the day I watched the fixture fearfully, afraid that the bare remnants of the filament might catch fire the next time the power came on.

During the morning I drank glass after glass of water from the tap to try to keep my stomach from aching and at noon ate another of the mint candies, sucking upon it at intervals and then setting it on a saucer to make it last, watching as the disk shrunk finally into a lacy host. After the light bulb exploded, I gobbled some of the cookie crumbs and chewed for a while on one of the dried leaves, which seemed to sharpen my vision.

I was starving and thus for much of the while that Camille was there I feared that Cedric would think I had hallucinated the event when he returned. She arrived unseen, during a moment I had left off looking out the window in order to fill up my water glass and to suck briefly on the hard candy. The knocking upon the door startled me and I was even more startled to see her at the door dressed in a full-length fur coat and tall fur hat, a pearl-beaded, silver-satin masquerade half-mask covering her eyes, and holding a quart basket of raspberries before her.

"Belated Kinswoman's Day!" she said. "May I come in?"

"How did you come through the curfew?" I asked. "I can't tell if you are real."

"If you let me come in, I'll show you," she laughed and the sound of it would have been proof enough. "I've missed you Daddy," she said softly.

It was not that I had forgotten that I was the bearer of Beckmesser's memory as much as that, among those memories, increasingly flashes of the contest for Elinor had come to the fore. Also I was beginning to suspect that the dark whirlpool of paralysis that now came over me at increasing intervals might owe as much to Beckmesser as to the memories of the life I called my own.

"Come in, come in," I said, trying not to disclose my wariness. My voice approximated one as chivalrous as the rider's, yet I was careful to back away from the door as she entered, almost as if fearing that a kiss or embrace from her might, if not transform me to a toad, sap the little sense of presence I had managed to summon since Cedric had gone away again.

In my pocket I pressed the keys of the pager hoping that summoning him might help me to determine whether her presence was real or an apparition.

Real or no, she sat at the table, after first folding her fur coat into a fat bundle and setting it upon the seat of the room's one arm chair, placing the hat upon it like a turret.

"Marco arranged an official car for me and we breezed through the curfew," she said. "He's been very tender, Daddy, since the accident." She rearranged her small mask as if to illustrate what was meant by gentleness, then gestured toward the berries. "And he brought these back for me out of season."

"Then he knows where we are?"

She slid the basket of berries across the table toward where I stood.

"Taste one," she said softly. "They are as sweet as kissing a baby."

The berries glistened so unreally that they might as well have been a basket of garnets and rubies carved to look like berries and yet when I held one in my fingers it was soft with fur and plump with juice and smelled sweet as violets.

"I do not like what is happening to me," I said. "If you loved me, you would try to help me find my way back."

"Taste one," she said.

It was the sweetest berry I had ever tasted, a rich smear of flesh studded with tiny seeds, an unctuous juice upon the tongue.

"They're delicious, but, as you say, out of season. Where did they come from?" I asked.

"There are no seasons anymore, Papa," she whispered. "Marco thinks the world of you. He loves you like a son."

This last assurance fell false on my ears, not just in substance but its actual audio quality, as if it were not a real human voice but a recording of something I had heard before. I felt surreptitiously along the outside of my pocket for the pager and pressed the button again and again; then patted the opposite pocket to locate the folding knife that Cedric had left me "just in case," a great dagger of a thing when flipped open from its wood and brass handle. I slid the folded knife toward the opening of the pocket without taking it out, making sure I positioned it so that I could release the lock and extend the blade quickly if I decided to wield it. All the while I studied the pale flesh of her face and neck below the pale mask, looking for the delicate stirring of her carotid pulse. Both face and neck were smoothed with an iridescent powder not unlike that which had rained from the exploding bulb, a festive look that suited the pearl and satin masquerade.

"What do you want of me?" I asked.

"I want you never to die."

She fed me another berry, holding it delicately between thumb and forefinger and extending her arm so that the sleeve of her dove grey cashmere tunic fell back to the hollow of her elbow.

She fed me like a mother bird, the nesting world inverted.

"Marco and I would like Cedric to come back."

"And what of me? Am I to remain embalmed here by myself?"

My fingers probed within the opening of the pocket feeling for the knife, the brass cool at its base.

She laughed as only a singer can, a lilting, lovely note.

"You can come back too," she said. "Or stay here as you will and play your games or have your own friends. I'd like you to come back. I want to know everything."

And thus was I not to die, I thought, to remain the perpetual telling.

"You could come in the car right now," she said. "The driver is waiting."

"I have to wait for Cedric," I said, somehow knowing what she would say next.

"He's with us," she replied, as I expected.

"Tell him Gurula has been asking for him," I said.

She looked momentarily confused, as if not programmed for this particular turn.

"I'm sorry," she said. "Is that a friend of yours? Yours and Cedric's?"

"A pet," I said. "A wild bird that comes around looking to be fed."

"Like your Franky?" she asked, still smiling below the mask.

Slipping my fingers into my pocket I cradled the knife, still folded, against my palm with my fingers, thumb upon the lock release.

Apparently Marco and his tests and swabs had succeeded in convincing her that the man she'd thought was her father was not who he said he was. If she made a move to detain me I would have to act quickly, I thought. But instead she relaxed, sat back in the chair and sang the flower duet, eyes closed behind the mask.

> *Sous le dôme épais*
> *Où le blanc jasmin*
> *À la rose s'assemble*
> *Sur la rive en fleurs,*
> *Riant au matin*
> *Viens, descendons ensemble.*

My own eyes were beginning to dim helplessly, the knife falling out of my lapsing grip, when Cedric returned.

"Oh you're here after all!" she said. "I was just telling Papa that you were with us."

I struggled to swim up to them from the darkening pool, pushing hard to surface.

"I didn't stay long," Cedric said. "Marco, I think, wanted me to stay longer."

Even in the face of the descending dark I could sense Cedric's coded irony. I knew he had escaped. More, he seemed to have gained some sort of upper hand.

"The woman you rented the shop to was there at the house," he told me. "It seems she knows Marco from another life. From way back as they say. She and her son both."

Now the ivory knight was standing before him, visor down, the barrel of the crusader's helmet polished like the buckler, the same face appearing there in the mirror surface, the face of the rider.

"Marco knows many people," Camille said.

"So she tells me," Cedric said, still talking in some sly code. He turned to me. "There was also another little fellow, the slimy older boy I had seen at the shop, who says he knows you."

"I mentioned Franky to him," Camille said.

"Whose side are you on?" I asked.

"The side of life, Papa, of course. *Ou descendons ensemble....*"

Suddenly she stood.

"I am afraid I have to go. Marco doesn't want me out after dark, even with the car and driver, given the unrest. I'll leave these for you."

Rather than slide the basket of berries across the table, she came around from her seat and set them before me, bending to kiss the top of my head, her hand pressing down against my own hand where it lay upon the knife in my pocket.

"You will have to trust yourself to events," she whispered.

"Goodbye for now, Cedric," she extended her hand to him and he raised it to his lips and kissed it.

"How charming," she said. "Did you know he used to be my body guard, Daddy?"

"Your assistant," Cedric said.

"All the same," she laughed and left.

And that was raspberry day. It was only when she was gone that I realized that the dimming had not taken me over after the onset of this last spell. I added a stone to the two on the windowsill and begged Cedric to tell me what happened. However by then he was weary from all the day's evasions and promised to tell me on the morrow.

Which was dry day, when the water stopped flowing from the sink and an unseasonable sun burned down relentlessly upon the walks and lawns outside. Instead of the hose trucks, troop carriers came by at intervals, the soldiers within them wearing masks with snouts.

"Like Ganesh," Cedric said, looking out. "Blasphemers. They are trying to move us all out by cutting off the water and power."

"Us?"

"Not just you and me but all of us," he said.

Cedric was angry with himself for not having anticipated the water being cut off. Had he thought of it, he said, he would have filled the sink and tub against that prospect and perhaps even hauled jugs of water back with him from the pond. As it was we had a little less than half of a stale plastic bottle from his vehicle and what was in the toilet, which Cedric boiled along with a drop of bleach from a bottle he found under the sink.

"Two days worth perhaps," he said. "Any more than that and we'll have to venture out, but so will everyone. They probably can't get away with it for longer than that."

"Why would they choke a city to flush us out when they know where to come and get us?" I asked.

"Not just us but all of us," he repeated. "It is like flushing rats from a building with fire—you collect them in a net as they run out shrieking."

My own lapsing energy left me far from being able to shriek, weary and hungry and increasingly thirsty in the way you get when you know there is little water. Thirsty for any certainty as well, I would give up all hope of slipping back through some knothole in the grain of time in favor of being caught up in it instead, its successive rings growing over me like an arrow sunk in a tree.

"Enough talk for now," Cedric said. "We have to conserve moisture."

It was hard to know whether this was a strategy of his or rather the habitual reticence of a retainer, always pausing at the edge of whatever revelation or story he had to tell.

Just as I longed for water I longed as well for his story, what had happened at the house to detain and free him in such a short span of time, why Camille or her simul had come to me, what the tenant woman held over Marco and, indeed, why and how she had suddenly appeared at the house.

And Franky, I thought, the reappearance of Franky.

Yet there was nothing to do but to doze and alternately wake and take my turn watching at the window, each of us watchers looking back at the other from time to time lest perhaps the other slip away, and, between turns, watching the changing light in its procession of hours across the room. Once as I was standing guard at the window, a young fellow darted from a house across the way looking back and forth as he began to run across the pavement. In an instant a soldier on a motorcycle appeared from nowhere and wrestled him down, holding him there until a troop carrier arrived and they hogtied him in plastic restraints and threw him in the truck between the feet of the soldiers.

"Look," I said, my throat surprisingly dry.

"I saw," Cedric said and handed me the plastic water bottle to wet my lips and throat.

During that long day I would probably have given myself over willingly to the limbo of the dark whirlpool if only to pass the time. However for whatever reason there were no further attacks upon me for the whole of that day. It was the first time I had been spared these episodes in exactly how long I could not remember, surely days and perhaps even weeks.

Nor could I remember whether I had added a stone to the sill to account for this new day. I held up a pebble to Cedric as if to ask, indicating my question by raising my eyebrows. He nodded, yes, and so I added the stone to the others.

How many stones would there be, I wondered, had I gathered one for each of the days of the lives I had lived, not even counting those that had looped back upon me again.

As the afternoon wore on toward evening, we witnessed a number of others captured and detained on the street, some older persons not even attempting to run, just walking out in the street and waiting with resignation for the trucks to gather them up.

"What will happen to them?" I asked, risking speaking aloud.

"Who can say," Cedric said, then added, "Nor will anyone ever tell us."

The rider had been bleeding for hours, his strength draining from him, when suddenly he felt the sting of the poultice upon the place on his forearm where the spear had pierced him. He looked up through dim eyes and saw that the ivory knight himself attended to the wound.

Eventually night came although there was an unaccustomed glow along the horizon as if some operation were underway out in the city illuminating the sky in a diffuse cloud. I slept, though whether Cedric did also I cannot say, since when I woke the next morning he was awake and at the window. Outside it the previous night's cloud seemed to have extended like a yellow fog across the morning and then the blood-red rain began, foul smelling, staining the pavement and lawns like rust.

"What is it?" I croaked, my mouth and throat drier than could be explained by the rationed water.

"An inversion of some sort. I've never seen it so bad." Cedric, too, croaked.

"Is it a war?" I asked.

"Not the sort with a foreign enemy," he said, his voice almost lost.

"A civil war then," I said, unnecessarily, my own voice now almost gone.

"No war is civil," Cedric croaked and drank a little from the reserve of water he had boiled the day before, handing the cup to me.

On the surface of the water lay a lace of oily iridescence.

"What——?"

"Stir it up and then drink," Cedric said. "It's an additive from my kit. Hopefully it might protect us from whatever's in this storm."

The antidote had a metallic taste but also an odor of walnuts and coffee. For a while it restored my voice and my will as well.

"What's happening?" I asked.

He was staring out the window at the yellow cloud and red rain.

"Who can say?" he shrugged. "For some things it is enough to say that it has happened, and not to trouble yourself thereafter with what it is or why."

There were no troop carriers or water cannons that we could see that day, perhaps because the poison rain accomplished the same control without the need for them. The rain started up and stopped without any sense of intermittence, as if by schedule, a sort of periodic stain upon the world outside the window. As the day went on, the rust collected upon the surfaces outside in a snow-like chaff. In the middle of the yard outside our window the chaff covered a dead raven in a mound over the black feathers.

We had all but run out of the boiled water when the open faucets coughed and then spurted with a water of an even darker rust color. "Let them run," Cedric warned unnecessarily. After an hour or so the water lost its color and he began to collect it in the tub and sink. The rain, too, had lost most of its color, turning into a light mist outside the window when I suddenly spotted a woman and a child hand in hand walking down the sidewalk under an umbrella stained rust from the rain without hurrying and without challenge. As they came just opposite our window she stopped and lifted the edge of the umbrella as if to look back along the walk to where we now both stood in the window. It was Irene and her child. She and the boy both gazed down the walk toward us for a while, and then she lowered the umbrella and they moved on.

"She's under more than one umbrella now," Cedric said mysteriously. "Or rather say she walks now under a cloud of her own making."

Mother and son trudged forward out of view.

I ran the faucet again to see if the water was still flowing clear and sipped some from my palm before Cedric slapped my hand aside. "Spit it out!" he ordered.

I blubbered out what little remained. It was the sweetest water I had ever tasted.

"We'll still have to boil it," he explained. "After this," he gestured toward the window.

"It's so sweet," I said.

"Like the berries?" he asked, a strange smile on his lips.

I didn't know what he was telling me.

He set to boiling a pot of water; even the steam from the pot was sweet.

"You'll have to see her when this is over," he said.

"Camille?"

"Not Camilla," he said, "but her, Irina." He nodded toward the window as if she were still there on the street.

"But why?"

"You're her landlord," he said slyly. Then, after a pause, he added, "I think she knows things you will want to know."

"About Marco?"

"About him, yes, but you as well. She has been places."

"I was afraid when Camille was here the other day," I suddenly confessed. "For a while I seriously considered slitting her throat. I held the knife beneath my fingers. I didn't think it was her beneath the mask. I was afraid."

Cedric studied me for some time without speaking. The water cooled behind him on the counter, the steam in the room misting the inside of the window and the blue-framed mirror before me on the table. It was a fright to see it there, since I didn't remember getting it out from my sack.

"Sometimes I am afraid of you as well, my friend," Cedric said. "Or at least afraid you will suddenly disappear like smoke."

We heard the music before we saw the trucks the next day, dove day, and Cedric knew exactly what it presaged.

"So once more they've declared victory over the forces of disorder."

The music came from a flatbed sound truck with soldiers standing under bright banners tossing wrapped candies to the pavement, gaily waving to empty streets, and from time to time releasing balloons and white doves into the air from wicker chests. It was like a dream circus.

One of the doves fell awkwardly to the still red-flecked lawn outside our window and waddled as if crippled. Cedric sprung from his chair and ran out to grab the thing before it could scoot away and then wrung its neck in full sight of the window. He cast his eyes about and found another and killed that one too, bringing them both back into the house where he slit their throats and drained their blood, then washed them in a solution of the purified water and detergent to free the feathers for plucking.

"We'll celebrate the grand victory with a lunch of roasted doves," he said, pulling the feathers.

The two denuded creatures looked pathetic, yellow skin mottled with blue dots where the feathers were. Cedric strung the two carcasses through on a wire coat hanger, tying it into a loop for a handle, and began to roast the sorry creatures over two burners of the hot plate, holding the wire contraption just far enough away to keep the skin from burning. Fat dripped on the glowing burners and they spat an acrid smoke. I began to open the window.

"No!" Cedric shouted. "The damn air has hardly cleared. That's why these two could hardly move."

Why then we ate them I do not know, except that the meat, surprisingly, was moist and sweet after Cedric's patient treatment, including rubbing the outer skin with crushed berries from Camille's basket once they browned and letting the berry smear caramelize into a sweet, blackened crust. The purified water we drank with it, though flat tasting, also retained some of its sweetness. And, of course, we both were ravenous.

We ate without talking, cleaning the two little birds to their bones and licking our fingers. Cedric had just begun to tell me about his adventures at the house and how Marco had found him immediately in the surveillance perimeter when I began to get violently sick and rushed to the bathroom. When I came back out, Cedric was outside the window vomiting upon the lawn. After a short time he reappeared at the door, his complexion ghastly white.

"You look like a ghost," I said, my stomach aching with cramps.

"You're seeing yourself then," he said, then railed at himself. "How could I be so stupid! Eating sick creatures and after such poison. These little fuckers are full of parasites anyway and then that fucking rain, and all of it on empty stomachs! Goddamn it, I swear I've lost all my common sense these last few days."

"On account of me?" I asked.

"On account of them," he snapped.

Then he began laughing rather madly.

"At least we didn't eat their fucking candies!" he said.

I would have laughed as well had I not felt so weak with illness that I could not even tell if the dimming had come back again. We each lay down in our beds for the rest of that day, rising up only to go to the bathroom though little came of our retching and bowel exertions. Each time he returned, Cedric forced water upon me.

"You have to hydrate, my friend, whether we've been poisoned or not."

On groaning day he decided that we had indeed been poisoned and that it may not have been the birds. That left the berries, I knew, but we were both too weak to pursue this subject and so groaning day disappeared into a twilight as real as the dimming or any loop in time, although one of our making. We lay there as if paralyzed, no longer strong enough to get up from the beds nor, once the water at our sides was drained, able to summon the energy to refill the glasses. Cedric moaned in a foreign language and half the time my mind kept running through a mad calculus wherein it weighed whether Cedric's suffering with me meant that he, too, was a prisoner and that what we were experiencing together was a strange kind of incarceration. In those moments of delirium when my mind was not trying to decide the undecidable, it—or rather Beckmesser's and my minds combined— kept us chasing after the ivory knight and calling to Rosaria in a dream world of vales and miasma-covered swamps.

And so when we heard the tea kettle whistling Cedric and I each in our own dream thought it a hallucination until the old woman appeared with the tray to summon us to the table, she too whistling, though her tune a lark's rather than a kettle's.

9

Cedric studied the cover of the holo with its intertwined limbs.

"Perhaps it's this that comes between memory and imagination, past and future," he said.

"Porn?"

"The image," Cedric said. "The event that leaves no trace upon us."

The old woman, Eleanor, the landlord's mother, had gone back to her house but left the cosy-covered teapot and the last of the arrowroot biscuits with us, promising to come by before evening with broth and water crackers.

When he had regained a little strength from the sweet tea and arrowroot cookies, Cedric asked her what had brought her to minister to us. She said that someone had telephoned to tell her that we were ill but who it was, or whether man or woman, she could not remember.

"At my age you recall only what you have to," she explained.

"And you," I asked, "how did you get through all this?"

"All this?" she asked, laughing. "You will be hearing of wars and rumors of wars. See that you are not frightened, for those things must take place, but that is not yet the end."

"Scripture," Cedric said.

"A long life," Eleanor responded. She turned to me.

"I keep a pantry like my mother did in the Great War, jugs of water, tins of sardines, biscuits, those awful things they call power bars, like eating silage, cans of sport drinks. It's all just a show, you know, they fight their wars with drones and robots, the soldiers are all actors."

"We saw them take people away," I said. "That seemed real."

"I did not say it wasn't real, young man, only that they are actors."

What she said stayed with me as Cedric and I talked afterward.

"What I don't know," I said, "is whether any of what we do is any different. Even now you and I seem no different than the soldiers, we're actors in a game that's real enough to have its costs and perils, but that unfolds no differently than the orgies on that holo or the tourneys of Ynys Gutrin."

"The difference between a philosoph and an actor is that the latter can and must act, while the former can lose himself among what the old woman's scripture calls those things must take place," Cedric said.

"Lose himself or lose his place?" I asked.

"This a question only for a philosoph: actors, lovers, and soldiers don't attend to such differences."

"Sometimes I think we are both prisoners," I said.

"Sometimes we are," he replied.

Still, whether I was an actor or a philosoph or a prisoner, I was out of place, I knew; the logic was not right even if I had fallen through a wormhole. If Cedric's information was correct, I had arrived at a point in Beckmesser's lived life well before he had given himself over to the events of Ynys Gutrin, including the fatal struggle with Franky over their beloved. Were Franky the ivory knight, as I suspected, my recent encounters took on the force of flashes forward, not imagination precisely, but rather memories of what would one day be imagined, fantasies of fantasies. The same would be true of Irene and Andy, or Irina and Candido if that was who they were to be. I could not hope to live to such a point that what I saw in parallax of my own life events would, like two eyes through binoculars, somehow focus into a single circle of stereopsis, merging who I was with who I am, my life moving forward again along some different path than the one that took me from Rosaria in anger and out into the alleys where my memories and imaginations were battered into a floating present.

"The real philosophs, the physicists, have a name for this anxiety you are feeling," Cedric said.

Once again it seemed that for however long I had swooned between thought and speech unknowingly, not certain how much of this I had said to him and how much of it merely thought to myself, whatever self was under these circumstances.

"It's called the pool ball paradox," he said. "You shoot a ball into a time tunnel and it emerges seconds before it was shot and headed directly for itself. What will happen?"

In truth notions of time travel and alternation bored me. I had no longing, I told him, to take an alternate path, even to loop back to one in the past, which would lead me to a future different than the one that I had lived. That was the stuff of games, with their alternate lives, or of the old woman's scripture and its afterlife. I wanted to be free of memory and imagination both. Perhaps Cedric was right and what I wanted was the solitude of the holo and the anonymity of its orgies, entanglements of limb and the disembodied erasures of individual genitals, breasts, bellies, and faces.

"And brains?" Cedric asked.

"And brains," I said, "if that's indeed where the mind resides, though I doubt that more and more."

"Then you need to think again, my friend," Cedric said. "Memories and imagination can be stored on a tiny needle and lost and found again in time, but the mind has its time and then ends, and that is different from a game or play. That's the real war against disorder."

Our conversation was haunted by a sense of expectation, a feeling of imminent collision as if in a car crash or Cedric's pool balls in a time tunnel. I had come to expect that times like these would be interrupted by some sudden intervention, a knock on the door and a basket of jewel-like berries, waking upon the floor of a huge kiln with another's face, or a night watchman's flashlight playing over the bare floor of an empty storefront. Instead for the first time in some time nothing happened, neither an atrophy settling upon me from some distant force switching off my consciousness, nor the half-hallucination liminality of vale and moor and knight. It was as if the poisoning had purged us alchemically and left instead a quotidian clarity that for once even events obeyed. The old woman's teapot rested, cool now, under a knit cosy; she would be back sometime to knock on the door carrying a pot of broth spotted with yellow fat and brown rimmed crackers, their white surface likewise pocked brown, whose sweet, benign flavor I could recall as clearly as the present.

"Like communion wafers," I said to Cedric.

"What's that?"

"So I wasn't talking aloud that time?" I asked.

"You may have been, my friend. Perhaps I was just daydreaming."

As we awaited the return of the old woman with her pot of broth, Cedric related more of the story of his visit to the house after Marco discovered him along the surveillance perimeter.

"Marco had night vision film that he was very proud of, green transparencies in which light and dark appeared in negative that he printed from a laser printer, a series of them. 'Look,' he said to me, 'do you know this creature? It's increasingly rare to see them here, he's known as the *Gulo gulo* or *Carcajou*—rather like a small bear, perhaps you know it as the wolverine—they're Northern creatures not native to where you come from, I suppose the palm civet would be closest to it. I have read that its winter coat glows a bright lavender color under ultraviolet light. That would be something to see, wouldn't it?' He flipped through the transparencies until he came to the one with the latest timestamp. 'And this would be you, dear Cedric. But you are no weasel, are you? Rather our trusted family retainer.'

"I heard him out without saying anything. Camilla was sitting in the shadows of the parlor where he was interrogating—or rather say interviewing—me. I could hear the clink of ice cubes as she sipped from a drink that, from its fragrance, I took to be gin and something. The doctor had offered me a drink as well but I declined under the circumstances, since it seemed clear that I had already been stunned or drugged. I had no memory of the time between when someone had suddenly come up behind me as I spied upon the house and when I sat before him as he showed me the green transparencies.

"'Yet it's very strange, isn't it?' the doctor went on, 'very strange indeed, that a trusted retainer would be discovered on the surveillance in much the same fashion as a wandering antelope or a civet tripping the cameras? How do you explain that, dear Cedric? My wife and I are both eager to know. Really. I mean, when one thinks of it, nothing at all has happened, has it? The person who says he is my wife's father has chosen to move away again, despite falling into harm the last time this happened; and you have chosen to resign to accompany him and look after him. That's totally in character, even routine in some sense, at least for a caretaker in this world of shifting allegiances. Yet there you are on the film!'

"His voice rose angrily then and he thrust the transparency before me, pointing to the bright form at its center. 'Look at yourself, my gluttonous one—that's what *Gulo gulo* means, did you know that? It's a very amusing name—what is it exactly that you are so hungry for?'"

Cedric was an accomplished storyteller, mimicking Marco's voice perfectly, building the tension of the interview in his telling, pausing now to let the doctor's questions hang in his account, letting the suspense build, his smile widening slightly in anticipation.

"Just then," Cedric said after a time, "just then exactly—you will have to believe me, my friend, though you will be certain that I am making this up or shifting the time to embellish the story—*just then* an alarm sounded and Marco turned to view the surveillance monitor where a small group of intruders appeared along the perimeter on foot. These three were, however, coming up the drive from the road as if proper visitors, albeit ones who somehow had managed to circumvent the gated entrance from the outer fence, a woman and two boys, one small enough to take her hand, the other marching untethered at her opposite side, the three of them appearing as chrome-green forms against the darker jade of the screen. Marco quickly printed off a transparency as if to make real what his eyes had seen. Meanwhile outside the guard dogs were barking. Marco was clearly agitated.

"'Who are they?' Camilla asked. She had come into the light from the shadows where she sat.

"'Wayfarers,' Marco said too quickly. 'Gypsies. Wanderers, beggars, whoever they are, the dogs will scare them off.'

"'But she has a small child with her,' Camilla said.

"Something had quieted the dogs, who whined now almost as if in pleasure."

Time unwound in the room where we sat, the light already lowering as Cedric paused within his story, its time and ours for the moment having merged into one.

"Do you see?" he asked after a time. "It was his past come visiting, his past itself imprinted upon the green transparencies of his night vision cameras, his past now present at his door, as the woman knocked patiently, then found the bell and pressed it, the sound of the past echoing in the vestibule beyond Marco's study."

But I didn't, I didn't understand exactly what he was telling me or how these events, however unlikely their complicity, however unlikely their coincidence, had conspired to renew Cedric's confidence and to bring him back here, albeit to find himself poisoned and perhaps nearly killed in the hours thereafter.

"You see?" he asked again but then rose up unsteadily and went to our own door rather than relate the events at the door in his story.

The old woman stood there, her tray before her, the smell of beef broth wafting.

"Hello Mother," Cedric said.

The woman smiled. "Hello dear, here's something to strengthen you as promised."

As far as I knew she had not knocked, nor could she have, I thought, laden as she was with the tray and mugs.

"How did you know?" I asked aloud.

"Suspense demanded it," Cedric said. "It was the moment in the story for it, a perfect parallel."

He laughed.

"Not to mention that I saw her coming through the shadows outside the window," he said, and then after a pause, "You're such an innocent, my friend, it's hard to imagine that you were ever a wayfarer."

The woman looked sharply at me, studying my face.

"You're a wayfarer?" she asked.

"Of one sort or another," I nodded.

"For a time I was once a wayfarer myself," she said. "My son was born into a wayfaring life, under the hedges as they say, although he would like not to remember that now that he has something to himself. He would like to think that the army gave birth to him."

Her complaint was more sad than bitter and Cedric slung a consoling arm about her shoulder as she doled out the broth, handing a mug first to me and then to him before removing the napkin covering the plate of water crackers.

"Are you not eating with us?" Cedric asked.

"I've had my supper," she said. "And you have been sick and need it more."

"Nonsense," he said and extracted a bowl from the cupboard, pouring broth for himself and handing the old woman the mug she had served him. "Take my chair." He patted it. "I need to make my legs work again."

I studied Cedric to see if he was testing her, whether he thought she, too, was an agent or a simul sent to poison us again.

"It's very kind of you," the old woman said to me across the table, as if the invitation had been mine.

"The kindness is yours," I said. "You've saved us. It's a sacrament."

She sipped at the broth.

"How long have you been a wayfarer?" she asked.

"Time, you will recall, is a strange substance for a wayfarer. It flows forward and back."

"My friend fancies himself a philosopher," Cedric teased. He leaned against the windowsill and sipped his broth from the bowl.

"What sent you out?" she asked me.

They had washed the afterbirth from her little corpse and the blue had drained away and left her snowy white and as cold as snow when they let me hold her once before wrapping her for the undertaker. I did not ask whether my wife had been able to see her, why I do not know except that I imagined that the Dutch nurse with her ample bosom and plump warm arms—who had told us before the baby came of her own family of six strong girls and two handsome boys—would surely have made some provision for another mother to settle her grief and hold her daughter against her own bosom before they took the small body off.

"I was running away from grief."

Her fingers trembled slightly against the mug of broth.

"And you?" I asked. "What sent you out?"

"The same," she said. "It is the same for all the wayfarers, is it not? Even the mad ones are full of grief and hungry for some kind of love."

She sipped her broth. "And what brought you back?" she asked.

"Out of nowhere, at some point in those years, a boy—a mischievous, maybe even a deceptive, creature—latched onto me as if a shadow and brought me to this city where he disappeared."

"How long ago? Can you remember?"

"Sometimes," I said, "I think it has not happened yet."

She turned to Cedric. "And are you two now looking for him? For the boy?"

"I suppose," he said.

"Sometimes you have to wander in the shadows to find what light there is," she said. "It's as if it gathers there upon the hidden branches."

She recited a verse again. "And when the children of Israel saw it, they said one to another, It *is* manna: for they wist not what it was."

"And you believe all that, Mother?" Cedric asked gently.

"I believe what I know," she said. "I have seen the light I speak of, hanging in clumps upon the underbrush."

She had a last sip from the mug and began to gather the tray of her things as Cedric moved to help her. He insisted against her wishing otherwise that we would not need the little bit of cold tea that remained, but he agreed when she urged that we keep the arrowroot biscuits and the water crackers since you could never be sure when the stores would reopen after one of these events. I rose to join them near the door and Cedric and I both thanked her profusely for getting us back on our feet again. Cedric offered to get the doors for her and walk with her to see her home and when I bade her farewell again she stopped and looked directly into my eyes.

"Perhaps it was your own shadow that latched onto you. Light and shadows get lost in time as do we. Sometimes, like us, they have to catch up to themselves."

They were gone down the stairs and into the gaining night before I thought that there was a question I should have asked her, although I couldn't for the life of me recall what I had thought it was. Something about a baby, I felt sure. I began to feel that perhaps I should chase after them in hopes that the question would come back to me before I never saw her again. Yet it seemed wrong, a kind of arrogance, to so mistrust time as to think a simple feeling of regret following a moment of forgetfulness was an omen of something worse.

I waited for Cedric in the dark but he did not come back that night or the next morning.

In some part of me I welcomed his not returning. For now the poisoning seemed to have suppressed the attacks upon my consciousness, while at the same time the interwoven layers of Beckmesser's and my memories, including the wooing of Elinor and combats with her champion, became easier to sort; and yet I felt no relief, for the anxiety I felt about having landed just short of a critical time in converging stories came more and more to the fore. I had not added to the stones on the windowsill, but despite the pageant of tumultuous events in the week that they marked, I nonetheless persisted there in that room, albeit in fragments, still locked in time and space and a bifurcated self, a man at both the middle and the end of days and increasingly in danger of living henceforth in what for the old woman was routine. Time spun like a wheel into wet clay while nothing and no one moved onward; stones or dawns or public disturbances were replaced by empty celebrations. These might mark a sequence, and the body itself might replicate it somewhere deep within its decaying cells, yet the world went on in the same muddy rut and meanwhile I had not made any progress toward anything I sought, or, in fact, even knowing what it was.

For an instant long ago hope had lain within my arms, the small thing snowy white and as cold as snow and I tried to warm her with my hands until the Dutch nurse gently pried the small body away from me and wrapped it in its white shroud. I should have run then, I should have run to her and held her and told her that life would go on, that we would be all right, that she should not try to run behind the snow white girl, that she should not die.

Against these deaths whether Franky had killed Beckmesser seemed a fruitless mystery to solve, even as it came closer to being an event I could witness—nay, suffer—firsthand in some alternate version of my life. It seemed obvious that Marco was a likely suspect in driving his father-in-law, or what he believed a simul of him, to lose his life, especially if he thought that life had already been snatched up into the zombie that I presented before him. The doctor was possessed by a fervent kind of justice that verged toward malevolence.

Yet say it was him who killed Beckmesser, I thought, who then could I tell? Who in what world would care about an event yet years off? Should I upload such a message to the orbiting Gurula, whisper it to Elinor, have the story tattooed in code upon a hairless shoulder or my wrist?

Your story, the ancient greeting, went back to a dim history beginning with the Greeks. The reply was always a series of monstrous births and malevolent deaths, an intricate series of interrelated mistaken identities and snuffed existences, sons-in-laws killing their wives' fathers, children sleeping with their own mothers.

Even if I found my way back, it wasn't clear who would care. Indeed there seemed every possibility that the authorities would reject any account of Beckmesser's death or my own existence that did not fit the story they had settled upon.

And who was to say they would be wrong should they reckon their own stories in this way? And what would it matter when the world was a field strewn with bones?

Caught up in these thoughts I was going mad with waiting and thus almost longed to feel the dimming come again. Instead I chewed at the remaining biscuits and gazed out of the window for hours.

The morning moved toward afternoon and a sullen overcast came over the world outside like a tarp, a thin nuisance rain seeping from it upon the increasing number of passers-by who moved unharassed under it along the sidewalk. I gazed out into the grey for quite some time, at first thinking Cedric would return and then that perhaps the old woman would return and bring something more to eat. Finally I rose and dressed, first washing my face with hot water and scraping at the whiskers on my cheek with the blade of the folding knife. Once I left the rooming house, I pushed the button of the pager, not so much to summon Cedric as to alert someone that I was out in the world. I took one of the flashkeys with me in the same pocket as the pager, slipping the small mirror in the other pocket along with the folding knife, the stones from the windowsill, and the turtle skull talisman. Were I to fall through the world again, even into Hades, I was ready. Indeed I wondered whether I had not gathered all these objects in some vague hope for transport.

Where to set off to, of course, was not so self-evident. What I could control was mundane—turn left or right, bear toward what I believed would be predictable landmarks despite whatever point in their own histories they were situated in. I would start toward the central square and from it navigate toward the commercial quarter where both the storefront and the copper-clad building were situated and where some past or future self and death itself, at least once upon a time, had resided together.

What I could not control was, I knew, a wide expanse, and who controlled it I could not say. All I knew was that, once, as a wayfarer even the mundane world seemed mine.

Still the truth is that what led me through the streets to find the square was not so much old memory as some proprioceptive instinct imprinted within me like a captionless GPS grid, the trace of a time when Rosaria and I spent mornings here together, walking these streets and looking for Mil.

Her lost son. Our search. And yet why, I wondered.

Then when I felt the warmth of the new sun upon my shoulders I wondered as well how it had so suddenly become spring and how the seasons could turn like pages.

The town square was a cinder patch of old benches with rusting iron brackets situated among scruffy grass, purple blooming nettles, and young milkweed sprouting amidst piles of shit from the dogs who roamed at will among the laughing anarchists and addicts and their molls, all of them looking like children, smoking cigarettes and drinking from unmarked bottles of schnapps. A police van sat idling along the street at the traverse walk, the cops, too, smoking and staring sullenly at the inhabitants.

I thought I saw Franky in the midst of the square sitting propped on the back of a bench.

"Halt!" a voice shouted before I knew I had moved toward the figure.

"Where are you going buster?" The same voice called from the van, where I turned to see a bored police officer.

"Aren't you—?" he said.

"I thought I saw someone I knew," I explained.

The cop was no more than a child dressed up in a brown leather jacket and cap like a video trooper. When he saw me, his tone changed.

"I'm sorry, Mr. B, you know it's a zoo in there. To tell the truth I'd doubt you know any of them."

B or D? I wanted to ask him. I couldn't be certain which since he spoke from deep within the van but also because the square was raucous. Yet I somehow knew it would not do to ask such a question.

"You know me then?" I asked instead.

"Of course, sir," he said. "I didn't recognize you at first."

"I've been ill," I said, "stuck inside for these past days during the disturbance."

"Of course," he said. "I just was afraid you might be harmed if you went in there."

I considered telling him not to worry, that I had a knife in my pocket, but then immediately reconsidered how it would seem.

"Which one?" he asked me.

It was confusing. I thought for a moment he had somehow read the question in my mind about the name he had called me by.

"Pardon?"

"Which of these animals did you think you recognized?"

I turned back and peered into the scabrous park. The fellow I thought had been Franky was no longer there.

"He was sitting on the back of the bench," I said, "just beyond where that girl with blue hair is wrestling with her dog."

The girl gripped a large branch at either end tugging the dog up on its hind feet by its jaws and twisting its skull back and forth, a froth of mucous spraying from its bared teeth as she laughed.

The policeman reached to the console that sat between him and his partner in the driver's seat, scrolling across a touch screen until he found something. He pressed a button and a small color printout emerged, still smelling of wet ink. When he handed it to me the ink stained my fingers where I gripped too far within the edge.

"Is that him?"

It looked to be, although the surveillance camera wasn't of very high resolution. I nodded and he pressed another button and waited, looking at his screen.

He turned to me. "Nothing," he said. "We have no information on this one. Probably a wayfarer. If we caught him on the street away from these creeps, he'd be gone."

"Gone?" I asked.

He looked blankly at me. I thanked him and handed back the printout.

"You can keep it as a souvenir," he said. Then his partner put the van into gear and they rolled slowly around the square, stopping at the opposite side of the traverse and idling there again.

"They don't know what to do with what they know," Irene said later when I told her the story.

It was easy to find the storefront from the square, of course, situated as it was just around the corner along a route I had taken any number of times, although in truth how many I did not know.

The storefront windows were still covered with newspapers although someone had painted the door and the outside window frames and trim with bright enamel. It was only as I stood there that I realized that the terra cotta identity chip was no longer embedded in my forearm and I could no longer open the door via the lock plate. Whether Marco or Cedric had performed the operation to remove it I could not say, and when exactly I was last aware of it there joined the many things I could not remember.

I banged against the window for a while with no response and was about to go away when I heard footsteps. The bored boy who opened the door seemed vaguely familiar to me, but it was not the tenant's son or someone who fit the description of the slimy fellow Cedric had seen previously. This one was well scrubbed and neatly trimmed, wearing black high-top sneakers and white tee shirt.

"He's here," he shouted back into the space of the store and waved me in.

The layout within now fit my memory of Irina's cyber café more closely, although the machines of course were a previous generation and the layout of the space slightly different, lacking the sofas and the game theatre and with a regular desk for the proprietress instead of the counter. Still it was much more self-similar than the town square had been.

"You like it?"

The warmth of her body and the lush perfume as she came up from behind enveloped me well before she spoke. This sensation of overcoming warmth was accompanied by an absurd longing to slip within it as one slips through a curtain.

And find myself where? I wondered.

"Yes, it's very impressive. How——?"

"I have an investor of course," she said and took my hand, her touch and smile both so warm that I readily let her lead me back along the corridor to the space where I had once lived and from which, despite the fact that it took place in a time yet to come, I long ago had fled.

This room was even more recognizable, with the same cloth hanging between the rooms, the same sofa, the same high-backed kitchen chairs and table where Cedric sat with the woman's son and Rosaria.

I felt myself begin to faint but Irene still held me by the hand and somehow kept me above the surface of the rising darkness.

"Do you know my sister?" she asked.

"I think we've met," I said.

Rosaria reddened modestly and looked down at her hands, gently turning back and forth the tiny dark blue ring on her little finger.

The boy, Andy, laughed. "She likes you I think," he said.

His mother swatted gently at him, still holding me with her other hand.

"Why wouldn't she like this nice man?" she asked. "Now go and play your new game."

"No, wait!" Cedric said and held up the shiny game disk folder. "Look here my friend."

It was, of course, Ynys Gutrin.

The feeling of faintness gave way to vivid fear. It was all too easy, as if the events of this table were a knot of complex strands suddenly sliding closed into a too symmetrical rosette.

"But you said...."

"It would be a year," Cedric intervened. "Yes, and it nearly has been. In any case Madame has certain connections in the industry, thanks to her investor."

"You can't do this to me," I said. "You are the ones I trusted."

Upon their upturned faces I could see the look of benevolence one shows to the aged when they are confused, a semblance of caring, perhaps even genuine, overlaid with their helpless inability to say anything that might penetrate the confusion of the one who stood before them. Irene shooed her son gently away from the table and freed her hold of my hand, letting me stand there by the table while she slipped into the seat where her son had sat. He joined the other boy who had let me in and who had stood patiently waiting for him at the doorway. They went toward the front of the store chatting with great excitement as if looking forward to the game as any normal boys would have.

Whoever had produced this spectacle was an expert, I thought, more gifted than any game maker. The sad eyes, the silence, the quiet breathing of the characters at the table were all perfectly rendered. What will happen next, I thought, is that the sister will address me with quiet affection.

"Would you like to take a walk together?" Rosaria asked, touching my hand softly.

I could see the small mirror embedded in the ring and upon my fingertip the image of a part of someone's face, the stain remaining from when I had smudged the inkjet surveillance printout.

"Do you see?" Cedric resumed his story seamlessly as if he had been telling it here all long and not in the rooming house. "It was his past come visiting, his past itself imprinted upon the green transparencies of his night vision cameras, Irene now present at his door, her voice echoing in the vestibule beyond Marco's study when Camilla got up to let her and the two boys into the house.

"It was as if she knew it all already as women so often do," he said and Irene allowed herself a little laugh while Rosaria's touch burned itself into my hand.

I felt neither faint nor the dimming but rather the intoxication of the spectacle. It was as if my body were weightless, about to float away, pinned to this time and place solely by the touch of the ringed finger.

"Marco sat there sullenly," Cedric continued, "he and Irene sitting in the silence and green glare of the surveillance screens, while Camilla went to the kitchen to bring back glasses of juice for the boys. Irene and Marco each declined a drink."

"It wasn't that I didn't want to accept her hospitality," Irene explained. "God knows, I was dying of thirst after the walk and the fright from the dogs. I just didn't want to cede any beholding to him. I wanted to match his strength."

"They heard Camilla singing as she returned with the drinks for the boys," Cedric said, "her voice echoing in the empty house, the glasses jingling on the tray, her scuffling footsteps. Just as she returned, Marco hissed 'Why are you doing this?' and she knew she had outlasted him."

"I wanted you to acknowledge your son," Irene said as if to Marco, now playing her part among us, her voice breaking slightly as she did.

Rosaria took her hand and we were suddenly a circuit, the three of us, a circuit of Rosaria's making. In the room beyond the open door, you could hear the distant music of the pageant at Ynys Gutrin and the boys excited yelping as the game began. Soon there would be the horns of heralds and the clang of swords, I knew, and perhaps the soft, sweet music of the voice of Elinor.

"Camilla gave the boys their drinks and then asked calmly, 'Are they both yours, darling?' but Marco said nothing."

"No, the other, the older one, is a traveler we took in," Irene said.

Rosaria pressed her hand to mine still more insistently, the circuit growing stronger.

"Camilla sat knee to knee with Irene," Cedric went on, "and they continued to talk together like sisters. 'They are both such handsome young men,' Camilla said to her. 'I can see your eyes in his.'"

"It was so brave of her," Irene said. "I began to feel bad about the pain I was causing."

"'Get them out of here!' Marco barked to me." Cedric took over the narration again. "It was as if he had forgotten that I no longer worked for him, as if I were still the trusted family retainer."

"Are you sure you aren't?" I asked and pulled my hand away, breaking the circuit. "How can I be sure this all isn't a production for my benefit, a way to tie me up into your stories? How can you be sure you're not being used for that? Although why Marco would bother with me, why any of you would care for the life of a wayfarer, I cannot understand."

They had that look upon their faces again, the three of them a silent jury. Could I have I would have ripped the visage of Beckmesser from my face like a rubber mask, wiping the remnants of him away like an actor's make-up. What I wished more than anything was that I could sit again in the green leather dentist's chair where the face of death presided and have him drain all alien memories from me. I wished that he or Franky or someone might return me to a self of my own, even that of a monkey-faced monstrosity.

"*Vaya*," Rosaria said, and took my hand again, getting up from the table and standing face to face before me. "*Venir, vamos a caminar*, come let's go for a walk," she whispered to me.

"But where?" I asked.

She made no reply but rather led me gently to the back door where we went out into the sun and shadows of the alleys, still not sure myself if any of this was real or whether I could trust her any more than anyone, the pager vibrating in my pocket as we went out.

10

The doctor speaks:

Every city, of course, has such a quarter whatever it is called: a series of alleys and warrens with loading docks, the so-called backstreets that house small manufacturing, offices of dubious enterprises, and warehouses of unknown provenance or purpose, all of them looking blankly upon each other. In some locales these corridors run along the innards of city blocks, alien courtyards clogged with dumpsters and refuse barrels that the denizens, rodent or human, must navigate among. Occasionally you can glimpse these spaces in shadow back along a narrow service walkway leading from a bright avenue. Sometimes someone emerges from one like a rodent, blinking in the light and moved to arrange himself no matter how orderly his appearance.

These spaces are not to be mistaken for the loft or warehouse districts along abandoned harbors or old rail yards that have long become urban malls and playgrounds for the young as well as a moneyed band of nomadic tourists in search of local color and a facsimile of history. What the backstreets house—if the verb suits them at all—is unclear; they are the underside of quotidian life, not the arteries but the veins, whose dark circulation is residue, what life casts off unthinkingly. Sometimes these spaces run in parallel through a city, like the dark vein along the prawn's shining back, a rough-toothed zipper of sorts.

Usually no one is tempted to frame these spaces in neurological metaphor, speaking of the corticospinal fibers and sensory fibers along the internal capsule, for instance; unless of course, one summons the plague of Alzheimer's as a trope for the city whose economy is choked by its own versions of myeloid plaques and neurofibrillary tangles.

In such a view the byways of the brain are portrayed as if a shadow image of the lower digestive system; and, indeed, the folds and convolutions of cerebrum and colon to an outsider can seem remarkably similar in medical illustrations of a naïve sort.

They, he, he and she, I—it is less and less clear to me anymore, despite my training, where identity resides—walked in such a space, perhaps for hours—temporality becoming no more clear than identity— apparently without talking at first. The gypsy woman, the sister to a woman I once knew well—I am told she is of Spanish origin and thus more properly called a Gitano, or perhaps Gitana—was according to her sister famously self-denying, an ascetic in other words, and as a fortune teller by trade thought by some to be a mystic or healer of sorts.

Thus one could say we were, and are, in the same business.

It isn't clear what she intended with my putative father in law, or the person he had so mysteriously, and abruptly, transformed into—not to say *become*. Perhaps she meant some sort of walking cure, a purgation, wherein the backstreet quarter through which they walked would function as a sweat lodge. My wife thinks instead that the woman meant to accomplish a sort of repatterning therapy, taking him through spaces he associated with traumatic events whether real or of his own imagination.

They have become quite close, in a way I would never have imagined, my wife, my one-time lover and her sister, which in some strange sense might have spawned a parallel affinity between me and my putative father in law to the extent that at times we each felt alien among them, subjects of their gaze and targets of their laughter.

Not that this affinity, in either case, excused my errings, of course.

In any case they walked—walking, as I said, for hours together—while my wife's former assistant—a man who worked as a retainer for me before coming to care for my father-in-law—sat and talked and tracked their progress through the backstreets along with the Gitana's sister. The two of them each possessed two different, previous generation tracking systems of some sort that ran under the radar—so to speak—of the kinds of work that I and others were accomplishing then on behalf of the commonwealth together with the public authorities, a way to assure that public order and freedom neatly interlaced.

Before long, however, the Gitana and my father-in-law were lost to their tracking devices as well and all that my former retainer and my former lover could do was to wait and watch the children, her child with me and another boy, Nim, a stranger she had taken in, as they played one of the new generation net games, a sort of pay-to-play medieval fantasy that my father-in-law was purportedly interested in as well, and which, in fact, came to be his abiding obsession in his final days.

But that is getting ahead of the story.

The thing about life is that there are no waste forms, at least to a scientist. Or to put it differently, even the most banal and peripheral of spaces, such as the maze of backstreets within which the Gitana and my father-in-law outran—or outlasted—these hermetic systems of tracking them, nonetheless have an internal syntax, a set of spatial gestures and architectural inclinations—however vernacular, even hemorrhagic or metastatic—that themselves comprise a spatiotemporal language, and which perhaps an adept can read in much the way that the labyrinth, whose form seems available only to birds-eye view of gods on high, nonetheless discloses itself to even the blind adept as she feels her way along its rough walls.

Or so I have come to believe.

More, I think that perhaps even the idlest of repeated encounters with such spaces holds the prospect of making anyone similarly an adept.

It is likewise with DNA, which is widely misunderstood even after all this time. Not a state of a substance or a being, or for that matter not strictly a biological constituent at all, it is instead a ground pattern, a set of inclinations, permutations, and random markings in the form of instructions, a map rather than a set of dwellings. A map of backstreets. One does not intervene in these instructions in the way an aspirin does by acetylating the COX enzyme to turn off its clotting powers. Instead one maps an alternate course for chemistry itself and, eventually, the race. Or so the story goes.

There was no question that my wife's father had been assaulted during the first episode when he left his home and moved away from us. The healing, wherever it had been accomplished—obviously under primitive conditions—left his physiognomy in outline beneath, a contoured armature upon which the scarring and post-contusion disfiguration settled in clefts and bloated hollows alike.

Yet she claimed she could see him there, that she knew it was he.

Error seeps into our understandings, scientific or otherwise, through an almost imperceptible set of assumptions, of defects in collection, of minuscule sample contaminations, or inept or overzealous—often these are the same—operations. Short tandem repeats and minisatellites that show themselves between DNA samples from a living subject and samples drawn from residue upon his purported toothbrush may themselves reflect any number of random and unaccountable events, coincidental interventions, and anonymous encounters. All of us live upon a public square in some sense and a forensic investigator comes to value the evidence preservation sack as much as the much more expensive and complex sequencing console.

Another way to say this is that we are each to some extent occupied by others.

I had implanted my father-in-law with a prototype monitoring device, not nanotech per se as much as extreme miniaturization. However, it had malfunctioned from the first, its biometric data intermittent—perhaps the result of physical or tech countermeasures on the part of his companion, who, as my wife's former assistant, can be expected to have certain suspicions—while the gross monitoring, especially the hyper-miniaturized UKW—that is, *Ultrakurzwellen*—microphone was, due to some malfunction, nearly useless, broadcasting only random fragments of conversations and ambients. From these data and his accounts and others there was anecdotal evidence that the implanted device had unfortunately brought on periodic episodes of syncope and asthenia in the subject, which is to say my wife's so-called father.

Remarkably, however, during the hours of this particular walk the ultra short wave microphone and transmitter functioned at least marginally where the other systems employed by both my former assistant and my former lover failed entirely. To be sure the transcribed transmissions are fragmentary and intermittent, but, taken together with the other data, allows one to propose at least a possible scenario of what went on during the couple's walk based upon these collected conversational shards.

Did I mention that the GPS tracking was, in this instance, excellent—thus, of course, providing reliable timestamps for the conversational fragments? Taken together with the higher incidence of audio transmissions, this suggests that this warren of backstreets is perhaps more permeable and transparent than one would think otherwise. Were I to hazard a guess, I would attribute this phenomenon to a hyper-compensation resulting in redundant installation of overlapping layers of radio antennae and cellular amplifiers by wary stakeholders in the quarter who are afraid to lose their virtual connection to the city beyond the labyrinth.

From the silence—and the garbled biometrics—I imagine that he may for some time have experienced another episode of syncope as they first ventured out into the backstreets. Aside from the few of her captured murmurs and what independent observers agree sounds like an anxious intake of breath from one of them in one burst of the transmission, I feel fairly certain of this, a certainty supported, of course, by anyone's ordinary experience of anxiety upon revisiting a site of previous trauma.

Also I think my father-in-law may have been a little in love with this woman, who by all accounts casts an alluring figure.

Since we do know that they left the establishment hand-in-hand, we may likewise imagine that she led him so through both the initiatory backstreets and this episode until he began to calm himself, if not yet trust her entirely.

At 00:34:50—times here given in seconds rather than hundredths—she is heard clearly to say, "*Calma, mi cariño, que bueno*," which loosely translated means, I am glad that you are more calm, my friend.

He says nothing.

In fact, he says nothing until 00:39:11, when he whispers, "I'm beginning to think…."

What follows is a relatively intact sequence of exchanges between them.

It is not unreasonable to believe that he may at this point have recognized some landmark or at least aspect of the locale.

For she immediately replies, "That's good, it's better when one can begin to remember" (00:39:20).

"What it is is I remember too much" (00:39:32), he replies, perhaps a curious locution but one my wife remembers as fairly common in his speech—and, as an aside, not so confusing a syntax in other languages, for instance Spanish, where one might translate, "*Lo que se es que me acuerdo.*"

After this they walk in silence again for some time, not surprisingly had it indeed begun to seem a particularly familiar place to him, since one could imagine him falling into a moment of reverie, or at least struggling to recall his prior experience and place it in memory.

Situating memory does not, of course, explain the almost hour-long gap that ensues between this initial exchange and perhaps the most curious and, in some way, telling interchange of the whole transcript.

This is why, given both the gap and the remarkable phrase that accompanies their emergence from it, it seems not unreasonable to suspect that a good deal of the intervening transcript was lost—perhaps because of radio interference—rather than to imagine that these two moved from an hour-long silent promenade into a dialogue as intense as the one that followed.

In any case it is she who prompts it, asking—in English, there is no evidence of her speaking in Romani or any language other than Spanish and English—"Do you love?" (01:36:07).

I am told by linguistic experts that my initial assumption that this was a malformation of a question by a non-native English speaker in the grammatical form of her native language is incorrect.

Had she intended to ask something like "are you someone who loves?" she would have said "*¿alguien que te ama?*" or "*¿eres la clase de persona que ama?*" I am told; while instead the actual English phrase as it is on the transcript would translate quite literally as "*¿Te gusta?*" or "*¿me amas?*," the former closer to "Do you like this?" and the latter to "Do you love me?"

Decades of machine translation, of course, make manifest that language, too, has its impenetrable backstreets, cul-de-sacs, and alleyways that for their practitioners are as native and effortless to navigate as the reticular hollows of coral reefs and wafting anemones are to the schools of fish that move effortlessly among them.

As with the genetic fingerprint, it is not enough to know the names of things as to understand that names, too, degrade, evolve, coalesce, migrate and intersperse. What someone is called changes over years or from place to place and yet never approaches the limit of the identity that came before the name or the one that will follow when our names themselves disappear into the final darkness.

In any case the question posed at this point of the transcript seems not to have been transitive, and thus the question before us is neither grammatical nor syntactic but rather philosophical. She was asking a question of his being.

What follows is remarkable. At first he stutters something unintelligible (01:36:29), but then pronounces carefully something that at first seems non-responsive.

"...am far from my own home" (01:37:01), he says, the halting pauses seemingly ones of calculation or considered thought rather than his being out of breath or a transmission error.

She replies with something that the transmission garbles.

Then there begins an extended segment of the transmission for which there is no satisfying technical explanation, the man's voice clear and lossless, the quality of the voice confident, younger sounding than elsewhere in the transcript.

"But could you love a monster?" (01:38:50), he asks, and continues at length, almost as if an aria:

"It's the beauty and the beast thing, yes of course, *La Belle et la Bête*, but for a mother something more, a question answered at some deep, almost cellular, remove, an evolutionary rather than an erotic or cultural matter. What stuff goes forward, if you will. Would a monster not father a monster? If so what then would be the cost? And how a woman would feel in the face of such sadness is impossible for me to understand: to sacrifice a child you've nurtured to evolutionary witness, accident or fate if you want to call it that, to have the whole prospect and pain come to nothing. How *could* you go on thereafter? How not hate the creature whose seed had in some sense authored such loss, his flawed genetic text overwriting yours, the weakened gamete helpless, evolution itself unable to see clear through the visual interference of this imbricated smudge. How can a woman go on? How would you?" (ends at 01:39:57).

One need not resort to psychology and notions of multiple personality to resist the suggestion that two persons cannot exist at once in any one being. Nor—to be quite open about one's own prejudices and inclinations—need one posit a technological explanation. The gamete itself, *opere citato*, offers perfect refutation, as does the Trinity for a believer. Witness a child plugged into a holo or a gameworld or an infant daydreaming at the breast. Nor are these matters restricted to the young: any lover embraces dissolution at the moment of orgasm and at that moment cleaves himself.

Yet these are matters of philosophy or theology, in some sense alien to one—such as the current investigator—trained in the natural sciences or medicine. The body is inalienable, it endures beyond what merges with or fractures from it. We enter into it—that is, take on an identity—as upon an uncontrolled motorway whose traffic presents us by chance with gaps of various extents and durations but whose openings diminish at any instant.

Yet this is a motorway without exits, a road that, when it ceases, the vehicle ceases as well.

Of course, my wife reminds me, another set of questions enters here as well, those of stylistics, the subjects of inquiry for those historians who turn themselves toward false accounts—literature and the like, or her own field, opera and the *chanson*. For her the discourse captured here does not comport with what she knows of her father's life and opinions. This makes it "not him" to her.

"He's more other to me in this speech than he is in your genetic analyses," she says succinctly. "Not just the discourse, but the situation. I can't imagine him giving advice about childbirth to a woman."

That we had no children is, for Camille, a source of profound sadness, a profundity even the most powerful of instruments cannot penetrate. That she is the last of her father's line as well adds a shadow upon a darkness.

In any case it is precisely her objection that the voice in the transmission addresses next.

First, however, there is a gap of several minutes.

"*Perdóname querida*" (01:47:22), his voice says, a moment which, in itself, adds to Camille's suspicions.

"Never in my life with him did he utter a word of Spanish," she said.

There are, of course, possible explanations, the simplest being that children do not know everything about their parents. Add to this that, walking with a woman who had some facility in the language, she may have served as an informant for him during some period of time that the transmission had dropped. That is, for instance, he could have simply asked her, "How do you say, I'm sorry dear?" Finally the medical literature is replete with instances—for example, coprolalia (Tourette's) or glossolalia (talking in tongues)—where unknown languages emerge from the swamp of the mind.

"It is just that I am tired of talking about myself" (01:47:35), he says. "Tired of talking, tired of thinking, tired of dreaming, tired of looking at myself. Tired of my own story. Yet I see such pain ahead for you if you fall in love...."

"Not fall in love, love" (01:47:46), she interrupts.

"*Lo siento lo siento lo siento, perdóname*," he says. "It is difficult to raise one's head above the horizon of self" (01:48:17).

It is not hard to believe that already at this point it was he who had fallen in love, not the love that she speaks of—the love beyond falling and pain—but a love nonetheless, one strong enough to lift his head up, to keep him from sliding into the veils of syncope or *sueño*.

This much is known of the history of the man who claimed to be my father-in-law:

Following the events of these days he continued to reside in the same rooming house, at first with our former retainer as his companion, but then, as far as is known—not only from the testimony of others at the rooming house, the landlord and his mother, now herself deceased; but also as well as from the player logs at Ynys Gutrin—he continued to live alone until his death. At the insistence of my wife and my former lover, all genetic investigations as to the identity of this man ceased, at least as matters of public record, during his life. However, when my private files were discovered and seized upon his passing, apparently in response to an anonymous allegation that I might be responsible for his death, there was an official inquiry which ruled the genetic evidence inconclusive and closed that case as moot, while also remaining inconclusive as to the identity of the so-called ivory knight who it was believed had manipulated my father-in-law's biometrics so as to cause a cardioembolic incident. All of this was, of course, complicated by the fact that—at least according to testimony at the coroner's inquiry—he had been cremated upon his decease and the ashes spread upon the lake before our house by the same fellow whose testimony it was, and who had become his caretaker and sometime companion, our former employee Cedric. As next of kin my wife would not consent to any further inquiry as to the place and circumstance of cremation, about which there remain questions in my mind. Likewise she would not agree to our pursuing a lawsuit to recover certain assets there were reasons to believe had fallen into Cedric's hands and others. We divorced almost immediately thereafter.

I try as well to imagine the moonless evening as Cedric rowed out upon the lake before my father-in-law's former house to cast his ashes upon its waters.

To begin with, the mere act constitutes a felony, since what is locally known as Beckmesser's Lake is in fact one of a number of reservoirs hereabouts that feed, not our little provincial capital, but the network of enormous aqueduct tunnels that lead a hundred and twenty two miles from here to the national capital. Both fishing from and fouling reservoir waters is forbidden, as also technically is boating upon its surface, although allowances have been made to us over the years as official caretakers. Even so there is no public access to its shores and only someone like Cedric could know how to reach it.

The lake, like its sister reservoirs, flooded over what had been living communities, their inhabitants resettled elsewhere along with their possessions, but the houses and barns, or—in the case of our lake—a handsome provincial church, were covered over by the waters.

Rumors, of course, immediately sprang up, as is the way of superstitious people. Some reported hearing sounds rising from the waters, lullabies and the cries of infants, the moans of the dying, an early recording of Frieda Hempe singing *Lola*, a dog barking. Others told of strange visions appearing below the surfaces, a lantern in a submerged window, an enormous squid with glittering silver flanks leaving a wake of white sparks, or—in the case of our waters—a glow emanating from a barely submerged church cupola from which organ music and hymns were heard.

Even for a skeptic such visions are compelling; one imagines ladies in ball gowns flirting over beaded fans in flooded ballrooms, the rustle of petticoats and the tiptoe whisperings of satin slippers, girlish laughter coming from the powder rooms. My wife—for so it is I still think of her—calls these the fantasies of an oligarch. "For the commoner, his monster squid; for the governor, his girls in silk stockings, *c'est la même*, it's all the same."

I wonder, however. Although there is no measure that I know of—save perhaps the slow descent of the sleeper from beta, to alpha, to theta and finally to delta—it would be interesting to study the relative values of imagination. Surely no one thinks that the brute who imagines bludgeoning or rape serves the human cause in any fashion equal to, say, Delibes' score to *Sylvia*. Such an argument, of course, makes a straw man of the brute; more interesting is to consider the finer differentiations—between *Sylvia* and *Coppélia* perhaps and their effects upon an audience. How are the illusions of the superstitious provincial hearing a sheep bleat from an abandoned meadow at the bottom of a reservoir any different that those of my former father-in-law—his blood pressure spiking, respiration rate racing—as he confronts an imaginary knight as much of his own making as anything real?

And what of your scans and slides and surveillance screens? someone might ask; how are the night and the dark screen and the black surface of the reservoir any different?

This is where, of course, one cannot fail to regret that the whole spectrum of instrumentation from the prototype monitoring device failed to function in ensemble as the Gitana and my father-in-law walked together. What might have then emerged could have been a *Gesamtkunstwerk* to rival any on a stage or in a holo. Imagine feeling the weariness of the muscles ease through a passive haptic interface as the endorphins are released; imagine a set of optic projections to rival the dreams of those ancient instrument builders who sought to create a color organ; imagine the confusion of intellect and senses as the monkey-faced *Bête* begins to think himself half in love with *La Belle Tzigane*.

Indeed imagine all sexuality enhanced in an augmented reality! The lover and the beloved finally one in a fully conscious—almost overwhelming—embrace of transcendent oneness. Not the syncope of the *petite mort* but the ancient explosion of the fireworks chrysanthemum over Changsha.

She laughed in my face when—just before the end—I risked sharing this.

"You want to make fireworks? Please spare me, Marco," she scoffed. "Was it good for you, baby? For me there were sparks."

She could not contain her laughter. I felt my temper rise and suddenly had a vivid recollection of how it was when I first courted her, the diva's faux smile in the dressing room mirror, her maid's barely suppressed laughter as she took the gaudy bouquets from my arms, the décolletage as Camille leaned closer to the mirror and wiped away the eyes of the romantic stage courtesan, leaving just another girl behind: complexion reddened into a faint rash from the greasepaint and the stuff she used to remove it, stained cotton puffs piling up in the little wicker basket next to the stool where she sat still in her silken slip. She delighted then in treating me like a boy before her, and—in the interim having honed the daggers she thrust in me—delighted so at the end.

"I have long thought that for you all of this is some sort of masturbatory fantasy," she told me then. "Whether you sit before the medical imaging or the surveillance instruments, you sit there diddling in your head, imagining yourself gifted with a vision that the rest of the world does not enjoy. That was what made it so funny, really, despite the pain, when Irina suddenly appeared there with your child in hand. Your little hard-on deflated into a worm, your randy breaths stuck in your throat and began to choke you. You wanted to make it all go away, erase the image from the screen and from your life at once."

It was no wonder, of course, that this episode for me summoned a recollection of the prima donna and her awkward suitor. She had lost her luster—even she could not deny this—and now it turned to venom. If—as she claimed absurdly—she felt an orphan with the loss of her father, the fact is that the parts for orphans fall largely in the comic opera repertoire nonetheless—Arrieta's *zarzuela* Marina or Donizetti's Daughter of the Regiment—which is to say that my wife, for all her drama, ends up playing foolish Micaëla to Carmen.

Yet, like any faded diva, she could not let up.

"What you want is to control things like the boy with the dick in his hand and impossible dreams in his head. It was an affront to you as one of the outer circle of guardians that you fell suspect in my father's death, but how could you think it would not have seemed obvious to anyone looking on over your shoulder as you played this grand game of yours?"

I will go to my grave believing that she spat on me then, although she denies it, and denied it from the first. I can understand, of course, that grief might have built to an anger of which she was unconscious, a controlled rage—to apply to the accuser the text of her accusation—that made her sputter.

Yet she spat upon me, there is finally no denying the evidence of the body's ejectamenta.

"You are as guilty as anyone!" she spat. "You sent him off to life in that room as surely as if your beloved guardians had banished him to exile and to death. Whether it was you who manipulated his heart from afar and made it burst does not matter. You killed with your claims upon all that he loved, his house, his daughter, and finally putting even his own identity under scrutiny in your instruments. He was a monster at the end, you say, a creature constructed from himself; so be it! You killed that creature as surely as whoever it was who engaged him in that imaginary clearing, draining his illusions and his life with them."

She, of course, burst into tears then and I admit with some shame that I was so hurt and callous as to applaud her, clapping my hands and mocking her with muttered cries of "Brava! Brava!"

I was wrong then, I admit it. No one should so prey upon the grieving, however deep his hurt or whatever injustice he may feel. There is no going back on that, I know; and yet I submit also that an impartial observer might have conceded that I was driven to this wrong.

Who killed the old man I would like to know as well, but I—more than anyone, alone in all the world—also ask when it was that the man was killed and whose ashes, if any, were strewn upon Beckmesser's Lake under the dim sash of light from the Akash Ganga flowing across the heavens above.

Cedric would perhaps know the answers to these questions, but he, too, is gone to some other life, although I know as well that—were he here—he would not tell me. In my eyes he was as much a suspect— and a more likely one—than I might have been; and after she had recovered from the violation of my mock ovation, I ventured to tell Camille so as well.

She dabbed at a tear with a handkerchief embroidered with tiny flowers and extracted a small blue mirror from the clutch upon her lap, a tortoise leather bag that I'd brought back long ago from Florence.

"If you start up again with that nonsense of the buried treasure," she sniffled, "I swear I will scream. If Cedric found something left in the ruins of that settlement before it was flooded over, more power to him. But to tell you the truth, Marco, this story of yours seems as much a fairy tale as the ones you make fun of when the townspeople tell them. What, please, is the difference between a silver squid pulsing through underwater ruins and a fortune upon a key ring of flash memory?"

"The difference is that I have held those keys in my hand," I said.

"And you know their worth because you read them with your instruments?" she asked.

I stopped there, of course, neither nodding assent nor making any gesture, careful to remain unreadable. If—as seemed likely—Camille and I were done, any admission would leave me open to a much more serious further inquiry, since the conversion of public treasure to private purpose leaves one open to charges of malfeasance and malversation. I would escape such charges as well, of course, but could not afford them nonetheless since the guardian council goes to great extents to keep its affiliates and their doings out of public scrutiny. Yet, if I knew that someone else still possessed the key ring with its flash memories, I would not hesitate to have him prosecuted.

Which is to say that it was likely as a pirate of sorts that Cedric rowed out upon Beckmesser's Lake—if indeed he did—bearing the ashes of that body of water's eponymous patron. One can almost imagine him in a little pirate hat and weeping copiously—bear in mind we are in the realm of comic opera here—just like the child that he often was while in our service. He was the child of a race of men as old as the great sailing ships of the explorers and whalers—what is it the imaginary historian called them? Isolatoes?—not acknowledging the common commerce of men, but each living in a separate economy of his own.

Indeed I always thought Cedric an oversized child, possessed by sentimentality and superstition, and, as such, capable of such exquisitely fine-tuned violence in the service of what he was called upon to protect: that is, myself, my wife, my father-in-law in sequence. Yet he would, I suspect, have been just as fervent—and as absolute—if asked to protect an orchid or a lark.

We need such men, of course, although need not be like them, except perhaps in the interludes that games such as that my father-in-law played into the end of his life provide. Indeed that is probably why such men play them, to think themselves innocents like Cedric, to imagine themselves likewise born to watery burial.

One can imagine how it may have been, if, that is, the story that Cedric tells is true. The container of the remains—I imagine a titanium cylinder with a closely fit screw top, although more likely it was cheap plastic—squeezed tightly between his thighs as he rowed, feathering the oars quietly so as not to disturb the dogs or the owls along the shore, letting the little boat glide between each stroke, looking back over his shoulder to gauge his course against some mark in the dim light, our house for instance, or—for the sake of the story let us say—a faery glow from the church tower whose top just skirts the surface of the lake like an island of bone.

Whatever the course and whatever the mark, at some point he would have let the craft glide, setting the oars aside quietly, then opening the container on his lap.

Whether he would have sprinkled the remains from the container itself or gathered the ashes up with his hand for this asperges might not seem in question for a less superstitious creature. With Cedric one cannot be as certain. He comes from a place where the dead are burned upon the waters themselves, floating out on barges that serve as platforms for their pyres rather than being calcinated by the fires within pyrolytic kilns of modern crematories. In a culture such as his one grows more accustomed to the intermixture of ash and bone and water—arguably the components of the mortar that first held together the rude stones from which human culture was constructed, although that is another story.

In any case it is hard not to imagine that he would at least have ventured to touch the ashes, finger still moist from sweat or perhaps having wiped a tear, feeling the silk and grit of it between his fingers, perhaps even marking his cheeks or nose or forehead with it in the way of primitive people, including, of course, Christians. A slick of the same silky grit would have draped itself along the surface of the lake behind the drifting boat as he poured it out, the dapple upon the surface perhaps briefly attracting small fish alert to any insect fall, the ash eventually dispersing, merging with the water and sinking albeit more slowly than the few stray minuscule bone shards. Perhaps he would have said some words, a prayer, a last farewell, or chanted some hymn or song.

I have watched snow fall upon the lake sometimes and it is a pleasant and calming sight, the wayward flakes like feathers in still air and settling briefly upon the surface of the water before they dissolve and disappear. It does not happen often, but is magical when you can see it.

11

I went on living long thereafter. I had to, really, if you think about it. After Beckmesser's disappearance and Franky's demise, there was no witness left but mine to their lives and reality, although in truth I shared as much as I could with Cedric before he, too, went away.

There was also the coming child and the promise of Rosaria's and my lives together, a pact that we had first formed almost without words, feeling it grow heavy in our bodies when we walked out that day, as if a sap of life rising from the maze of walks and pavement itself and then slowly inhabiting us no less than the child inhabited her belly.

"Like a seed in a sweet melon," I said, nuzzling there just below her breasts.

Our love was no healing miracle; our walk that day was no pilgrimage to Compostela. In fact the episodes of weakness assailed me worse than ever thereafter, as if whatever unseen force that controlled them resisted my pulling away just as particles resist severing a molecular bond, not wanting to loose and lose the cement of the world.

More surprisingly the interludes of the woods and courts and tournament fields likewise grew stronger again. It was as if submitting to love in one corner of my being left me open to all the illusion and hopes that swirled about me; so much so that I gave myself over finally and sought to register as a character at Ynys Gutrin in order to see for myself what was happening to Beckmesser and perhaps who had eventually killed him. But when I sought to register, I discovered to my surprise that I was already there.

I pressed my finger against the biometrics scanner on the screen to complete the registry but it was refused.

ONLY ONE CHARACTER PER BIOMETRIC SIGNATURE

SAY "RESUME PLAY"
OR "KILL OFF CURRENT CHARACTER"
OR "EXIT"

"Resume play."

I was at the edge of a pond veiled with mist, a woman walking before me in veils of lavender voile as thin as the mist. She was singing a haunting and wordless song and strumming an instrument which altered the tones.

"It's called a *guimbarde*," Irene's son, Andy, explained. "Some say it is the oldest human instrument."

"A Jew's harp," I suggested.

"Some call it that," he said.

He and the quiet boy, Nim, sat with me at the game console. It was a day or two before Irene was about to open her establishment, the first such in the city according to her and Camille, although as yet a mere skeleton of what she would eventually flesh out into Madame's café.

The women were out seeking last minute trappings to fit out the establishment before the opening, leaving me and Cedric to look after the boys.

On the screen the woman was about to disappear into the mist ahead along the shore.

"You have to keep walking," Andy chastised me, moving the game controller for me. "You can't just attend to one of your worlds and ignore the other."

He made me laugh. "You are a true Candide, aren't you?" I said.

"What's that?" he asked.

"Yet another world," I said. "Like the garden of Eden."

"Be careful!" he hissed. A huge tree trunk fell with a thump and blocked the path before me.

"Did someone do that? Or was it an accident?"

He didn't answer at first. The sound of the woman's voice and the plaintive overtones of her instrument grew more distant. Mist swirled.

"You'll have to decide whether to climb over this thing or find a way to go around," Andy—my Candido—said. "If you choose to climb you may have to unburden yourself of some of your possessions in order to be able to get over. But if you do so, you risk ambush if someone has set this obstacle before you. Let's see what you have."

He manipulated the controller again and a semi-transparent fan of objects veiled the top of the screen, the pastel procession of my possessions arrayed like a rainbow.

"Ah, a *guiterne*!" he exclaimed. "So you are a musician as well. Perhaps you can avoid all this and make her linger by playing something to woo her."

"How do I know that is what I want to do?" I asked. "Who says she wasn't leading me to this ambush? And who am I anyway?"

"You have to keep playing! You have to keep playing!" he admonished again, this time manipulating the controller so that the game paused and the screen dissolved into darkness. The other boy giggled nervously.

"There is no other life here," Andy said. "You can't buy one, you can't win one. You lose and you are out."

"I know someone who really died there," I said.

This provocation didn't shake him. He didn't seem surprised or even especially bothered by such a prospect; he simply looked at me as if awaiting what I would say next.

"How do I know who I am?" I asked him. "I mean my role there."

Nim suddenly spoke, his voice studious and earnest. "That's very hard, actually. Even if you see yourself in someone else's armor plate or spy your reflection in the surface of the water when you drink from a well, what you see may be one of the disguises you've taken on or the result of a spell someone has cast over you. It can even be a dream. To really see yourself you need the blue mirror."

"He didn't have one," Andy interrupted.

"He has one in his pack back in the room where we stay," Cedric said, having come into the space at just that instant.

"That won't work here," Nim said.

He and Andy were clearly fond of Cedric, looking on him as if a court jester.

"I was about to woo or be ambushed," I told him.

"It seems you've done your wooing already, my friend," he said and laughed.

Cedric had taken to spending some nights elsewhere during those times when Rosaria stayed with me, explaining the future to me, talking and holding each other through the night.

"What else can you discover on that screen of yours?" I asked Andy.

He ignored me.

"What do you mean?" Nim asked.

"Could you find a character with a certain name in a gameworld?"

"The character or the person?" the boy asked.

"Any gameworld or Ynys Gutrin?" Andy added, his tone a little dismissive.

Without warning I began to weep. Naturally it surprised them; it surprised me as well how sad and lost I suddenly felt, not the lostness of the technologically inept, but rather an echoing, transcendent sadness, the kind of loss someone must feel after having had a stroke and unable to summon body or voice, unable to signal to an outside world that glimmers high above the depths he floats within.

The boys were gentle with this awkward sign of weakness.

"We can take time to learn these things together," Candido—Andy— said quietly. "Really."

The other boy merely leaned his head against my shoulder.

"He's just tired, aren't you, Alex?" Cedric placed his palm upon my back.

"Tired and lost," I said.

With Rosaria, however, I was less lost and, although I say we talked nights, it was the speech of silence as well as words, a deeper version of the consolation I felt with Nim's head against my shoulder. I don't think Rosaria understood my situation as I explained it to her, with all its geometrical details of intersecting identities and time. This was not because she was unschooled; far from it; she was among the wisest and most learned persons, man or woman, whom I had ever known. Rather

I was literally incoherent, a torn flag whose faded rags flapped in a cosmic wind.

"I don't understand where you want to go or who you want to be, except yourself now here with me," she said to me that day when we walked out together through the hidden city.

"But I have to know—"

"*Tu sólo tienes que saber lo que puedes*—you only have to know what you can, *querido*," she hushed me. "What was, and what is to come, you can only know in memory or imagination, and they are volatile substances, transforming into each other in an instant."

We were walking near a place I thought I recognized, the dizzying upswell of brick facades broken by a tall chimney that rose well beyond the top stories of the surrounding buildings. A thin stream of white smoke rose from it like a magician's knotted scarves, dissipating in the glare into dove-white patches.

"You think you know where you are?" she asked.

"I think so."

"*Bueno*," she said simply and we walked on.

She did not ask me to tell her what I thought I recognized, but instead seemed content that I had placed myself this once and might therefore do so again. Her calm was a comfort to me.

Still I felt a deep need to look upon my own visage in Ynys Gutrin, to know who I was there at least. My opportunity came one night not long after the opening of Irene's establishment, when I had stayed over with Rosaria rather than her coming to me. That night both Irene and the boys slept on the floor in the as yet unfurnished rooms along the corridor. Irene had given up her place in the big bed that normally she and Rosaria shared and slept instead upon a pile of the cardboard shipping cartons from the terminals, the nest covered over with a thick Peruvian blanket. The boys slept as usual upon foam pads under bedrolls but in different rooms because Andy had contracted some kind of fever, perhaps from the comings and goings of the initial customers.

As soon as I heard the soft, rhythmic breathing that marked Rosaria's sleep I rose up, moving quietly down the corridor to where the dimmed screens of the machines hummed in the large front room, slipping on a headset to keep from waking anyone.

"Resume play," I whispered, worried that the microphone would not pick up the command.

I was there at the fallen tree immediately, the mist seeming to have dissipated from what I recalled. I felt someone looming behind me, heard the sound of his breath huffing beneath the visor of his helmet.

"Will you strike an unarmed foe without warning?" I asked, not turning. "Will you attack from behind unchivalrously?"

The wonder of a game is that you can know at some instant, if not exactly what has happened, at least the logic of the array of events that has brought you where you are and thus have some understanding of those that will follow as well. I knew at that instant what had happened to me.

You have to play, Boss, a voice said.

This voice was my own, it had come from within me I knew, an internal being within the character stopped there on the screen before the fallen tree trunk. The voice, my voice—Franky's—was within him and not that of the adversary behind him.

Myself a voice within me.

"Franky," I whispered.

Yes, Boss. You're back again.

It's you who are back, I thought.

It's the same.

And I'm the ivory knight then?

You'll need a mirror to find out.

I have one.

You may not like what you see there.

It is I who kills him?

Of course. There's no way out otherwise.

And you? Have I imagined you, my friend?

You have to keep playing, the voice said again.

"Behold the Rider," the figure looming behind me beckoned. "Behold me and then show yourself, knight, and be recognized. Thereafter we will be equally armed."

Then who is playing Beckmesser's part? I asked.

Somewhere someone was moaning in pain. I heard him crying and then someone rising to go to him.

You have to keep playing.

I wiped across the controller pad and the screen dimmed and went black but then I restarted it immediately, pressing my finger against the biometric scanner, waiting until the registry warning message appeared again.

ONLY ONE CHARACTER PER BIOMETRIC SIGNATURE

SAY "RESUME PLAY"
OR "KILL OFF CURRENT CHARACTER"
OR "EXIT"

"Kill off current character," I whispered.

Rosaria knelt with her back to the door before the naked Andy, shivering as she sponged him from a silver bowl to bring the fever down. Gently she lowered him to the bedroll again, sponging his limbs and forehead once more, never looking back at me.

I went out through the back door and lost myself in those same alleys that we had walked one afternoon together, turning this way and that until the pre-dawn light began to seep across the darkness and I knew I had to get back to the room to rest and think through whatever next steps to take until we could escape this place that had trapped me into its litany of names, events, and confusing visions.

Cedric awaited me at the table as if he had advance warning.

"There is Ceylon tea in the kettle, my friend," he said. "Dimbula exactly, with hot milk. It's very good for you."

"How did you know?"

He reached into his pocket and extracted the pager. On its four-line screen there was a rudimentary map with a set of crosshairs blinking next to a small bright circle.

"I watched you coming from my vantage perched upon the wings of a great bird," he said.

"And before that? Could you track me into Ynys Gutrin?"

Cedric showed a rueful smile.

"That you would return to that place was more certain than these satellite coordinates," he said. "But no, the coverage does not extend into other worlds."

"Not yet," I said.

"You are probably right, sahib," he said. "Not yet."

He listened judiciously, sipping tea and nodding, as I told him of my encounter at Ynys Gutrin and my decision to kill off the character bound to my biometric signature, the one whom I took to be the white knight.

"Maybe you can revisit the space as a mendicant, perhaps some sort of monk or wayfarer," he said.

I knew he was teasing me but I needed certain things of him. There were things I had to understand. If Beckmesser were The Rider, as I thought he was, that would mean that he still lived somewhere on this earth. Yet if I removed Franky from both worlds in killing off our shared character, that would mean he could not have killed Beckmesser in either world.

"A hall of mirrors," Cedric said much too enigmatically, annoying me with the obvious.

"Damn it!" I snapped. "I'm too tired for all this. Where's Beckmesser then?"

"He lives here," Cedric said in the same enigmatic tone.

"You?"

"Not physically, not in the biometrics, no," he said. "But I can play a part as well as anyone. It's a small thing to fill a man's memory, small enough you can hide it like a needle. A small thing especially if you can keep someone you love from pain."

I was beginning to understand. I poured myself some tea from the copper kettle. It was strong and fragrant, sweet with milk and honey, an elixir for a body battered too long.

"And if we leave now, Rosaria and me, what will you do then?"

"Me?" he turned to me with a look of amusement. "Or Beckmesser? Him, he will go away again. Camilla will grieve but she will eventually understand. For her he's become something of an old chief from the stories now, looking for somewhere to lie down and die. Whether on the shores of the lake with his name or Ynys Gutrin little matters."

"And that makes the deception worthwhile?" I asked.

I offered the question without malice and he took none.

"That I think you understand, my friend, more than anyone I know. You begin these things for reasons that make sense at the first; you tell yourself a story, that you are protecting her, she whom you love as something more than your employer, that you are giving her time to come to terms with what will break her heart eventually, time to gather the strength she needs and, perhaps, to rid her life of burdens and the interlopers within it, before she has to face that which she does not wish to face. The truth is I do not know for sure where Beckmesser lies now, whether he is dead or truly alive. In that sense the story as we will live it, as we have, is a true one."

"In that sense the game is real as well," I said.

"Do you think so?" he asked.

His was a genuine question for which I had no answer and so said nothing. Nor did he say anything more that morning.

Instead we sat for a while in silence and then I went back to bed and slept as well as I had for months, without any dream that I could recall.

Rosaria and I left not long thereafter, travelling in the company of a small band of musicians who had been expelled along with many other aliens following the last campaign against civil disturbance. Because Rosaria knew the musicians' language we were able to fit in with them easily. She looked the part, of course, much more than I, although when covered in a blanket and a straw hat and smeared with make-up by Rosaria and her giggling sister, I made a credible enough appearance to be deported. Andy had recovered from his fever by then and he and Nim did their part in fitting me out. We waited until a day when Camille had called to say she would not be stopping by. She was not to know that we were departing.

Andy gave me a small stringed instrument, its curved back a shell I thought at first was turtle.

"A *guiterne?*" I asked.

"No, a *churango*. It's the word for the creature, the armadillo."

"How did you find such a thing?" I asked.

"This one's a shaman," Irene said. "A healer like his father. And he doesn't need your *Ayahuasca* brew in order to see things."

"Candido," I said. "That's my name for him."

"It's a good one," she said.

Nim presented me with a counting stick that he had made from the branch of a birch tree.

"It's better than a calendar, boss," he said. "Better than lining up pebbles."

Irene stood between the two boys and twisted their ears until they howled and squirmed, making them promise before their aunt and uncle that they would never disclose what they knew of our leaving.

Me, Irene kissed goodbye, thrusting her tongue bawdily into my mouth in a way that made everyone laugh, then took my head between her hands and whispered in my ear rather than twisting it.

"You stick it to my sister like that and you'll make babies," she whispered, then kissed me more chastely again.

She and Rosaria held each other in silence for some time, briefly touched each other's cheeks, then Rosaria left so abruptly I had to hurry to catch up with her.

"That's the way! Make him run behind you!" Irene called after us but Rosaria did not look back.

We caught up with the musicians at the edge of the city. I inquired of them whether they knew Manco's band, his mother Mayra, her boyfriend Wenceslao, and his uncle Miguel Angel. The leader of this one, Don Alejandro, said he thought he knew them but if they were the same band he remembered, that Wenceslao had not been on the road for years. Rosaria told me later that he would have said he knew them as a mater of pride whether or not he did. She also said that Don Alejandro had told her that he was impressed by the quality of the weave in the small blanket I carried as a sack, which he said had to be the product of a famous weaver.

I worried because we had neither papers nor identity chips but the bored border guards waved us through without either any questions or any of the insults that Rosaria had steeled me against in advance. For some reason I thought we might see Marco among the authorities watching over the deportations but of course he was not there.

Of the time that followed there is a time that I remember most, an event of such unaccountable novelty and normalcy at once that it forms for me a lasting portrait of Rosaria.

Some months after we had departed together to our new life we were on a train. Remarkably she said this was only the second time in her life that she had been on a train. The first had been when she rode one as a little girl in the company of her auntie she called Tíanita, riding for a full night and a day across a vast plain only days after her own mother died. "She called me her little *huerfanito*, making it sound pretty to me," Rosaria told me. "I remember very little. Distant lights at a crossroads in the middle of nowhere and then—*milagro del cielo!*—in the middle of nowhere a star streaming across the night sky. I was very excited and shook my Tíanita awake and told her, hoping there would be more to see in the sky. '*Tu madre*,' she whispered sleepily to me, '*tu madre*.'"

The railroad car that Rosaria and I were riding in was in daylight, a commuter line along an undistinguished river between two small cities, each of which was the twin of the other across the river in another country. The baby had been showing for some time in her belly and Rosaria wore a great round blue skirt with a print of yellow and blue flowers, its tie string waist fastened above the mound where our baby stirred and, from time to time, tumbled, making Rosaria catch her breath.

"She's a big one," she said.

On the river a tug pushed three black barges lashed together, their cargo, if any, hidden below decks. Wake spread behind the barges in the shape of a fan fringed with white lace at its edges. A deckhand picked his way among the cables and hatches, walking slowly along the barges to the prow of the most forward of them. Rosaria gazed upon the scene, her deep brown eyes filled with gentleness. Her hands rested upon either side of her belly, the fingers also fanning out, spreading and closing in a gentle rhythm.

"It is a very nice train, isn't it?" she asked me. "The cars are clean and it is not at all noisy. I'm very happy, aren't you?"

We both were very happy and before long there would be three of us together and happy as well or so one hoped, although never said in so many words. Enough valuation was left on the four flash memory keys to take a train when we needed to and to make a life together. Where we were headed was a district where it was said that we could buy a small house and register as lawful immigrants and establish an identity, not just for our daughter, but together.

Things turned hard for Rosaria toward the end but she never lost patience. Well before the baby was due the midwife who was attending to her told her she should not exert herself but rather stay in bed and so I moved the bed next to the large front window of the house where it looked out onto a meadow and a hill of houses leading up to the town center and where she could see the world coming and going. She especially liked to watch the children dawdling their way to school, her eyes glazing over with thoughts too complex to tell me and too simple to need to.

I would sit there and watch out the window with her. Sometimes to amuse ourselves we gave names to the creatures, human and animal both, which passed outside the window. A particularly waifish boy who was always sniffling trailed every day just behind a pack of chattering girls his age. Him, we called Romeo. A shorthaired hound that Rosaria baptized Veshjuk moved in a half-gallop sideways along the meadow. One evening, just a day or so before the labor pains began, we saw a small band of musicians with their blankets and straw hats climbing up along the path toward the center of the city. Even from that distance I could tell they were neither the band we left with as refugees nor Manco's band. Them, we called *almas de los perdidos.*

After a day and a half in labor the midwife told Rosaria there were situations where it made more sense to have all the instrumentation and drugs and oxygen present and so she thought it was time to go to the hospital. Rosaria was in such pain that she agreed, first asking me was I sad that she would not deliver our baby before the window in this house. She was like a ragdoll by then, her whole body soaked with sweat, eyes glazed after the hours of recurrent labor, waves of dark hair plastered against her forehead and face like a wreath.

When they let me hold the baby before wrapping her, I did not ask whether my Rosaria had been able to see her but when I came back to the floor I knew that Rosaria would see our child now in heaven. The Dutch nurse slid from behind the nurses' station and met me the moment I stepped out blinking from the elevator, trying to recall which way to turn. "You don't know, do you?" she said, but then I did of course and began to weep. She put her arm around my shoulder, cradling my head against the top of her head as we walked to a waiting room just down the corridor that I had not seen before.

"Poor man," she whispered. "One time is a hundred times too much for any man, yet twice that is an infinity."

Racking tears choked me, tearing away the linings of my lungs, burning my throat and searing my eyes and the woman held me saying nothing.

In time this wave of tears gave way to forlorn whimpering and a weariness in my limbs. My own breath caught and choked just as Candido's had during his fever. I could not bear to think of her as she had been then, so gentle and caring, the very image of a mother, the moon itself in the silver bowl of water before her.

"Why?" I moaned.

"It was her heart. She's such a little thing, her heart burst from love I think," the nurse whispered.

I cried aloud again.

"There is time enough to see her, time enough for everything in its time," the nurse comforted me.

She led me to a bare room, not a morgue, but some intermediate place reserved for such viewings, its walls bare, no apparatus or furnishings but the chrome gurney where the body lay beneath a simple sheet, peaked where the feet were, small contours at the knees, belly, breasts, and then the crease above the shoulders under which the face.

Brown as a fawn in life, Rosaria in death was ivory, a snow-white bandage at her throat where the nurse told me they had cut at the last moment to try to help her breathe.

"If you want to lift the sheet, you can," she said. "Sometimes people wonder if that is allowed. But I have to warn you there's no bandage where they opened her up to go after the baby and the sutures will seem rough to you since they don't take quite the same care when a patient is lost."

Where was she lost, I wondered? In what world could I find her? I smoothed her cheek and ran my hand along the outside of the sheet, cold along the flesh of her belly where the baby had been, and then the Dutch nurse helped me tuck the sheet around Rosaria once more before I kissed her face.

I walked with the orderly as they moved the gurney from the receiving room to the morgue and the Dutch nurse gently lifted her from it onto the silver tongue of the morgue shelf. The stainless steel drawer closed on noiseless hinges leaving her to lay yet again among other lost creatures.

They gave me her ashes in a sleek metal canister with finely fitted threads where its cap screwed closed. Inside it the pasty white ashes were the consistency of coarse sand and crushed shells and left a feeling like talc when you touched them. I pressed my face to the opening of the canister but there was no odor except the absence of odor, a bland minerality and something vaguely metallic, likely from the canister.

The baby was born without a name but I called her Maria Elena on the certificate. I was alone when I buried them, alone I carried the little coffin, the canister balanced on its top. I remember the weight of the white box in my arms, the white enamel surface like a sugar glaze, grasping it at both ends with the little silk handles of twisted white rope, afraid the baby would jostle within the satin blankets. The undertaker wanted to walk with me but I would not let him. We would walk this path alone, Maria Elena, Rosaria and me like a family. I whispered to them that I loved them, whispered to them the whole of the while that I set the white box in the ground and spread her mother's ashes around it, the white powder falling like mist upon the darker ground where the coffin lay. When they were settled, I retrieved the pager Cedric had given me from my pocket and pressed the button, then laid it in the grave along with the blue mirror. As I turned away someone came out from the trees and began to shovel the clay upon the opening.

After that, time itself slipped again and again like a gash in a mirrored disk, a flaw that the lasers cannot penetrate and the correction algorithms cannot fathom. It wasn't I but time itself that had been marred by this slit in the earth into which hope sank like a white lozenge. Some form of who I am began to veer away from all I knew and led me toward a place where I was lost in what I had lost and where I stumbled out on the road again, a wayfarer.

MICHAEL JOYCE

In the early 1990s *The New York Times* called Michael Joyce's novel *afternoon* "the granddaddy of hypertext fictions." *afternoon* has since been anthologized in *Postmodern American Fiction: A Norton Anthology* and translated into various languages. Other hypertext fictions include "On the Birthday of the Stranger" in the inaugural edition of *Evergreen Review* online, as well as *Twilight, A Symphony*, and *Twelve Blue*. His most recent print novel, *Was: Annales Nomadique*, was published by Fiction Collective 2 in 2007. A very early (1994) e-book, *Going the Distance*, will be reissued in print by SUNY Press in 2013. In recent years he has taken more and more to poetry, with poems and translations published in various journals and a book-length sequence of poems, *Paris Views*, published by BlazeVOX in 2012.

His collaborative multimedia work with LA visual artist Alexandra Grant includes *Lost Hills Hokku* (2009), text for her paintings and for her one woman show, *Bodies*, at Honor Fraser Gallery (2010); and *The Ladder Series* (2007), text for four paintings for her one-woman show, at LA MOCA. With Jay David Bolter and Maria Engberg he is working on an augmented reality fiction regarding the Swedish painter Anders Zorn. An earlier augmented reality fiction text, "Joyce in Berlin," for *Osmotic Minds: Berlin Alexanderplatz 5.0*, by Stefan Schemat, Hilmar Schmundt, Michael Joyce, and Isabella Bordoni, won Honorable Mention at Ars Electronica in 1999.

He lives along the Hudson River near Poughkeepsie where he is Professor of English and Media Studies at Vassar College.

Steerage Press

~ where good books are given berth ~
_____

Joe Amato, *Big Man with a Shovel*
Chris Pusateri, *Common Time*
Michael Joyce, *Disappearance*

Made in the USA
Charleston, SC
21 October 2012